GIRLHOOD

Novels by Cat Clarke

ENTANGLED

TORN

UNDONE

A KISS IN THE DARK

THE LOST AND THE FOUND

GIRLHOOD

CAT CLARKE

GIRLHOOD

Quercus

QUERCUS CHILDREN'S BOOKS

First published in Great Britain in 2017 by Hodder and Stoughton

3 5 7 9 10 8 6 4

A CIP catalogue record for this book is available from the British Library.

ISBN 978 1 78429 273 7

Typeset in Perpetua 14/17 pt by Palimpsest Book Production Limited,
Falkirk, Stirlingshire

Printed and bound in Britain by Clays Ltd, St Ives plc

The paper and board used in this book are
made from wood from responsible sources.

Quercus Children's Books
An imprint of
Hachette Children's Group
Part of Hodder and Stoughton
Carmelite House
50 Victoria Embankment
London EC4Y 0DZ

An Hachette UK Company
www.hachette.co.uk

www.hachettechildrens.co.uk

For Cate, Ciara & Caro
There ain't no party like a C Club Party . . .

ONE

We always have a midnight feast on the first night back. Because that's what you do at boarding school, right?

When we were younger, Jenna and I were obsessed with boarding school books. We desperately wanted to be the twins at St Clare's. Almost every night I'd sneak over to her bed after Mum turned out the lights. We'd put the duvet over our heads and take turns reading to each other by torchlight. Two peas in a cosy little pod.

Somehow I ended up at Duncraggan Castle, just like in the stories.

But Jenna's not with me. I had to come here alone.

I wasn't alone for long though.

'Would you rather . . . have muffins for hands or squirrels for feet?' Rowan leans back and crosses her arms, smug as you like.

1

Lily snorts with laugher while Ama clinks her mug against Rowan's.

'Well, that depends,' says Ama, now mock-serious. 'Do the muffins regenerate? Can I choose what flavour? Can I choose *different* flavours, depending on the day? Oh, and are the squirrels red or grey?'

Rowan's ready. 'They regenerate on a daily basis. You can choose any flavour. Grey squirrels. Those poor little bastards have such a bad rep.'

Lily starts on a rant about the plight of the red squirrel, and I put my hand over her mouth to shut her up.

I think I've decided, but I have a question that needs answering first. 'Can you control the squirrels though? Like, with a tiny pair of reins?'

Rowan gives that some thought. 'Yes. But they don't come already trained. It's a lot of work, you know. Squirrel-training is a very serious business.'

'Then it's easy! I'm Team Squirrel. Ama? Lil?'

Lil votes muffins (as long as they're made with organic flour). Ama goes for squirrels 'because it would be like having pets with you WHEREVER YOU GO.'

I ask Rowan what she'd choose. 'No idea,' she shrugs. 'It's a really stupid question.' I throw a pillow at her head.

'I've got one!' Lily pipes up. 'This one's for Ama.'

'Uh-oh,' says Ama. 'This is never good.'

Lily stands up, between the two beds. She coughs as if clearing her throat. 'Allow me to set the scene . . . It's the night of the Christmas concert. The packed auditorium is hushed. The audience has sat through screeching violins and off-key oboes, but now things are looking up. Ama is set to take the stage, to dazzle and delight with her peerless piano playing . . .'

'Bit overboard on the alliteration there if you ask me,' Rowan stage-whispers.

'Hush!' Lily kneels down in front of Ama and takes her hand. 'Ama, my dear, very bestest friend in all the world, would you rather . . . play your piece while your parents have sex on top of said piano . . .'

I can hardly hear Ama's disgusted retching over our laughter.

'*Or* would you rather have sex with a person of your choice up on stage, while your *mum* plays the piano?' Lily's 'Would you Rather's are *always* about sex.

The laughter escalates and I'm half worried Miss Renner will come knocking on the door. But last year Rowan somehow managed to find out that Miss Renner listens to *Sounds of the Rainforest* on her headphones to help her sleep. Maddox wouldn't be too happy about that if she found out.

'You are disgusting, Lily Carter. Disgusting and depraved.'

3

'That may be true, but I'm afraid I'm going to need an answer. You know the rules.'

'I can't!' Ama wails, but she knows we won't let her get away with that. 'OK, OK! I just . . . waaaaaah!'

'Got any supplementary questions *this* time, Adebayo?' Rowan asks, an eyebrow raised.

'OK, first of all, I'm pretty sure my parents never, ever, ever have sex.' Ama grimaces. 'But I'm going to have to go with Option A. There is no way on earth I would ever have sex in front of anyone. ANYONE.'

'But you're perfectly happy for your parents to go at it like rabbits while you play Rachmaninov?' I smile sweetly, but I've crossed the line. Ama hates Rachmaninov.

Our midnight feasts aren't so much 'lashings of ginger beer' as 'whatever booze we can smuggle in'. Sometimes – if someone remembers – we even have food. Tonight, we demolished a whole tin of yakgwa made by Rowan's mum. Whoever invented deep-fried biscuits was a genius, no question.

Lily grimaces every time she takes a sip from her tiny bottle. 'I fucking hate whisky!'

'It's better than nothing!' Ama pouts. She was the one who managed to blag twenty miniatures on her flight back from Lagos.

'Well, you should learn to love it. We are in

4

Scotland, after all.' I can't stand the stuff either, but loyalty to my country wins out.

'I'll start liking whisky when Ama starts liking haggis,' says Lily with a grin.

'Aw, come on, Lil! It's hardly the same thing! A sheep's innards should stay on the inside as far as I'm concerned. And I know you agree with me, Little Miss *I was a vegetarian before I could even spell the word*.' Ama's not exactly slurring her words, but one more bottle and she will be.

'I'm sure the *sheep* agrees with you,' Rowan says, leaning past Ama to take one of the bottles. She opens it and sniffs deeply. 'Ah, can't you just picture the purple heather in the glens? The noble stag surveying his kingdom . . .'

'Right before he gets shot by some idiot banker who thinks that killing defenceless animals makes him more *manly*.' Lily's voice drips with disdain; it always does when she talks about her dad.

'I bet Sharp-Shooter Kent over here could teach your dad a thing or two. She's fucking deadly.' Rowan jostles my shoulder.

'Clay-pigeon shooting isn't quite the same thing, Rowan. And I'm crap at it anyway.' This isn't strictly true. I'm now approaching the dizzy heights of 'mediocre', although Miss Whaite prefers to describe my skills as 'solid'. Dad was appalled to find out the activities I signed up for when I started at Duncraggan. *'Shooting?! Why did it have to be shooting? And rock-climbing? What's that all about? Don't they do any normal things there? Like . . . rounders?'* He had a point, but I'd made a promise to myself when I came here. I wanted to do the kind of weird shit you only get to do at boarding school. I gave up on the climbing after a few months, but I still shoot every week.

By two a.m. the whisky is gone and Rowan's eyes are drooping closed every couple of minutes. 'Come on you, let's get you to bed.' I drag her up into a sitting position. 'Tomorrow's going to be brutal.'

We say good night to Lily and Ama and creep next door to our room. The corridor is dimly lit – just enough light so you can find your way to the toilet in the middle of the night. The green 'emergency exit' sign glows incongruously above the door to the stairs. I wish they didn't have to have things like that – fire doors and official-looking signs and strip lighting really don't belong in a building like this one. So many changes and additions have been made over the years that it's only in certain places that the building still feels like a proper castle. Those are the parts that get photographed to death and plastered all over the website. Those are the parts that made me want to come here.

'Home, sweet home,' I say, turning on the bedside lights. Our room is slightly smaller – Lily got the pick of the rooms after being elected head girl last year. And Rowan managed to convince Hozzie and Sylvana to swap so that we could stay next door to Lily and Ama for our last year at Duncraggan. It felt right. The four of us have been a little unit since Rowan took me under her wing when I arrived.

I think about that day a lot. How I felt when the car pulled up in front of the castle, tyres crunching on the gravel. How Dad patted my leg and said, 'Well, this is going to be an adventure, isn't it?' even though the look on his face said otherwise. How everything seemed so strange and new and not like something a person like me should ever experience.

On my first night, lying awake and listening to the wind rattling against the windows, I wondered if I'd made a terrible mistake. I looked across the gloom towards the other bed and everything about the silhouette was wrong.

Jenna should have been there, sharing everything with me, like always. That's what twins do. That's who we *are*.

We all have our reasons for being at Duncraggan; some are more interesting than others. Most people are just here because their parents are filthy rich, and apparently the first thing you do when you're filthy rich is make sure your children live as far away from you as possible.

Bonus points for remote location in the wilds of Scotland. Terrible weather builds character, apparently.

Ama wanted to come here because of the reputation of the music department, but Lily had no choice in the matter. Rowan, Lily and Ama all have rich parents, but it's not something we talk about. The clues are there if you pay attention. If you look at the labels on their clothes and listen closely for key words like 'trust fund' and 'driver' and 'yacht'. I try not to hold it against them – the fact that money is meaningless to them, no matter how much they try to convince themselves otherwise. They don't care about money because they've never had to think about it.

Rowan's parents moved to South Korea when she was eight years old. Most kids would be upset by that, but apparently she had no fucks to give. She went to another boarding school in London before transferring here for senior school. She stayed here even when her parents moved back to Surrey last year, saying she'd never dream of abandoning us. 'Together till the bitter end,' she said.

Rowan's the only one I talked to about why I came to Duncraggan. I asked her to tell Ama and Lily, because I thought they deserved to know but I couldn't face telling them. It's too tiring, telling the story over and over again. Working so hard to make sure you don't tell the *whole* truth.

I hate talking about it, and the girls understand that. If one of them finds herself veering into dangerous conversational waters, the others will yank her back to safety. Rowan's usually the one to do the yanking; I don't know what I'd do without her. Sometimes I feel bad that I've never told her all of it. The worst of it.

The worst of it is simple. You can strip the excess flesh of the story down to the bare bones. You can shrink it and starve it and whittle it down to almost nothing.

That's what happened to her.

Jenna died of heart failure. Other things too: a perforated ulcer, a collapsed lung. But it was the heart that gave up on her. It couldn't do the job it's supposed to do; it didn't have the fuel.

My twin sister was fifteen years old when she died. She weighed just under five stone.

It had started as a post-Christmas diet.

A diet that was my idea.

TWO

It was my fault she died.

People say that losing a twin is like losing half of yourself, half of your soul. They're wrong. You lose yourself. Everything that makes you *you*. You lose everything you've ever known to be right and true.

But Jenna's death is not the whole story. It's the bit that strangers know about, because it was in the papers. Mum and Dad insisted on going public, so that people could learn from our tragedy, and other parents could watch out for the warning signs before it was too late. I was against the idea from the start. Jenna was *mine*. I couldn't bear to think about sharing her with the world like that. My parents listened to my arguments, patiently and sometimes tearfully, but they did it anyway. Mum said she was sorry, but it was the right thing to do.

It might have been the right thing to do for them, and for all those parents out there – a cautionary tale they could read about with their morning coffee, dusting crumbs of toast off the paper before turning the page.

But what about me? I couldn't turn the page. Ever. And what about Jenna? My sister would hate the fact that you can google her name and read all the lurid details. She would hate the school photo that ran in all the papers – the one they used to illustrate how lovely and normal and healthy she looked *before*. She's smiling in that picture, even though she hated having her photo taken. When we brought our photos home from school that day, Mum told me off for not smiling in mine. She thought Jenna's photo was 'just lovely' though. She couldn't even see that Jenna's smile was fake. *I* could see, of course, because our fake smiles were identical.

They found the *after* photo on her phone. She'd sent it to one of her 'ana' buddies a couple of months before she died, and this so-called friend had congratulated her on how amazing she looked, sending a photo of herself so they could compare and contrast. The measurements were unfathomably tiny.

There's no way to look at that photo and not be appalled, and the thought that millions of people could do just that by reading the newspaper or looking online was poisonous to me. They would never know her like I did. They would never know the girl who thought the fact that she was twenty-three minutes older than me made her infinitely wiser. The girl who had tried and failed to save a baby sparrow that had fallen out of its nest. The girl who had cried at the solemn sparrow funeral we held, sacrificing her best shoebox as a coffin. The girl who, in her 'I want to be an archaeologist' phase a year later, dug up the shoebox to examine the bird's remains.

Jenna was a person – a wonderfully messy human being, with faults and hopes and fears – but she'd been reduced to a morality tale.

The only blessing was that my parents managed to keep me out of it. They did four interviews in all, with journalists coming round to our house and sitting on our sagging sofa, beady eyes no doubt darting around the room to take in the family photos on the mantelpiece, the stains on the carpet, the ancient TV. My parents told them that Jenna had a twin sister, but that was it. When the journalists inevitably asked to talk to me, my parents refused. My dead sister was fair game but I was off limits.

The newspaper stories mentioned that my sister's anorexia had seemingly started with a 'harmless New Year's resolution' to eat better and exercise more. They didn't know it had been my idea, and that I'd pressured Jenna into doing it with me. I knew if I did it by myself I would give up after a few days. I told her it would be fun, something we could do together. She wasn't overweight, not even close. Neither was I for that matter, but I was a little heavier than her and I couldn't accept that. Identical twins are supposed to look the same.

Mum knows it was my fault. She saw me persuading Jenna to get off the sofa and come for a run with me on New Year's Day. She saw me raising my eyebrows in disapproval when Jenna overfilled her cereal bowl in the morning.

We've never talked about it. Mum has never actually come out and said that she blames me. Perhaps because she saw me doing all those things, and she did nothing to stop it.

I did my research, when things started to get really bad with Jenna. It was months after I'd lost interest in watching my weight, and my sister was steadily shrinking away. I was scared. It turns out that twins are more likely to be anorexic. I didn't need further confirmation of my culpability, but there it was on my laptop screen. My very existence was to blame for Jenna's illness.

The rest of the story is supposed to be the yin to the yang of Jenna's death. It's so ridiculous and painfully ironic that people don't know how to react when you tell them. You can see their eyes flicker in a sort of panic, because they can't react in the way they would normally react to such news.

It happened the day after my sister died, but we didn't find out until the morning after that. Dad had switched his phone off because he couldn't face talking to anyone. It was all down to Mum, ringing people to tell them that Jenna was dead. She didn't say 'dead' though; she said 'gone' or 'passed away'. 'Dead' feels more honest to me. The word itself sounds final, like a full stop.

We were having breakfast – or rather, sitting at the breakfast table, drinking coffee, eating nothing – when Mum's phone rang. 'Don't recognise the number,' she muttered. Dad told her to leave it, but she picked up.

After a moment or two she held out the phone towards Dad. 'It's Jan,' she said. Jan worked with Dad. No one at the sorting office knew about Jenna yet. He'd taken the week off when it was clear that she didn't have much time left.

He sat up straight, cleared his throat and took a deep breath, as if he was summoning all his strength. 'Hi. Jan. How are things?' His voice sounded unnatural.

Then Jan talked – a lot. Dad said 'OK' and 'I see' a few times before hanging up. His facial expression didn't alter once during the exchange.

He put the phone down on the table and took a sip of his cooling coffee.

'What did she want? You really should have told her, you know. You'll have to call your boss today. I think we should see if we can arrange the funeral for next Friday. That way people can stay over and travel home on the Saturday. What do you think?'

Dad's fingers were tracing the pattern of the worn wood on the kitchen table. His thumb grazed over the place where Jenna had carved her initials when we were ten years old. I'd carved mine too, but on the underside of the table. Mum was furious, shouting at Jenna for ten minutes straight before sending her to our room. She never told though – that I'd done the same but been a bit more subtle about it. She never told.

'Sam?'

'What?' He looked up into Mum's eyes and she must have realised that it was something major. But the worst thing that could ever happen had already happened, and we were still there, sitting at the table, trying to not to look at the empty chair next to the window.

'We won,' he said.

'What are you talking about? Won what?' Mum was clearly exasperated and I had a sudden, horrible thought – a premonition? – that she wouldn't stay with him. They would get divorced. Maybe not soon, but one day.

'The syndicate.'

Mum sighed and leaned back in her chair. 'What is it this time? A hundred quid? Because in case you hadn't noticed we have more important things to worry about, and I could really use your help.' She stood and picked up her mug and mine. I'd only had a couple of sips; the coffee sloshed over the edge of the mug, fat splashes of brown landing on the table. 'Shit! SHIT!'

Mum was losing the plot, anyone could see that.

'Twenty-one million. Just over.'

He had to repeat the figure three times before Mum finally understood. She sat down at the table, ignoring the coffee dripping on to her shoes.

'Oh,' she said.

He'd been a member of that syndicate for eight years, along with six other postmen and women. Jan was the one who'd set it up years ago. The most they'd ever won before was £144. This time they won £21.2 million. Dad's share was just over £3 million.

My father became a millionaire. The day after his daughter died.

THREE

The whisky hangover is almost exactly as bad as expected, but it's the kind of hangover that needs food so I hurry down to breakfast, my hair still wet from the shower.

'How many pieces of bacon is too many?' I ask Rowan.

'No such thing as too much bacon this morning. There's not enough bacon in all the world for how I feel right now.'

The queue moves far too slowly; there should be an express queue for emergencies like this one. I'm almost at the front when Rowan nudges me. 'Looks like we've got ourselves a newbie this year after all.' I turn to follow her gaze and see a girl I don't recognise, sitting at a table with the kind of girls who got an early night last night because lessons start today and this year is IMPORTANT.

I subtly check out the new girl. She looks normal

enough, which may mean that she's sitting at exactly the right table with exactly the right people. But you never know, people have hidden depths. You can't necessarily tell where someone belongs just by looking at them. Lily, Ama, Rowan and I aren't exactly homogenous; Ama reckons that we look like the world's worst girl band.

Over breakfast, Lily tells us that the new girl is called Kirsty Connor. She arrived late last night after her flight was delayed. She's in our year and in the same house as us, which means she'll be living on our corridor.

'So, Lil, what do you make of your first victim? Reckon she can hack it?' I ask Lily, who seems to think that granola and natural yoghurt is enough to banish her hangover.

Lily stares unashamedly at the new girl. 'Hard to say. It'll be good to have someone to practise on before we officially get started next term though. Antonia left me notes but I reckon I'm going to shake things up a bit. Make it my own, you know.'

Rowan, Ama and I share amused glances. It's typical of Lily to want to put her own spin on the head girl's most important duty. 'Don't worry! I promise it will be just as traumatic as it was for us lot.' She casts her eye over the new girl again. 'Let's do it tonight.'

We try to talk her out of it – especially Rowan,

who thinks the whole thing is barbaric — but Lily says rules are rules. It's strange to hear those words from her mouth. Maybe being head girl is going to transform her from anarchic eco-warrior into . . . God knows what. Power can do strange things to people.

'Will you and Ama help? Might as well get it over with, don't you think?'

Ama shrugs but I waver for a second or two. I have to help at some point, so it may as well be tonight. With someone I don't know. I'd feel worse doing it to one of the girls in the year below. Starting next term, each and every Year 12 girl will be victimised in turn. It's only fair that new starters in our year get the same treatment.

The head girl picks two deputies each time. By the time the year is over everyone in our year will have had a hand in it, and some people will have helped twice. It means that everyone is complicit. Everyone is equally guilty, so if the teachers ever found out, no one individual would take the blame.

The new girl passes by our table on the way out of the dining hall. Her eyes meet mine but I quickly look away. I feel terrible; she has no idea what tonight has in store for her.

We didn't go public after the lottery win, obviously. None of the journalists who came to interview my parents about Jenna knew anything about it. No fur coats or chandeliers or giant plasma TVs in our little terraced house. If they'd found out, the story would have been huge: *tragic irony . . . twist of fate . . . the Kents would give up every penny if it meant they could have their daughter back.*

Things were bad after Jenna died. Very bad. The money made no difference. It sat, untouched, in a special bank account that Dad's financial advisor had told him to open. The fact that Dad now had a financial advisor was the only noticeable change. He was the only member of the syndicate who didn't quit their job. Jan booked herself on a three-month round-the-world cruise before the cash had even hit her bank account. Meanwhile Dad still trudged off to work at five every morning.

Mum didn't give up her job either. She became obsessed with 'keeping busy'. She went into this bizarre frenzy of doing stuff *all* the time. Before, she had her little morning ritual of a cup of coffee on the bench in the back garden – no matter the weather. She'd sit out there huddled under an umbrella, wearing one of Dad's big coats. She called it her thinking time. There was no more of that after Jenna died. Thinking time was to be avoided at all costs, because the only thoughts now were sad ones, waiting to swamp you when you least expected it.

When I finally went back to school, I didn't tell

my friends about the lottery win. I didn't have a best friend, like all the other girls seemed to. You don't need a best friend when you're a twin, because you have something better and closer and unbreakable. But it turns out there's no such thing as unbreakable.

It wasn't even hard to keep the secret. People thought the only thing that was going on with my life was grieving. The only questions they asked me were 'How are you doing?' and 'Do you want to talk about it?' (The answers being 'Pretty fucking terribly, thank you,' and 'Not with you.') I wanted to talk to Jenna about it, to say how messed up it was that girls who'd never even talked to her were claiming to have been her friend. It would have amused her, I think. She'd have laughed and said that it didn't matter, not really. Because *we* knew the truth. She'd have told me to let them say whatever they wanted if it made them feel better about themselves. Jenna always did have a bigger heart than I had. It shouldn't have broken like it did.

School without Jenna was unthinkable and unbearable. It took everything I had to get through each day without screaming. I pictured doing it: standing up in Maths or English and opening my mouth and screaming and screaming until my throat bled raw.

Home was even worse than school. As soon as I put my key in the door I could feel it. A heaviness, as if the air inside was filled with a dense cloud of poison.

It was hard to breathe in that house, but somehow the three of us kept on inhaling and exhaling, our hearts pumping blood around our bodies. We kept on living, which didn't seem right. How could we live in a world without my sister in it?

Dad's workmates all moved into fancy new houses, because that's what people do when they win the lottery. But my parents wouldn't hear of it. It was as if they thought Jenna might come back to us one day and would need to be able to find her way home. They didn't ask my opinion. They didn't ask what it was like for me to lie awake at night staring up at the ceiling, doing everything I could not to look at the empty bed on the other side of the room. The bed was neatly made up, with the corner of the duvet folded back. I don't know who folded the corner, or why, but I wish they hadn't. It was as if the bed was waiting for her.

Four months after Jenna died I sat my parents down at the kitchen table and told them I wanted to go to boarding school. The plan had been brewing in my mind for a while, but I'd been waiting, biding my time to see if things would get better. I wasn't expecting miracles – just a tiny sign that life wouldn't be this unremittingly awful for ever. But if the signs were there, I must have missed them. I couldn't help feeling that my parents weren't even making an effort. I felt crushingly guilty for thinking that, and I tried *not* to think it, but it was futile. They still had one daughter left, but it felt like they'd given up. As if there was no point in trying to be a family any more.

Mum was more shocked than Dad, especially when she saw how much research I'd done. I had all the facts and figures at my fingertips, all the answers to every possible question. They had *a lot* of questions, but only one that really mattered: why?

If I'd told the truth it would have broken them. I couldn't bear to be around them any more. I could not stay in this house without Jenna – not when they could afford to send me away.

Instead, I talked about the opportunities that a place like Duncraggan Castle would provide. The extracurricular activities and academic excellence. I said that I wanted to reach my full potential, whatever that was. I talked about my future.

Dad couldn't get his head around it. '*Boarding* school though? Why boarding school? There are plenty of good schools around here.'

It was true, and I floundered. Mum came to the rescue, much to my surprise. 'Oh, you remember, Sam . . . the girls used to love those boarding school stories when they were younger, didn't they? Jolly hockey sticks and all that.' The faintest smile flitted across her features at the memory.

Dad shook his head. 'But this is real life – not

some kids' book. I don't know why you'd . . . I don't want to lose . . .' He shook his head and I was glad he didn't finish that sentence.

Mum patted his hand, but she was focused on me. 'Is this what you really want, Harper?'

I ignored the tidal wave of doubt and said yes. Then I delivered the final blow. 'I want to do this for Jenna. Have new experiences and meet new people and do all the things that she can't.' Dad flinched, as if I'd struck him. 'I feel like I owe it to her.'

I worried I'd gone too far, that they might not buy it. But Mum nodded thoughtfully. 'Still, you have to do what's right for *you*.'

I kept quiet! The wrong words now could ruin everything.

Mum said that they would need to talk it over, and find out more about Duncraggan. She said it was quite a long way away, and that it was just a bit of a surprise, but they *did* have the money now, didn't they?

That was when I knew I'd won. I felt faint with relief.

We left for Duncraggan a few months later. We stopped at a motorway service station for lunch and Mum cried. That was the only time I wavered and wondered whether I was doing the right thing. I suddenly felt like I was abandoning ship, leaving them to drown in their sadness.

'Are you two going to be OK?' I whispered, hugging her even tighter.

'Don't you worry about us, love.'

She hadn't really answered my question, but I didn't ask again. It was too late for that. I didn't want to drown.

FOUR

The Hole is not as bad as it sounds. In the grand scheme of things, it's definitely not a big deal. But it's a tradition, and traditions *are* a big deal in a place like this.

And if, to an outsider, it sounds a little bit like torture, all I can say is that boarding school can be a bitch.

The teachers would flip their lid if they ever found out, but that's never going to happen. Even when things go slightly wrong, there's a code of silence surrounding the Hole. Ama was the first one of us to be chosen, and she told us exactly what to expect – in excruciating detail. It didn't exactly put our minds at rest.

It was my turn a few days later. I'd thought boarding school was going to be all mugs of hot chocolate before bedtime and hockey games on crisp winter mornings. I should have known better. I should have known that the cruelty of girls is intensified here, living together 24/7, hundreds of miles away from home. Everything feels more concentrated, like orange squash that hasn't been diluted with water.

It's close to midnight when Rowan hands me a tiny torch.

'Thanks, but I've already got one.'

'It's not for you. It's for the new girl.'

It takes a second for me to catch on. 'But how am I supposed to . . .?'

'You'll find a way. Just make sure Lily doesn't see. Or Ama for that matter. I've put fresh batteries in so it'll definitely last the night.'

'I don't see why she should get help. No one helped *us*.'

'Give the girl a break, Harper. She doesn't have anyone to tell her what to expect.'

I sigh and take the torch. I know it's the right thing to do. Rowan *always* does the right thing; it's massively annoying.

When Miss Renner showed me to my room that first evening, I had no idea what to expect. Duncraggan students are divided into three houses: Fairclough, Balmedie and Roundhouse. I'd been put in Fairclough, which meant my room was in the castle proper, rather than one of the newer annexes. Miss Renner explained her role as house mother, and showed me her apartment at the end of the corridor on the third floor. She had her own little sitting room with two comfy sofas and a tatty old armchair that reminded me of Dad's. Miss Renner mentioned the monthly pizza parties she hosts for Fairclough girls.

'I like pizza,' I said, for want of something better to say.

'Who doesn't?' she laughed. But then she got that look on her face, and I knew what was coming. 'If you ever want to talk – about anything – or if you're having any problems or difficulties, my door is always open. It's important that you know that.' She seemed almost embarrassed, as if she knew full well there were things I would never think of discussing with her. At least now I was sure that she knew about Jenna.

I liked Miss Renner straightaway. Her granny-style glasses made her look friendly, and she was dressed casually in jeans, flip-flops and an oversized jumper. As she led me along the corridor, I glanced through doorways to see girls sitting at desks amid piles of books. Miss Renner explained that it was homework time, or 'banco' as they called it. She laughed at my confusion. 'Sorry, we have our own little language here at Duncraggan. It takes a bit of getting used to at first!' She wasn't kidding about that – I'm still not used to it.

Every girl turned to look when we passed, apart

from one who had a pair of giant headphones on. I felt scrutinised. Judged.

All I knew about my new roommate was that her name was Rowan Chung-Black and her previous roommate had moved to Switzerland over the summer. My hopes were reasonably low: I wanted my roommate not to hate me, and I wanted to not hate her.

She was standing at the window with her back to the door, definitely not studying or banking or whatever. Miss Renner had to cough to attract her attention. When she turned round I saw that she'd been looking through a pair of binoculars.

'Arctic terns,' she said, as if that meant something to me. She was East Asian, with short black hair that could politely be described as haphazard. She was slightly shorter than me, and curvier underneath her *Star Wars* T-shirt and board shorts. She wore furry green slippers that looked like monster feet. It was quite the first impression. 'They're migrating south for the winter. To the Antarctic. You have to wonder why they're not called *Ant*arctic terns, don't you?'

Miss Renner introduced us. 'Rowan's our resident ornithologist, not to mention the owner of the most unusual collection of slippers in Fairclough.'

'Aw, Miss, I bet you say that to all the girls.'

I accidentally snort-laughed, and Rowan smiled at me. Miss Renner looked from Rowan to me and back again and said she'd leave us to it. 'I have a feeling you two are going to get along just fine.'

When the door closed behind her, Rowan sat down on one of the beds. The right side of the room was plastered in posters and fliers and photos. The left side was bare.

'We can swap sides if you want.'

'This is fine. Thanks though,' I said, even though I'd have been grateful to swap. I always slept on the left side and Jenna slept on the right. I wanted things to be different here.

I manoeuvred my way past my suitcases and sat on the empty bed.

'OK, some things you should probably know . . . I like to keep the window open as much as possible – fresh air helps me think clearly. I only listen to music on my headphones. I've been told that I snore like a mammal of considerable size – but that's only when my allergies are playing up. What else? Oh yeah, I'm a lesbian, so if you're not cool with that, you might as well say so now.'

I focused on the interesting bit. 'Do I look like someone who wouldn't be cool with that?'

She narrowed her eyes as if I was trying to trick her. 'I'm not sure what you look like yet.' She paused. 'But people can be assholes, even when they don't look like assholes. My last roommate freaked out when she found out – reckoned I was going to jump on her in the middle of the night . . . can I just say she *wished*! Anyway, so I thought this time I'd go for full disclosure. There's just no easy way to drop it into conversation, is there?' She stopped and took a breath. 'Sorry. Too much, too soon?'

'Full disclosure works for me. I'm bi.' It was only the third time I'd said it out loud. As Rowan said, it's not something you just drop into a conversation.

Rowan's eyes lit up and she pumped her fist. 'Excellent! Duncraggan's queer quota was badly in need of a boost. I'm president of the LGBTQIA+ Society if you want to join? No pressure. Actually, fuck "no pressure". You have to join Queer Soc. It's your roommately duty.'

'I don't know . . . I've never really been into societies or clubs or whatever.'

'How about you join just so I can prove to Miss Maddox that it's not a pointless waste of time? You don't have to come to meetings.'

'Deal.'

'And if you could wear a pair of rainbow shoelaces every once in a while, that would be great. And a badge.'

'There are badges?'

Rowan pointed to her chest but I wasn't close enough to read it so I had to lean forward: 'Do I look straight to you?' was written in rainbow letters.

I laughed, and Rowan smiled. 'And if you don't like that one, there are a few other options . . . I may have got a bit over-enthusiastic when I found the website,' she said sheepishly.

She reached under her bed and pulled out a cardboard box full to the brim with round metal badges. After much deliberation I picked one with the bisexual pride flag on it. 'You can take a unicorn one as well, if you like? I think there are a couple left – everyone likes fucking unicorns.'

'Really? I always find their horns get in the way. They can take someone's eye out if you're not careful.'

Rowans laughed for longer than the joke deserved. I was surprised; it usually took me a lot longer to be myself around people. But Rowan was blunt and weird and like no one I'd ever met before. I didn't know it then, but she would turn out to be exactly what I needed.

FIVE

At 11.50 p.m. I head to Lily and Ama's room with the torch tucked into the back pocket of my jeans. I open the door and stifle a scream at the leering clown face in front of me. 'Get your mask on, Kent. I want to take a photo . . . for posterity,' says Lily, voice muffled under the plastic.

The three of us pose for the creepiest selfie ever: a clown, a zombie and, most terrifying of all, Donald Trump. I was actually glad I got the Trump mask, because it meant I didn't have to look at it.

We creep along the corridor to the turret room – the only single on our floor. The door creaks when Lily opens it. We tiptoe over to the bed and look down at our victim, curled up tight like dormouse. Kirsty Connor is frowning in her sleep and making these strange little distress noises. Perhaps she'll be glad of the wake-up call.

Lily switches on her torch and shines it in the girl's

face. She taps her on the shoulder and waits for the eyes to open. I've never asked the others, but I'd imagine most people's reaction would be to scream, or at least try to. I did, when it was my turn. A hand was placed over my mouth to stifle it. The hand smelled of lotion – coconut and lime. It's strange, the things you notice when you're scared out of your mind. Kirsty doesn't try to scream, although her eyes nearly pop right out of her head in shock.

Lily starts the spiel, about Duncraggan's long and illustrious history and how when the time comes, every girl must prove herself. 'Tonight, you are the Chosen One. Rule One: no talking. Rule Two: no screaming, shouting, struggling or biting. Rule Three: no crying to the teachers tomorrow morning. Understood?'

The new girl nods. We whip the duvet off her to see that she's only wearing a T-shirt and a little pair of shorts. 'Give her a dressing gown at least – she'll freeze,' I whisper to Lily.

Lily's leering clown face turns to me. 'Did YOU have a dressing gown? Look, I didn't make up the rules. She'll be fine.'

It's Ama's job to do the blindfolding. Tonight's blindfold is one of those eye masks you get in First Class on a plane (apparently). Kirsty doesn't look particularly scared or worried. Her face is curiously blank. It occurs to me that maybe she thinks this is a dream.

We propel Kirsty through the castle with no problems, other than Ama banging her elbow against the suit of armour at the end of the corridor. (Rowan loves that suit of armour; she calls it Ralph in homage to Judy Blume, which is doubly weird because Rowan definitely does not like penises.)

The three of us let out a sigh of relief when we close the library door behind us. The library is one of my favourite places. It looks like the set of a costume drama: rich red velvet curtains and Persian rugs and fancy old furniture. I even like the slightly fusty, musty smell. Only senior students are allowed in – Maddox says it's a privilege for us to be in the midst of all these boring old books about nineteenth century flora and fauna of the Western Isles and biographies of the Earl of this and the Lord of that. The books that anyone might ever want to actually read are kept in the other library, in the east wing. The best thing about this room is the enormous fireplace. I like it best when it's just me and Rowan in here, sitting on either side of the fire like characters in a gothic novel. We manoeuvre the new girl over to my favourite chair – one of those green leather wingback ones that make you feel like you should smoke cigars. Ama sets her torch on a side table and angles it to face one of the bookcases.

Lily and Ama leave me to guard the prisoner while they get to work on the bookcase. I tuck the torch into the waistband of Kirsty's shorts. She flinches at my touch.

The bookcase is supposed to slide away from the wall but the girls are struggling. 'Well, don't just stand there! Give us a hand!' Lily the Clown sounds stressed.

I grab a shelf and pull. When the bookcase finally starts to move, Lily elbows me in the side. 'We totally loosened it for you.' She runs her fingers around wooden panelling on the wall, until her fingers find the catch that loosens the middle panel. She removes it and sets it aside, revealing an alcove carved out of the stone wall. The Hole. It's tiny. Not high enough to stand up in, not wide enough to lie down in. All you can do is sit and wait for the enemy soldiers or religious persecutors or whoever to give up their search so you can go about your business, ordering your servants around or kicking peasants.

We manage to get the new girl inside and sitting down on the little ledge. 'Put your hand out,' Lily orders, and Kirsty obeys without hesitation.

Lily takes the matchbox from her pocket and places it on Kirsty's palm. 'Right. Please don't go freaking out or anything. No one will hear you if you scream, we know that for a fact. There's nothing to be scared of, it's just a little. . . test. We've all done it. There are forty matches in there. They reckon it says a lot about you, how many matches you use . . . but I wouldn't worry too much about it. Loads of people use all the matches so it's nothing to be ashamed of.' No prizes for guessing that Lily was one of those people. 'There's a bottle of water in there just in case you accidentally set fire to yourself. We'll be back in the morning . . . Um . . . sorry about this . . . and welcome to Duncraggan Castle.'

We remove the blindfold and seal her into the Hole. Rowan's right: it *is* barbaric. Thank God she has that torch. Still, it feels like we're burying the new girl alive.

SIX

At six a.m. on the dot, Ama and I remove the wooden panel and Lily says, 'Wakey, wakey! Rise and shine!' in a too-loud voice. She's impossibly cheery, as if we haven't just subjected a total stranger to a horrible ordeal.

Kirsty's sitting with her knees drawn up to her chest, face buried in the crook of her arms. She finally looks up, blinking and shying away from the torchlight.

We help Kirsty out of the Hole. Her legs give way but Ama and I have hold of her elbows. We sit her down in the chair by the fire and I wrap a blanket around her shoulders. Her feet are a strange colour – almost blue – and she's shivering badly. I wonder if the other two are feeling as guilty as I am.

'Right, let's see how you got on.' Lily holds out her hand and, with some difficulty, the new girl unclenches her fist to reveal the matchbox.

Lily shakes the box and a frown creases her

features. Then she empties the matches into her hand and starts to count. 'Forty! She hasn't used any!'

I manage to dial down my smile to the appropriate level. 'No one's ever done that before, have they, Lil? Rowan holds the current record, doesn't she? I mean *held*.'

Lily crouches down in front of Kirsty. She introduces herself and explains about the Hole, and that we all had to endure it last year. She even apologises, saying she didn't really have any choice in the matter – traditions are traditions. Then she cracks a smile. 'Anyway – you're going to be a bit of a legend after this. Just wait until word gets out that you didn't use a single match! Talk about badass! You're OK, aren't you? You'll be fine once you've warmed up. Nothing a few minutes in a hot shower won't fix . . . right?' She smiles hesitantly. She's *definitely* feeling guilty.

Kirsty stares at her for a few seconds, then she looks up at Ama, and finally at me. Something about her gaze makes me want to look away, but I don't. She licks her chapped lips and says, 'I'll be fine.'

Most people cry when they're let out of the Hole. I did. This girl is acting like nothing untoward has happened – at all. Lily and Ama both smile, relieved.

'I'm sorry about . . . well, everything,' I whisper to Kirsty while the other two are putting the bookcase back in place. 'My name's Harper, by the way. You're Kirsty, right?'

She nods.

'Duncraggan's not always like this, I promise. We're actually not a bad bunch . . . when we're not torturing people.'

She doesn't smile, but that's OK. I wasn't in the mood for smiling either, when they hauled me out of the Hole.

We creep through the castle back to Kirsty's room. Lily and Ama are in the lead, making sure the coast is clear, with Kirsty and me a few paces behind them. I feel her fingers brush against mine, and for the strangest second I think she's trying to hold my hand, but then I feel the cool metal of the torch. I jam it into my back pocket.

Back in Kirsty's room, Lily's conscience starts to get the better of her. She makes sure Kirsty gets straight into bed to warm up a bit before having a hot shower. Then she asks Kirsty if she wants one of us to stay with her, or maybe bring her a cup of tea. Antonia Fletcher wasn't nearly as nice to any of us lot last year.

Kirsty shakes her head. For the first time I noticed that her eyes are bloodshot, either from tiredness or crying.

'OK then,' Lily says in that same bright, shiny voice she used earlier. 'We'll see you at brekker then!

Um . . . congratulations on surviving the Hole. You did . . . really well. You won't tell anyone, will you? Teachers, I mean.'

Another shake of the head.

'Great. Cool. Bye then.' Lily looks at me and shrugs before she and Ama leave the room.

I linger, feeling that there's something else that should be said. If only I had a clue what that something might be. Kirsty is sitting huddled in the duvet, staring into space; the poor girl probably just wants to be left in peace.

My hand is on the doorknob when I realise something. 'How did you know it was me who gave you the torch?'

She looks up at me, eyebrows crinkled.

'How did you know it was me? I mean, you heard Lily's voice so you knew she was moving the bookcase. But it could have been Ama. So how did you know it was me?'

Her confusion clears, and there's a tiny hint of a smile. 'I just knew.'

Something tells me there might be more to Kirsty Connor than meets the eye.

SEVEN

Kirsty doesn't appear at breakfast, but I'm not overly worried. She's probably still in the shower, trying to get some warmth back into her bones. Word starts to spread straightaway, mostly through Ama's stellar efforts. By the time I've finished my second cup of tea, most people in our year are well aware that the new girl is hard as nails. Lily posts a picture of the full matchbox on Instagram (#legend).

Kirsty's not in the same classes as me, so I have to wait till break-time, when Ama reports back that Kirsty missed their first lesson. She turned up to French with a note from the nurse, and Ama overheard her telling the teacher that she had really bad period pains. Apparently Miss Welsh was *très compatissante*, and let her sit quietly for the whole class. Welsh is such a soft touch.

At lunchtime, I look up from my food to see Kirsty standing in the doorway. The clatter and chatter on our side of the room dies down straightaway.

A clap sounds out, echoing off the high ceiling. I crane my neck to see who it is: Marcy Stone. I hate that girl. She's doing this weird, sarcastic sort of slow clap, and it's clearly aimed at Kirsty: like, big deal, you spent a night in total darkness, so fucking what? But then something brilliant happens, and it's all down to Gabi, who (God bless her) starts clapping too, either not realising or not caring that Marcy is trying to take the piss. And even more amazingly, the applause spreads. Rowan's the first to start it up on our table, and of course she has to go one step further, standing up and whooping. Ama, Lily and I join in too, just for the hell of it.

The younger girls on the other side of the room are all looking at each other and gawping at us, completely clueless. Kirsty stands frozen in place in the doorway for a few seconds. She looks around at everyone who's clapping, and everyone who's clapping is looking at her (except for Marcy Stone, who is now doing her best to focus on her lunch), then she just walks over to the queue as if it's no big deal at all.

'That was weird,' I say, spearing a piece of fennel with my fork.

'That was *excellent*,' says Rowan. She pauses, realising the three of us are staring at her. 'I mean, you know I massively disapprove of the Hole – obviously – but still.'

'Still what?' A sly smile creeps across my face.

'Got yourself a little crush on the new girl, is that it?' I'm only messing with her, but then I realise it actually makes sense. *That's* why Rowan wanted me to give Kirsty the torch.

'Yes, you're right. I've fallen madly in love with the new girl.' Rowan fake swoons, putting the back of her wrist up to her forehead. Then she sits up straight again. 'No, dumbass, I do not "have a little crush on the new girl" as you so adorably put it . . . Why? Do *you*?'

I shrug. 'Nah, she's not really my type.'

Ama and Lily are watching us, amused. They're used to this. 'You two are so cute. You would make the *best* couple.' She's talking about me and Rowan, not me and the new girl. Ama suggests this at least once a term, usually when she's drunk.

Rowan jumps in before I can say anything. 'How many times do I have to tell you?! Just because we're both queer does not mean that we fancy each other, right, Harper?' She usually laughs it off, but she seems annoyed.

'Right.'

'God, straight people get on my last nerve sometimes.' Rowan says this – or variations of it – a lot. Mostly to wind up the other two. She starts on this big rant and my attention wanders; I know this stuff off by heart now.

I can't see her at first, but then I see Gabi staring intently at a table in the corner. There she is, alone. I wonder why Kirsty didn't sit next to the same crowd as yesterday. She doesn't look bothered at being by herself – she's not gazing around the room longingly, or anything. She sets about eating her lunch, not looking up even once.

Rowan leans over and whispers, 'You should ask her to sit with us.'

I shake my head.

'Why not?'

'*Why?* I don't even know the girl.'

'Yes. That's kind of how it works with strangers. You talk to them – or, you know, torture them in the middle of the night – and then you get to know them. And then – voilà! – they're no longer strangers.'

'Hilarious. Really. Are you *sure* you don't fancy her?'

'OK, you are allowed to say that one more time – just once – before I officially lose my shit.'

'Sorry,' I say, but I'm not. 'Do you really think I should go over there?' People will look at me, and Kirsty might say no, and then I'd have to traipse back over here looking like a loser.

'Yes! No one should have to sit by themselves like that. It's not right.' Rowan looks over at Kirsty again, then something else catches her eye. 'Go go go! Gabi looks like she's ready to make a move.'

Sure enough Gabi's standing up, laser eyes aimed directly at Kirsty. I can't sit back and let that happen. Gabi means well, she really does. She's a nice girl, but the trouble is that she never wants to be left out – of anything. And the unfortunate consequence of that is it has a tendency to make people *want* to leave her out. Her nickname says it all, really. Gabi Get Involved.

I move fast to head her off. 'Hi . . . me again!' I'm blushing, which makes me furious. How dare my face let me down at a time like this? 'Um . . . I was – *we* were wondering if you wanted to come and sit with us?'

Kirsty cuts a roast potato in half with precise movements. She pops one half into her mouth and chews – one, two, three, four times – before she swallows. She's going to blank me, isn't she? Just because she can't take a joke. Uptight little . . .

'Sure,' she says, standing up with her tray.

She follows me back to our table and I refrain from looking in Gabi's direction, because I've had enough of feeling guilty today.

I sit down first and Kirsty sits next to me. It ruins the symmetry of our little group; four is such a neat number. But I tell myself that Rowan was right –it's the right thing to do. And it's only this once – it's not as if she's going to sit with us every day. She'll find her own friends soon enough.

The introductions are over quickly enough. Rowan insists on shaking Kirsty's hand in an oddly formal gesture that makes Lily and Ama roll their eyes.

'So how are you settling in?' Rowan asks, kindly.

Again with the systematic chewing before Kirsty answers. It makes me think of Jenna. 'Fine, thank you.'

'It's OK, you know. You can tell us the truth.'

Kirsty smiles. It would be exaggerating to say that her face transforms, but it almost does. The smile makes you notice things you might not have noticed before, like the fact that she has blue eyes. They are startlingly, vibrantly blue. Too blue, almost.

'Well, last night wasn't exactly what I was expecting.'

'I'm *so* sorry about that,' says Lily. 'You know, maybe Rowan's right and I should put an end to the Hole, at least for this year. Next year's head girl can do whatever the fuck she likes, but I'm out.' I'm almost certain she's just saying this for Kirsty's benefit and that she'll have forgotten all her apparent fit of conscience as soon as next term rolls around.

Rowan takes her at her word. 'Better you put a stop to it before someone *dies* in there – anything could happen . . . panic attack, asthma attack. Pretty sure that would fuck up your chances of getting an interview at Oxford, don't you think?'

'I was elected head girl at my old school, but I

left before I even got my badge.' Kirsty doesn't seem like typical head girl material, but then neither does Lily, I suppose.

'Watch out, Lil, sounds like you've got competition,' I tease. 'Don't forget Kirsty didn't use a single match in the Hole . . . She's clearly not someone to mess with . . . particularly in dark, confined spaces.'

Kirsty says nothing, but her smiling eyes meet mine. I glance sideways at Rowan, feeling a twinge of guilt for taking credit for her kindness. Rowan doesn't look annoyed though, and you can usually tell. She's the most open of open books. Still, I make a mental note to tell Kirsty that the torch wasn't my idea. Credit where credit's due.

'So why did you leave your old school?' Ama asks, fixing Kirsty with her friendly-yet-interrogatory stare. She likes collecting people's stories, wheedling information out of them so that before you know it she knows the name of the imaginary friend you had when you were five.

'I wanted a change of scene,' says Kirsty, shrugging.

'Well that's vague. We'll get the truth out of you though. Just like we did with Harper – *eventually*.'

'Ama!' Rowan is appalled. I am too, but I hide it better.

'Sorry.' Ama winces, and I can tell she's trying to catch my eye, but I won't let her.

Rowan forces out a laugh. 'Anyone would think we're in prison, the way you talk about it! "What are you in for? Drunk and disorderly, nothing major."'

Kirsty has stopped eating now. Her knife and fork are placed neatly on the empty plate. 'Why did you come to Duncraggan, Harper?' she asks.

'I . . .' There's no way I'm telling her.

Rowan slaps her hand on the table, hard enough to rattle the cutlery. 'Why don't we talk about something else? Like . . .'

'Recycling!' Lily comes to the rescue, in her own way. 'I've got a meeting with Maddox tomorrow about the bins in our rooms. It's ridiculous that all that stuff just goes to landfill when most of it can be recycled. I found these bins online the other night. They've got different compartments and they're not that expensive if you buy in bulk.'

Kirsty raises her eyebrows, clearly intrigued. Not about recycling, but about my friends' blatant attempts to deflect attention from me.

I look down at my plate. A single roast potato sits there. Too pale. Roast potatoes should be golden, and crispy round the edges. It was the roast potatoes that did it. And the turkey. And the sausages wrapped in bacon. And the million other side dishes that Mum insisted on serving up for Christmas dinner.

Dad said it was tradition – over-eating at Christmas.

49

He said 'it's just what people do, isn't it?' But when I lay down on my bed after lunch, my stomach bloated and aching, feeling sick and fat and ashamed, I knew he was wrong. Jenna hadn't eaten too much. She'd refused a second helping of roast potatoes, hadn't had any bread sauce, and left some of her turkey. It was just Dad and I who'd completely pigged out. That was exactly the right word. Pigged. I was a disgusting fat pig. There was no way I would fit into my favourite jeans in time for Jackson Frith's party. It was only a couple of weeks away and I was really, really hoping that his older sister was going to be there.

Jenna came upstairs to tell me that Dad was passed out on the sofa, and that we should draw on his face. It was a bit of a Christmas tradition in our house. At least, it had been until Jenna accidentally used a permanent marker to draw teardrops on his cheeks a couple of years before.

She found me lying in the dark, crying. It didn't take long for her to get the truth out of me. I could never lie to Jenna.

'You're *not* fat,' she said, stroking my hair. 'Annoying? Yes. Fat? No.'

I got out of bed and put the light on. I took off my top and stood in front of my sister. 'What do you call this, then?' I pinched the fat between my fingers, so hard that it hurt.

Jenna shrugged. 'Um . . . skin? Flesh? Stuff that covers your skeleton?'

She had no idea what it was like. It might be OK for normal people, but not for twins. I was well aware of the looks people gave me. They'd look at me, then Jenna, then back at me. *Oh, so you're the* fat *twin*. You try walking around next to someone who's exactly like you in every single way, apart from the one that people always notice. There wasn't *that* much difference between us, I knew that. A few pounds at most. But it was enough.

I let Jenna talk me round, or at least, I pretended to. I nodded and smiled when she said that I wasn't fat and that I was perfect the way I was. She said I was just a bit more muscular than she was. And when I confessed that I was worried about what to wear to Jackson Frith's party, she said we'd use our Christmas money and go shopping together in the sales.

We went downstairs and drew on Dad's face (Harry Potter glasses and lightning bolt scar). Later, when Mum brought a plate of turkey sandwiches through just in time for the Doctor Who Christmas Special, I said I wasn't hungry.

By bedtime I was starving. When everyone else had gone upstairs I stood in front of the open fridge, eating slice after slice of ham. That was when I decided: I would allow myself one more slice, but then I was

51

going to do something about this. I reassessed: there were three family parties to get through between Christmas and New Year. So there was no point starting now. It would have to be New Year's Day.

It wouldn't be a diet; diets were for middle-aged women who drank too much wine and ate too much cake. It would be a health regime. Just for a few weeks, to get me back on track. Now all I had to do was persuade Jenna to do it with me. Looking back, my logic was flawed. I could have kept quiet – exercised more and watched my eating habits in secret. Then *she'd* have ended up being the fat twin. It never even occurred to me.

But Jenna was always more driven than me. She got better grades because she studied more. She had more friends because she made the effort to keep them. She *cared* more, it was as simple as that. If this was going to work – if I was going to lose enough weight to fit into those jeans – I was going to need her help.

EIGHT

'You must be insane.' A grinning face looms over me, eclipsing the morning sun. I'd forgotten she was here; there's something about swimming lengths that lulls me into a trance-like state.

I smile back as I take off my goggles and shake the water from my ears. 'You should try it sometime.' I boost myself out of the pool and Kirsty hands me my towel. I rub my arms to try to get some feeling back into them.

'No chance. You look colder than I was in the Hole. How can you stand it?!' She shivers even though she's wearing a red school hoodie and jogging bottoms.

I must be the only person at Duncraggan who prefers this pool to the indoor one. Most girls treat it like it's some kind of punishment. They squeal and shriek and scream when they're forced to do a couple of lengths. They don't understand that the cold is part of the joy of it. Those few seconds after you get in, when you're sure you can't bear it and your body will shut down if you don't get out immediately and get yourself into a hot shower. That's why I do it. The shock to the system, the shortness of breath, the awareness of every single part of your body. Feeling awake and *alive*.

Swimming always makes me think of Jenna. She loved it, even when we were little. I was scared of the water, but she had no fear. I can still picture five-year-old Jenna standing on the side of our local pool, decked out in her pink and black polka dot swimsuit, hands on hips, orange inflatable armbands circling her upper arms. It's the deep end of the pool, and Dad's treading water a few feet away. She jumps without hesitation, making an enormous splash as she sinks and then bobs to the surface, giggling. Dad would try to get me to do the same but I refused to stray from the shallow end of the kids' pool.

Jenna stopped swimming when she was twelve, suddenly self-conscious of her body. I was glad, because it didn't feel right that she loved something I didn't enjoy. It made us too different, and we weren't meant to be different.

I only became interested in swimming when I came here and saw this pool. They call it the ducker, because they have weird names for everything here. Of course I thought of *Malory Towers*, and Darrell swimming in the pool cut out of the rocks by the sea. The ducker isn't quite as cool – it's just boring old concrete – but the setting is incredible. Close enough to the cliffs that you can float on your back and watch the herring gulls swoop and circle overhead. I looked at the pool and thought of Jenna and knew that I had to swim here. Rowan came with me the first few times – even the strongest swimmers in school aren't allowed to swim alone. Student drownings have a tendency to put off parents thinking of sending their little darlings to Duncraggan, apparently.

At first the outdoor swimming was an obligation – doing something she never got the chance to do – but I grew to love it. My technique is sloppy but I don't mind. I'm not doing this to be good at it. Mr Tovey keeps trying to get me to train with the swim team and I keep telling him it's never going to happen. 'But you clearly love swimming!' he says, exasperated, and I tell him that that's the point. I love it for what it is; competition would ruin that. I've never been a competitive person. Not like Jenna.

Kirsty and I dash to the green hut that serves as a changing room for the ducker. We don't even stop to admire the rampant red sunrise, peppered with wispy cirrus clouds.

When we reach the hut, Kirsty puts a hand out to

55

stop me. A spider has woven its web across the porch and sits right in the middle, at head height. A face full of spider is never a good start to the day.

Carefully, Kirsty puts her hand through the side of the web, the silken strands catching on her fingers. She draws the web to one side, depositing it against the wooden post. The spider scuttles to safety under the eaves. Meanwhile, I'm freezing my arse off.

'You could have just killed it.'

'I like spiders,' she says. 'I don't understand why everyone hates them so much.'

'Because they're creepy little fuckers who have a tendency to lurk in dark places?'

She laughs. 'That's one way of putting it, I suppose.'

I head over to the worn wooden bench with my stuff on it. 'Thanks so much for coming with me. You really didn't have to.'

'It's really no trouble, honestly.'

Since Rowan decided sleep was more important than solidarity, Lily's been the one coming with me in the mornings. She sets out her yoga mat next to the pool. On colder days she switches to tai chi. Last night we were making tea in the kitchen after banco when Lily told me she thought she'd pulled a muscle in her leg and probably wouldn't be up for yoga for a while. Plus, she said, the early starts were killing her this term.

I'm not going to lie – I was kind of annoyed. I couldn't go without my morning swim. But of course I said it was fine, and she should get matron to have a look at that leg, maybe see if she could see a physiotherapist in town.

'I can do it,' a voice emerged from the hallway. Kirsty came in with an empty mug, and squeezed past us to get to the sink. There was barely enough space for the three of us, so I backed out into the doorway.

I was tempted to ask how long she'd been out there, listening in. But maybe Lily had just been loud. Her voice does have a tendency to carry. (Rowan describes it as 'braying', but only when Lil's not around.)

Lily was delighted to be off the hook. 'Nice one, Kirsty,' she said, and left with her steaming mug of peppermint tea.

There was nothing for me to do but accept the offer. I'd even let Marcy Stone come with me if it meant I got to keep swimming. I gave Kirsty one last chance to get out of it. 'Are you sure? I'm usually in the pool by six-fifteen.'

'I know. My room overlooks it, remember? And I wake up early too. I . . . I don't sleep all that well. Anyway, I can bring a book or something. It'll be nice to get some fresh air before breakfast.'

I didn't correct her. Everyone – apart from me

— calls it brekker here, making already posh people sound extra posh. I thanked her, and said I'd knock for her at ten past in the morning. I went back to my room, feeling oddly exposed. Had she been sitting on her window seat every morning, watching me glide through the water below?

I did like her, even though I wasn't quite sure at first. She was a little quiet, especially the first couple of times she sat with us in the dining hall. I *definitely* liked the fact that she didn't just assume she could sit with us after that one lunchtime. At dinner that day she took her tray and went over to an empty table. The four of us quickly conferred and decided that it would be OK for her to sit with us. Everyone thinks we're too cliquey anyway.

It was strange at first, getting used to someone else being with us at every meal. Some of the conversations were a bit stilted, and we had to go easy on the in-jokes. But it got a little easier, a little more comfortable, every time. She was still quieter than the rest of us, but it can be hard for anyone to get a word in when we're in full flow.

Kirsty sits on the bench as I dry myself properly and attempt to get the blood flowing again. There's no heating in the hut, and the single shower isn't even worthy of the name. I bet they never show *this* to the parents on Open Days; it's not exactly in keeping with Duncraggan's reputation of 'state-of-the-art facilities in an idyllic historical setting'.

It's quiet in here, and suddenly I feel awkward in my swimsuit while Kirsty is fully dressed. I hurriedly pull on leggings and a hoodie over my still-damp swimsuit.

I'm leaning across Kirsty to grab my flip-flops when her hand reaches up towards my face. I automatically flinch but try to disguise it, brushing my hair from my face.

'I just wanted to look at your necklace. It's so pretty.'

'Oh, right. Yeah, thanks.' I sit down next to her and start rolling up my towel.

'May I?' Her hand reaches out again and there's nothing I can do but sit still. I feel trapped.

She lifts the pendant and holds it for a second or two. Her face is close to mine. Finally, after too long, she lets go and sits back. I resist the urge to check that the pendant is fine. Of course it's fine.

'Where did you get it?'

I'm so tempted to lie. I would definitely lie if she were a stranger, or some other random, but Kirsty's not going anywhere so I might as well get this over with now. I don't need Rowan to help me out this time. Perhaps that's progress.

'It was my sister's.' I concentrate on the floor, my wet footprints still visible on the cracked concrete.

I expect Kirsty to ask if my sister gave it to me or whether I nicked it from her jewellery box, something like that. But she must have noticed my tone of voice. I didn't even try to hide it, like I usually do whenever the subject of sisters or families comes up.

'What happened to her?' she asks.

'She died.' I manage to force out the words without a hitch in my voice or tears in my eyes. Definitely progress.

'I'm sorry.'

It used to infuriate me. I wanted to shout WHAT HAVE YOU GOT TO BE SORRY ABOUT?! IT'S NOT YOUR FAULT, IS IT? But that was before I realised that they're just words that people say. They're the words you're supposed to say, and *not* saying them makes it look like you have no shits to give.

After the 'I'm sorry' and the appropriate amount of time (usually around four or five seconds), most people ask what happened to her. They want to know *how* she died. I used to think it was downright nosiness, but now I think it's not quite so simple; it's morbid curiosity too. When someone old dies, people aren't that surprised. Old people die all the time, after all. But a teenage girl . . . there must be a juicy story there, surely?

Kirsty *doesn't* ask, and that's why I tell her. It doesn't take long; I don't go into detail or anything. I certainly don't tell her about my role in it.

She exhales. 'That's fucking awful.' And something about the way she says it – so brutally honest and not trying to gloss over it – makes me laugh out loud, the sound echoing off the floor and around the glossy green tiles.

Kirsty laughs too, just a little. 'Sorry, was that the wrong thing to say?'

There are tears in my eyes and I suddenly worry that she must think I'm a freak, laughing when I talk about my dead twin. I try to rein it in a bit. 'No! Not at all! Sorry, I know it's not funny – at all – but . . . I don't know . . . it *is* fucking awful.'

My laughter trickles away down the drain when I see Kirsty's face change. Any trace of a smile is gone now.

'Are you OK?'

'I'm fine.'

'What is it?' I lean forward and down a bit, trying to catch her eye.

She shakes her head.

'OK, if you're sure . . .' I leave that hanging in the air for a little. Just in case she changes her mind. She does.

'I lost my sister too.'

NINE

'Oh.' That's the best I can do? I've been expecting people to say the right thing despite the fact that there *is* no right thing, and *that's* what I come up with? Try again. 'God, I'm sorry. That's . . . wow.' I really am as useless at this as everyone else. I never appreciated how hard it is.

I want to ask what happened. Of course I do; it's only human after all. I manage to resist, and she tells me of her own accord. A car accident, four years ago. Kirsty was thirteen when her sixteen-year-old sister died. Is that better or worse than what happened to me? Losing a twin is hard to beat in the Trauma Olympics.

Kirsty asks me not to tell anyone else – not even Rowan. As if she somehow knew that would have been the first thing I'd have done when I got back to my room. I don't ask why she doesn't want anyone else to know. It's up to her, just like it was up to me not to say anything when I got here.

'What was her name?'

Kirsty takes a long shaky breath. 'Rhiannon.'

'It's a pretty name.' I'm going to have to dig myself out of this cliché hole right away before I say something like 'She's in a better place'.

I decide to go with humour – an attempt, at least. 'So I guess that means we're the founding members of the Dead Sisters Club.'

She doesn't know how to react to that, which is fair enough.

'DSC is *the* most exclusive society at Duncraggan Castle. Current membership: two. I wonder if Maddox would give us funding for trips and stuff. I heard the junior ski team are getting ten grand to go to the world championships next term.'

She finally gets it, and laughs. 'We may have to recruit some new members first.'

'Hmm. You're right. That's going to be tricky. Dead sisters is quite a niche market. Maybe we should branch out? Dead Mums? Dads? Goldfish?' It feels strange to be joking about this, but it also feels good. Like a pressure valve has been released somewhere deep inside of me.

As we're walking back to the castle, the wind whipping our hair around our faces, I decide that I want to be friends with Kirsty Connor. The Dead Sisters Club thing may have been a stupid joke, but

I'm glad I said it. There aren't many people who really get it. Rowan tries, but she doesn't *know*. It's not her fault – how could she possibly know what it's like? She doesn't even have a sister in the first place. Kirsty knows though. And as sorry as I am that her sister had to die for this to be the case, I can't help feeling a little bit grateful.

What is it Dad always used to say?

Misery loves company.

On Saturday afternoon, most of Fairclough is helping out in the gardens. The houses take it in turns, and we all end up doing two or three hours every week. I don't mind. I like being outside. I like how the earth feels when it crumbles under my fingers.

Actually, a lot of the girls are surprisingly enthusiastic about gardening duty. Surprising, that is, if you've never seen Marek Koslow, who magically appeared last Easter, after the previous head gardener retired or died or something. I have no idea what Maddox was thinking. Although I suppose she has to hire the best person for the job, whatever he happens to look like. It just so happens he looks like he was genetically engineered to appeal to ninety per cent of straight girls. He's tall and muscular and tanned and his favoured attire is a white vest and cut-off jeans and big black boots.

I don't fancy him; I agree with Ama that he's too

obvious-looking. Lily, however, practically starts panting whenever she sees him. She was the first to volunteer to help Marek with the digging for the new flowerbeds he's planning.

Rowan's at an away match with the lacrosse team, which means we're at least spared the terrible 'lady garden' jokes. Ama, Kirsty and I are weeding the vegetable patch, but I can see Marek and Lily from where we are. Marek's showing Lily how to mark out the flowerbed with twine before they start digging. Maybe it's my imagination, but Lily seems to be bending over a bit more than is strictly necessary, ensuring Marek has the perfect view of her arse.

I tell the other two and we stop to watch.

Ama shakes her head. 'Man, she's got it bad. And check out the look on Marcy's face! Jealous or what?' Marcy and Tatiana are glaring in Lily's direction, and I want to cheer when Lily pulls her hoodie over her head, exposing her tanned stomach.

Ama makes this big show of turning her back on Lily and Marek. She leans on her hoe. 'Let me know if they start boning in the begonias. What do you think, Kirsty? Would you?'

'Would I what?'

Ama's surprised that Kirsty doesn't understand, but she doesn't take the piss out of her at least. 'Would you have sex with Marek?'

Kirsty grimaces. 'I . . . um . . . isn't he sort of like a teacher?'

'It's purely theoretical, of course.' Ama grins wickedly. 'Besides, if the answer's *yes* you'd have to get to the back of a very long *theoretical* queue. That's assuming you do like boys. Not that I would ever assume such a thing. I've been on the receiving end of Rowan's lectures about the evils of heteronormativity enough times to know better.'

'I like boys.'

'*Just* boys?' Ama slings her arm around me. 'Or are you also partial to the ladies like our friend Harper here?'

'Ama!' I shove her away from me, not altogether playfully.

'What? It's not like it's a secret!' She's laughing, not remotely bothered that I'm blushing. I have no reason to blush but that doesn't seem to make a difference.

'I never said it was!' I look at Kirsty who seems entirely baffled by the conversation. 'Sorry, Kirsty, Ama isn't exactly known for her tact. All that time practising piano instead of interacting with people – it takes its toll, I guess.'

Ama chucks one of her gardening gloves at me, so I chuck a handful of weeds at her face. She squeals, which catches Marek's attention and he shouts at us to stop messing around.

'He's so *commanding*,' Ama says under her breath, making me giggle.

It's not till later when we're washing our hands at the sink behind the greenhouse that Kirsty tells me she doesn't fancy Marek. She says it awkwardly, so instead of making a joke, I say, 'That makes two of us.'

'I won't tell anyone. About you being . . . you know . . .'

'Bi? Oh God, don't worry about it. Ama was right – it really isn't a secret. Anyway, people round here have got better things to do than gossip about me – I'm far too boring.'

'I don't think you're boring,' Kirsty says, painfully earnest. 'You're one of the most interesting people I've ever met.'

I shake my head, smiling. 'You are far too nice for this place, Connor.' I don't say what I'm thinking, which is that she really needs to get out more.

'Lily's leg seems to be OK,' she says.

'Mmm?'

'She thought she'd pulled a muscle, didn't she? I was worried when I saw her doing all that digging. I'm glad she's feeling better.'

I walk on in silence. I should have known Lil was just looking for an excuse to get out of chumming me down to the pool. Actually that's not quite fair – she did say that the early mornings were starting to be an issue.

'If it's OK, I'd be happy to keep coming with you in the mornings.'

'Of course. As long as it's not too annoying?'

'Not at all. It's . . . peaceful.'

I warn her that it's going to start getting cold soon – *really* cold. 'You'll need to wrap up warm.'

'Thanks, *Mum*,' she says sarcastically. Just as I'm starting to laugh, she frowns and hurries on ahead of me. She can be odd like that, sometimes. Good thing I like odd.

TEN

Term rolls on, the leaves start to fall from the trees, and all anyone can talk about is university. Lily's busy working on her Oxford application and equally busy trying to get Rowan to apply too. She knows Ama's a lost cause because there are better places to study Music. She knows I'm a lost cause because my grades aren't good enough.

I'm not even sure I want to *go* to university, but that's not a thing you can say at Duncraggan. Every time I sit down to start work on my UCAS personal statement, I feel overwhelmed. How do you sum yourself up in four thousand characters? My parents are on my case – every phone call and email mentions it at least once. They don't say it, but the implication is there: now that you're going to this fancy-pants school you'd better do something decent with your life. It's enough to make me want to bury my head in the sand for ever.

Lily's started her yoga again, but she gets up later and goes to the dance studio. I don't mind, because Kirsty and I have established a nice little morning routine. She always brings a book with her, but whenever I look up from the pool, she's never reading.

After my swim, we usually sit in the changing rooms and talk. Sometimes I cut my time in the pool short so that we have longer. Rowan's noticed and moans if I'm late for breakfast. I tell her that she doesn't need to wait for me, but she always does, even when she's starving.

The changing room may not be warm, or welcoming, but it's private and you soon realise that privacy is the most precious commodity at boarding school. It turns out that Kirsty and I have more in common than I thought – not just the dead sister thing. We like a lot of the same bands and the same films and TV shows. It's funny how I might never have got to know her if the guilt of putting her through the Hole hadn't pushed us to invite her to sit at our table. She could have become best friends with Gabi Get Involved and I would never have known that the quiet girl on the other side of the dining hall was a potential friend.

We talk about Jenna a lot. I find myself glad when Kirsty asks about her; the others never do. It's actually nice to show Kirsty the photos on my phone, and tell her about the stupid stuff we used to get up to, like the time I came up with a whole secret language for the two of us and Jenna flat-out refused to use it because it was such a twin cliché. Kirsty asks a lot about the twin thing – I've never understood why people are so fascinated by it. I suppose things always feel normal from the inside.

It feels like Kirsty's one of us now. Sometimes she's so quiet at mealtimes that you almost forget she's there, but then she'll ask a question or make an observation and you realise that she brings something to our little gang. She looks at things differently, as if she's seeing us all through a brand-new lens. Which is exactly what she is doing, if you think about it – bringing fresh eyes to the absurdity of Duncraggan life. I suppose I did that, once.

She's genuinely interested in what people have to say. She quizzes Ama about her volunteering at the equestrian centre (the rest of us make a point of yawning whenever Ama talks about horses). She'll ask Lily about the latest Marek sightings. Maybe the questions serve to deflect attention away from herself, but so what? It's not easy being shy here – Duncraggan girls seem to have more than their fair share of self-confidence. It was one of the first things I noticed. There's never a shortage of volunteers for anything involving public speaking, and oral presentations seem to be second nature for most people. Things were very different at my last school. People were normal there.

Yesterday I finally told Kirsty about the lottery win, mostly because of something Lily had said the night before. We'd been watching *The Apprentice* in the TV room and ended up talking about jobs. Lil mentioned that the starting salary of her brother's job down in London was 'barely enough to live on'. Forty-six thousand pounds, for fuck's sake.

I didn't say anything, since everyone else was murmuring their agreement. But that night I went to bed thinking of all the things I could and should have said. Sometimes it's hard being around people whose families have always had money. They tend to forget that I'm not like them. We never went on holiday to St Barts or Dubai or the Maldives; we went to the Trossachs or the Yorkshire Dales or camping in Brittany (once). Rowan is better than Ama and Lily at remembering that I'm different. She's always ready to tell Ama to check her privilege if she whines about the fact that her parents won't buy her the latest MacBook Air even though hers is '*well* over a year old'. But Rowan wasn't there that night because she would never be caught dead watching reality TV, and I didn't mention it to her when I got back to our room. I knew exactly what she'd say: Lily didn't mean anything by it and would be horrified if she knew how upset I was. Rowan would have been right – she usually is – but sometimes you just need to vent. I knew Kirsty would listen without judging me, but I needed to tell her about the lottery win so that she could see where I was coming from.

I cut short my swim by ten minutes to make sure I'd have enough time to offload. I started off by telling Kirsty what Lily had said, and that it frustrated me that she had no concept of the value of money. Then I explained about the lottery, and Dad being a postman and that time the ancient TV broke and we couldn't afford to get a new one for six months.

Kirsty listened attentively and didn't act all excited about the lottery thing. Instead she said it must have been terrible, that happening right after losing Jenna. I could have hugged her. Some people are spectacularly tactless about it. ('*Such a shame about your sister dying, but at least you're really rich now, yeah*?' No one's said those exact words, but not far from it.)

I felt so much better that everything was out in the open, but I realised I'd essentially just been talking *at* Kirsty for fifteen minutes. 'You don't have to keep doing this, you know? Coming down here. I won't be annoyed.'

She looked taken aback. 'Why? Don't you want me to?'

'No! I mean, yes! I just meant that I don't want you to think that you *have* to.'

'I *want* to. I just . . . it's nice to spend time with you, without the others. Does that sound really bad?'

'No, not at all.' I felt oddly flattered, almost a little embarrassed.

'Don't get me wrong, I like the others. I really like them. But I feel like I have more in common with you.' She was fiddling with the bookmark lodged in her book – the same book she'd been reading for a good two weeks now. It was a short book.

'There's nothing wrong with that,' I said. 'Dead Sisters Club secret handshake?' I held out my hand and we made up a stupid, elaborate handshake and the laughter glossed over any awkwardness between us.

After lessons, Kirsty walked with me to the clay-pigeon range. She was thinking of signing up for it as one of her extracurriculars, but she wanted to try it first.

The winding path through the woods is straight out of a fairy-tale. The first time I saw the red and white speckled hats of the fly agaric mushrooms sprouting from the moss I could have sworn they were fake. When Rowan tires of scanning the skies for seabirds, she sometimes comes down here with her binoculars to look for deer and red squirrels. She usually finds girls smoking weed instead.

I was telling Kirsty about the time Rowan spied on some Year 8s dabbling with Wicca when she suddenly said, 'My parents aren't rich either. Not even close.'

It took me a second or two to process the subject switch. 'Did they win the lottery too? Or rob a bank so you could come here?'

'I got a scholarship.'

'Really?'

She nodded. 'Otherwise there's no way my parents would be able to afford it.'

'Did you have to do some kind of test or something? Or did they just go by your grades at your last school?'

'It was a combination of both, I think? Anyway, I don't want anyone knowing about it. The scholarship, I mean.'

'It's nothing to be ashamed of. No one's going to think any less of you just because your parents aren't loaded.' That wasn't strictly true. Off the top of my head I could think of at least five girls who *would* think less of her.

'I know, but it's just . . . it's private, you know? It makes me different, and I don't want that.' Her voice was thick, full of tears about to spill.

I put my hand on her shoulder and we stopped walking. 'Different is good,' I said gently.

The wind whispered through the branches above our heads and Kirsty was silent, staring at me. 'Do you really think so?'

'Definitely,' I said. And I meant it.

*

Rowan and I are lounging on our beds, throwing a tennis ball lazily back and forth. Rowan says that it helps her think, the rhythm of it. I only join in because otherwise she'd just annoy me, chucking the ball against the wall by my bed.She's been quiet all day, but I haven't asked what's up. Rowan has a tendency to clam up if you push her.

I try to get her talking by telling her about a video I found online about intersectional feminism, but she's not biting. She nods and says she'll check it out sometime. I know it's only a matter of time before she tells me what's bothering her, so I wait.

'So,' she says, after a couple more minutes of ball-chucking.

'So what?' I said, throwing the ball a little too hard, nearly hitting her face. She manages to catch it though.

'You and Kirsty.' Rowan keeps the ball, throwing it from one hand to the other.

'You know that totally doesn't count as juggling, right?' She gives me a withering stare and I laugh. 'Me and Kirsty what?'

'I dunno . . . you two are spending quite a bit of time together.' She's embarrassed; Rowan doesn't really *do* embarrassed.

'And . . .?' I say, but Rowan just shrugs. 'Are you *jealous*? Is that it?' I smirk.

'No!' Rowan drops the ball, which rolls across the

floor and under my bed. She crawls to retrieve it. 'You really need to hide that booze better, Kent. I know Renner's pretty lax on the room inspections, but still.'

I wait.

She flops back on the bed. 'OK, OK! I'm a *tiny* bit jealous,' she says. She holds her thumb and index finger a few millimetres apart to show exactly how tiny her jealousy is.

I want to laugh, because the idea is so absurd. But one look at her face tells me it wouldn't help the situation.

Before I can say anything, Rowan makes a sound of disgust. 'Sorry. I know it's pathetic. Completely and utterly pathetic. Forget I said anything. Anyway . . .' She gets up and busies herself rearranging the folders on her desk. 'I need to finish my essay and *you* need to start working on your UCAS form. Just write any old bullshit and I can polish it for you.'

I wait until she's sitting at her desk, shoulders too tight, before I sneak over and hug her from behind. 'I think it's *adorable* that you're jealous.' I ruffle her hair for good measure.

'I hate you,' she says, but I can hear the smile in her voice.

'I *love* you,' I say, ducking my head to try to get her to look me in the eyes. 'I'm sorry if I've been neglecting you . . .'

She swivels her chair round to face me. 'You haven't been "neglecting" me. I'm not some orphaned puppy, you know. I shouldn't have said anything.'

'I'm glad you did. I'm sorry.' I'm not entirely sure what I'm apologising for, but it seems to smooth things over with Rowan. It's easier to say those two words than to explain why I enjoy spending time with Kirsty. No one else knows how much the two of us have in common. And for some reason I like it that way.

ELEVEN

'Happy Friendiversary!' Kirsty says when I get out of the pool.

'Happy *what*?' I say, shivering. There's a biting north-easterly wind blowing in off the sea. It's dark, too. In a few weeks the ducker will be closed for the winter, so I have to make the most of it while I still can – even if it feels a little bit like torture.

'We've been friends for a month. If you count from the day of the Hole, when you gave me the torch . . .' I must look baffled because she suddenly frowns and mumbles, 'We are friends, aren't we?'

'Of course we are!' It's quite sweet, how awkward she is. 'Friendiversary, eh? Have you bought me flowers? Gonna put a ring on it?' I say, holding up my left hand.

'Um . . . I . . . what?'

'I'm kidding!' I laugh and after a beat or two she does too.

'I'm such an idiot,' she says when we're back in the

relative warmth of the hut. 'You must think I'm ridiculous.'

'I don't think that.'

My hoodie gets stuck as I try to pull it over my head. Kirsty helps me out, pulling on the hood and patting it down. 'It's just that I've never really had a friend like you before, and I woke up this morning and realised the Hole was exactly a month ago and time has gone so quickly. Don't you think? It feels like I've known you a lot longer than a month.' She pulls on one of the drawstrings so that both are the same length. 'I hope you don't think I'm weird.'

'I think you're just the perfect amount of weird, as it happens. Happy Friendiversary to you too.' I say the next words because it feels like the right thing to do, even if the others will be annoyed. 'I think I know *exactly* how to celebrate.'

I refuse to elaborate, even though Kirsty begs me to. I tell her she needs to wrap up warmly and be ready to go at one a.m. Of course she immediately thinks it's a rerun of the Hole, or something similarly traumatic. I reassure her that she's got nothing to worry about. 'It will be fun, I *promise*.'

Rowan takes a little convincing. 'But it's *our* thing! Just the four of us. What if she tells someone?'

I say that I can vouch for Kirsty; there's no way

she'd tell anyone. So Rowan's tries a slightly different tactic, saying it's too big a risk for Lily as head girl. But Lil says she's cool with it – probably because she's still feeling bad about what we put Kirsty through.

I hound Rowan all day. I even trail her to the theatre after lessons and help her paint the forest backdrop for *Into the Woods*. 'Look, Harper, I appreciate the help, but your attempts at bribery are *not* subtle.'

'I am good at painting branches though, aren't I? I think I've found my calling.'

Rowan shakes her head and we carry on painting in silence. After a while, she speaks. 'Why are you so keen for her to come tonight?'

I think carefully before answering. 'I think it would be nice. For her, I mean. And . . . I don't know . . . It's not easy to come here when everyone already knows each other. It wasn't easy for me, but you let me in. You, and Ama and Lil.'

Rowan sighs. '*Fine*. Bring her along.' I knew she'd cave; Rowan's sense of decency is off the scale. 'And don't think for one second that I don't realise you just played me like a cheap violin.'

At five minutes past one, the five of us are standing in front of the fire door in the kitchens.

'Are you sure?' Ama asks for the second time. 'What if they've fixed it over the holidays?'

Rowan doesn't seem worried. 'Why don't we open it and find out?' She gives the metal bar on the door a shove and the door opens. Ama and Lily wince, but the alarm doesn't sound, and Maddox doesn't come tearing round the corner in her nightie, ready to expel the lot of us.

'When are you lot going to learn to trust me?' Rowan asks with a smile as she steps back to let us pass.

'Where are we going?' Kirsty whispers when we're all safely outside. She hasn't moved from my side since we collected her from the turret room.

'You'll see!' It's better if it's a surprise.

Rowan props the door open so we can get back in later. 'Follow me. And Kirsty? Try not to fall off the cliff.' She takes the lead, moving in a low, crouching sort of run.

'Um . . . please tell me you're not going to push me off a cliff,' Kirsty whispers when we're past the tennis courts and it's clear that we are, in fact, headed for the cliffs just north of the school. I squeeze her arm to reassure her. We hurry across the astro pitch and duck behind the spectator stand that was erected last year. I'm pretty sure Rowan's dad paid for it so that more people could watch her kick ass at lacrosse, but Rowan denies it. From here it's plain sailing because we're no longer visible from any of the windows.

The cliff steps are strictly out of bounds; there's

an iron chain barring the way and a red 'DANGER' sign. Plus Maddox makes a point of mentioning it at the first assembly of every term. It's annoying because it's by far the quickest way down to the beach.

Kirsty looks dubious when Rowan hops over the chain and starts down the steps, followed by Lily and Ama.

'It's safe,' I say. 'Promise.'

Thankfully the steps are dry tonight. When they're slick with rain and bird shit, it's a whole different story. Even now it's not exactly easy going – the treads have been crudely carved into the cliff face, each one not quite deep enough for your foot. Whoever did the carving was either in a hurry or had tiny feet.

About halfway down, a ledge juts out from the cliff. Rowan was down here one day on the lookout for some lesser-spotted wotsit bird when she noticed it.

Getting from the cliff steps on to the ledge is the ever-so-slightly tricky bit. It's not a huge distance – sixty centimetres at most. It's a decent-sized step that wouldn't be a big deal under normal circumstances, but it feels a little different when the moon shines down on to the rocks below.

Kirsty doesn't even hesitate. She just follows Rowan's lead as if it's the most natural thing in the world. I watch as she disappears into the rock face.

TWELVE

'Pretty cool, right?' I say, taking a bottle of vodka out of my rucksack and placing it on the bar – a grey piece of driftwood that Rowan wedged into a nook in the wall. She even carved the word 'BAR' into it for good measure.

We keep our coats on because the cave is freezing, even though it looks cosy with all the fairy lights. Those were Ama's idea. They make the place look a bit more festive and a bit less like we should be skinning a sabre-toothed tiger as we crouch in front of the fire. Not that we have a fire. What we do have is a pile of glowsticks that Rowan arranges to look like one. Never mind the fact that it doesn't give off even a hint of heat.

It's quite sheltered here though. The gap in the rock is narrow – just wide enough to squeeze through if you turn sideways.

'What is this place?' Kirsty asks, running her hand over the wall.

'This,' says Rowan, stretching her arms out wide, 'is our little secret. Never to be discussed with anyone outside the group – ever.'

Lily and Ama sit down on their usual rocks and Kirsty sits on the ground. I sit next to her, instead of my usual spot next to Lil. Rowan starts sorting out the drinks, muttering about the fact that no one thought to bring a mixer.

'Hey! I brought the vodka! I can't be expected to think of everything. Plus I had to do some hardcore flirting with Creepy John to get him to serve me.' I shudder at the memory. Creepy John is notorious among sixth-formers at Duncraggan, but as the owner of the only off-licence within walking distance, he has a certain power over us. He never stops looking at your tits long enough to ask for ID.

Rowan hands Kirsty a plastic cup full to the brim with vodka. It suddenly occurs to me that maybe she doesn't drink.

'You don't have to drink if you don't want to,' I say, earning an eye-roll from Rowan.

'Thank you, Rowan,' Kirsty says, ignoring me and giving the cup a tentative sniff. 'And thank you for letting me come along. You don't have to worry . . . your secret's safe with me.'

Rowan touches her cup to Kirsty's then takes a sip of her vodka. Kirsty downs her whole cup in one go and we all stare at her in shock before bursting into laughter.

'*That* was unexpected,' chirps Ama in a perfect New Zealand accent. It's a line from one of our favourite films – *Heavenly Creatures* – and judging by the blank look on Kirsty's face, she hasn't seen it. She waits patiently while the rest of us join in with our own quotes and take the piss out of Lily's terrible attempt at a Kiwi accent.

The *Heavenly Creatures* chat goes on a little bit too long and I'm suddenly horribly aware of the discomfort of being on the outside of an inside joke. 'Sorry, Kirsty! It'll all make sense when you see the film. Let's watch it together sometime.'

'Just save it for a day when your mum's being particularly annoying,' says Rowan.

Kirsty's face clouds over. 'What do you mean?'

I explain that the film is based on a true story about two girls who murder one of their mothers.

'My mum isn't annoying,' she says and we all stare at her again, because surely there's no such thing as a mother who isn't annoying.

'Well, aren't you lucky,' says Rowan and it sounds so sarcastic that I flinch even if Kirsty doesn't. Rowan and her mother don't exactly see eye to eye on a lot of things – Rowan's sexuality being top of the list.

I glare at Rowan and she says, 'What? What did I

say?' All I can do is shake my head and hope that she starts playing nice. I know it's not her fault. She doesn't know what Kirsty's been through.

I think we're all grateful when Lil breaks the tension with an enormous burp.

It's definitely not the same, having Kirsty here. Lily and Ama are acting normally, but Rowan is on edge, even after two cups of vodka. If I'd known she was going to be like this I wouldn't have insisted on inviting Kirsty.

The first time they brought me here was magical. I was clueless, like Kirsty, and so afraid of breaking the rules. Not afraid enough to say no; I wanted these girls to accept me. I needed to prove there was a place for me in this world without Jenna. When I entered this cave with Rowan and Ama and Lily, it felt like the start of something. And I knew, even then, that it could be something great. It was the first time I'd felt hopeful since Jenna died. The guilt of it made me cry myself to sleep after we'd crept back to our rooms at three a.m.

'TRUTH OR DARE!' Ama shouts, startling me.

'Boring!' shouts Rowan.

'Can everyone stop shouting, please?' I ask. 'And Ama, Truth or Dare? *Really?*'

'It's fun!' she says, pouting slightly.

'It's dull as fuck. At least Would You Rather allows for a bit of creativity,' Rowan says.

'And surely we don't have any more truths to tell?' says Lily.

She has a point. We've played this game so many times that we know each other inside out and upside down. I've found out all sorts of things: Lily used to steal money from her grandmother's purse on a regular basis and felt so guilty about it she dropped three twenty-pound notes into her coffin at the funeral home; Ama occasionally writes One Direction fan fiction to de-stress; and Rowan fancied Justin Bieber when she was younger because she thought he was a girl.

'But we haven't played with Kirsty yet! So it won't be boring at all. You want to, don't you, Kirsty?' Ama nods a bit too vigorously in Kirsty's direction.

Kirsty shrugs. 'I don't know . . . I've never played it before.'

'Whaaaaaat? How is that even possible? OK, now we *have* to, right?!'

Rowan surprises me by agreeing. Lily was up for it in the first place. I don't mind either way, so Ama explains the rules to Kirsty.

It's fairly tame stuff at first. Lily chooses Truth and Ama asks what she dreamed about last night. Lily cheerfully announces she dreamed about going down on Marek. 'Tell them the rest!' Ama crows.

Lily refuses, saying there's nothing in the rules that says you have to elaborate on your truth. But of course we push her and Ama says that if Lily doesn't tell us, she will. So Lily admits that her sex dream also involved Miss Maddox. Watching . . . and then joining in.

Rowan and I burst out laughing, and after a beat, Kirsty laughs too.

When it's Ama's turn, Lily cackles, and says, 'Revenge is sweet.' She pretends to hold a mike in front of her face. 'So, Miss Adebayo, would you care to tell the group how old you were when you first masturbated?' She holds the invisible mike up to Ama.

Ama screeches, 'BITCH!' and shoves Lil's hand away.

'We're waiting . . .'

Ama takes a deep breath then collapses in a fit of giggles. Her voice is muffled by her hands when she speaks. 'Eight.'

'EIGHT?!' Rowan shakes her head in disbelief. 'Fucking hell, Ama!'

Ama shrugs. 'I didn't know that's what it *was* . . . obviously.'

'Wait for the best bit!' Lily can hardly breathe for laughing.

'There's more?!' I ask, casting a quick glance at Kirsty. She's not laughing or smiling. I want to ask her if she's OK but maybe she wouldn't appreciate me drawing attention to her.

Ama fake glares at Lily, but you can tell she doesn't really mind. 'OK, first of all, I am never telling Lily anything ever again. Ever. And second of all . . . I . . . um . . . used my teddy bear.'

Laughter consumes us – Kirsty too – and it takes a while for everyone to calm down.

Rowan's up next and she chooses Truth. We let Kirsty do the asking, to break the cycle of best friends trying to embarrass the hell out of each other.

Kirsty doesn't have to think long before coming up with her question. 'Who do you have a crush on?'

It's a pretty dull question, but the girls are kind enough to act like it's not.

Rowan smirks and says, 'No one.' She gets shouted down for that. 'It's true!' she protests, laughing.

I make a noise like the wrong answer buzzer on a quiz show. 'FAIL! I think you should ask her another question, Kirsty. Either that or give her a dare.'

'OK. If you had to kiss one of us, who would you choose?' She's getting the hang of this.

I can tell Rowan's not happy, even though she's still smiling. 'I'll go for a dare instead.'

Lily slings her arm around Rowan's shoulders. 'Too late! You *have* to answer. Come on . . . I bet I know the answer anyway.' She kisses Rowan on the cheek with a drunken flourish. 'So . . . who's it going to be, Rowan?'

Ama starts a drumroll on the tops of her thighs and the rest of us join in.

The smile has slipped from Rowan's face and she's staring at Kirsty. I'm not sure what her problem is. It's still a pretty tame sort of question compared to the others.

'Fine,' she says, her voice taut. Her eyes stay firmly on Kirsty. 'Lil. I choose Lily.'

'YES! I *knew* it!' Lily stands and dances on the spot. There's a lot of gyrating.

Ama laughs and says that she can swap rooms with me so that Lily and Rowan can share. Lil pretends to be up for it even though she's the straightest person I know. When I told her I was bi, she said, 'I used to wonder if I was bi before I realised that I'm ALL about the penis.'

When Lily sits down, Rowan pats her leg and says, 'Sorry to have to break it to you, but you do realise this doesn't mean that I actually fancy you. Best of a bad bunch, that's all.' At least she seems to have recovered her sense of humour.

Rowan turns to Kirsty. 'Your turn, new girl. What's it going to be? Truth or Dare?'

'Dare,' Kirsty says without hesitation, taking a huge gulp of vodka.

'New girl's got guts. OK, let me think for a minute . . .' Rowan strokes her chin like an evil genius.

'Go easy on her,' I say, worried about the glint in Rowan's eye. 'It's her first time after all.'

'Well, that settles it then,' says Ama. 'You know what the dare has to be, right, Rowan? We've all done it.'

Worry prickles up my spine. But Rowan will say no, I'm sure of it. Kirsty isn't one of us yet – it's not fair.

Rowan's sense of fairness must have deserted her, because she nods. 'I suppose that'll do. Kirsty, I dare you to take off your clothes and dance around the fire for a minimum of sixty seconds.'

THIRTEEN

Kirsty half laughs. 'You're not serious?'

'Deadly,' says Rowan, splashing some more vodka into her cup and necking it back.

'I can't do that,' Kirsty says quietly.

'Aw, come on!' Lil says. 'There's no need to be shy! We're all friends here.'

'Yeah, Kirsty,' Ama joins in. 'You should have seen when Harper did it – it was too funny.'

'Harper?' Kirsty looks at me, and I don't know what she wants me to say.

I glance at Rowan and I realise this is some kind of test – for me, not for Kirsty. 'It's only for a minute. It'll be over before you know it.' Whatever she wanted me to say, I'm sure it wasn't that.

Kirsty looks at each of us in turn, but when she speaks, it feels like she speaks only to me. 'I don't want to do it.'

I wish she'd just get on with it.

Ama and Lily start booing, but they're just messing. No one really cares if Kirsty gets naked or not. It's the principle of the thing.

'Why not?' I ask. I figure if she can come up with a decent answer they'll let her off the hook.

'I just . . . I *can't.*' She looks utterly helpless.

I look at the others, waiting for one of them to say something. It can't be me; Rowan would be so pissed off with me. Surprisingly, Rowan's the one who comes to the rescue. 'It's OK, you don't have to do anything you don't want to. We're not monsters.' She looks at her watch. 'We should probably be getting back soon anyway.'

Ama chimes in with a jaw-cracking yawn. 'Yeah, Rowan's right. I need to get up early to fit in some practice before brekker.'

Lily stands and stretches, and Rowan gathers up the empty cups and puts the half-empty bottle on the bar for next time.

I thought Kirsty might protest, say that she'll do the dare after all or ask to do truth instead, but she says nothing.

The mood is muted on the way back to the castle. I hang back to walk with Kirsty while the other three go on ahead.

'I hope I didn't ruin everything,' Kirsty whispers

when we're crossing the grass to bypass the gravel of the driveway.

'Not at all,' I say, even though I know that's what the others are thinking. It wasn't her refusal to go through with the dare, I don't think. We've all refused dares before. It was that she took it so seriously instead of just laughing it off. I don't know about the others, but it made me feel as if we were doing something wrong somehow. It made a simple, stupid game feel like something sinister.

We pass Kirsty's room first and the others whisper their 'good night's and do a decent job of acting like everything's fine. I turn to go but Kirsty puts a hand on my arm and leans in close. 'I'm sorry I couldn't do it.'

I shrug. No one cares about the stupid dare.

'I didn't want them to see the scars,' she says softly.

'Scars?' I hadn't noticed any scars when we hauled her out of bed for the Hole.

'From the car crash.'

I freeze.

'Good night, Harper.' She starts to close the door.

'Wait! Can I come in for a second? Do you want to talk about it?' I look over my shoulder, in case Renner's decided to go for a late-night wander down the corridor.

'I'll see you in the morning.' She closes the door,

leaving me standing there feeling like the world's worst human.

It hadn't crossed my mind that Kirsty might have been in the car when her sister died.

'I knew it was a bad idea to invite her,' Rowan says as soon as I walk into our room.

I'm still too stunned to speak. I peel off the layers of clothes and brush my teeth at the sink.

'What's with the silent treatment?' Rowan looms behind me in the mirror.

'You shouldn't have dared her to do that,' I say, dropping my toothbrush next to hers in the mug.

'For fuck's sake, Harper. It was just a stupid dare.' It doesn't help that those were my exact thoughts. 'And it wasn't even my idea! I don't see you blaming Ama.'

I'm too tired for this. We're *both* too tired, too drunk. 'Forget it.'

'No. I won't. I *said* she didn't have to do the dare. That was what you wanted me to say, wasn't it? Anyway, I didn't see you standing up for her.'

I can't win this argument. Not without telling Rowan about Kirsty's sister, and I'm not going to do that.

'I don't want to fight with you, Rowan.'

She laughs and it sounds hollow and wrong. 'That's

funny because it seems like that's exactly what you want to do.' When I don't respond she rolls her eyes in disgust and says, 'Fine, but she's not coming with us again.'

Rowan doesn't need to worry about that. I wouldn't put Kirsty through it again.

Ten minutes later we're in our respective beds and the lights are out. I know I need to sleep but I just can't leave it alone. 'I saw the way you looked at her when she asked who you'd kiss.'

Rowan's duvet rustles as she turns to face me in the dark. 'And?'

'Why don't you like her?'

Just when I'm sure she's not going to answer, she speaks. 'I don't dislike her. But I don't understand why you like her so much.' She doesn't sound annoyed or drunk. She sounds sad, and lonely.

I say nothing, turning my back on my best friend.

FOURTEEN

Mum texted this morning. A line of x's instead of words, because words are unnecessary. Jenna died three years ago today.

I'd planned to call home, but this made it easier for all of us. Maybe my parents don't want to hear my voice today. My voice is her voice, after all. They must hear the ghost of her whenever I speak.

I texted Mum back with exactly the same number of x's.

They'll go to the grave today. Mum will buy red and yellow tulips from the florist on the corner of Hawthorn Road. I don't see the point; they're just going to wilt and die.

I searched for Jenna in the mirror when I was brushing my teeth this morning. Sometimes I see her straight away, but lately it's not so easy. More and more, it feels like she's hiding.

We looked nothing like each other at the end. Jenna was made of shadows.

It started at seven a.m. on New Year's Day when I dragged Jenna out of bed after five hours' sleep. She stood there, swaying like a drunk zombie while I rummaged in the bottom of the wardrobe to find her trainers. I'd bought new ones on Boxing Day, blowing half of my Christmas money in one go.

'I hate you,' said Jenna, when I chucked a pair of tracky bottoms over my shoulder.

'I really, really hate you,' she said, when I helped her pull a hoodie over her head.

'Yeah, yeah, of course you do.' I was raring to go. New year, new me, and all that bullshit.

We didn't bother warming up. We just started running. Side by side, our feet slapping the icy pavement while the rest of the world was asleep.

I felt as if the cold air was cleansing me, scouring away all the crap that I'd eaten over the past couple of weeks. Jenna struggled to keep up, moaning about having a stitch in her side. I laughed and ran faster.

I took pity on her when we reached the park gates and stopped and ran on the spot to let her catch up. 'Sadist,' she gasped.

'You'll thank me later,' I said, smiling. 'Race you to the bandstand?'

I didn't give her the chance to answer, setting off at a sprint.

'Bitch!' she shouted. But I knew my sister. She never let a challenge go unanswered.

I heard her gaining on me as I crossed the bridge over the river. I tried to run faster but I had nothing left. She overtook me, slapping the side of the bandstand a full five seconds before me, her laughter dissolving into a coughing fit. 'So what's my prize for kicking your ass?' she asked.

My legs felt wobbly, my heart was thumping hard and I felt more than a little bit dizzy. 'Your prize is . . . the chance to beat me again. Tennis courts!' I set off again, determined to win this time.

She won again. She always won.

We ran before school every morning. Sometimes we saw Dad on his rounds. He would call out something like 'You two are mad!' but we would just laugh and run faster.

We started off having smoothies for breakfast. Carrot and kale and things that don't belong anywhere near breakfast let alone all whizzed up in a blender. Mum moaned the first time I asked her to buy loads of vegetables. She said, 'Who do you think I am? Jamie flippin' Oliver?' But she was happy that I wasn't raiding the fridge at all hours, and she let us cook a few meals a week even though Dad complained about having to eat 'rabbit food'.

I weighed myself every day and wrote my weight in a little notebook that I carried with me everywhere. I kept a food diary too. For the first two weeks or so, Jenna didn't do either of those things – the exercise and the healthy eating were enough for her. She said she didn't want to get obsessed.

I don't remember the exact words I said. Something about wishing she would take it seriously. Why did I say that? Jenna didn't need to take it seriously. She didn't even need to lose any weight in the first place. She was perfect.

I think that was when it changed for her. Maybe it's arrogant of me to assume that my words made a difference. Maybe it was just a coincidence that the next day she got us up fifteen minutes earlier so we could run for longer, and that she said she only wanted half a glass of smoothie for breakfast.

If I could rewind my life and go back to that moment in time, with my sister looking at me and smirking as I wrote in that notebook, charting my weight down to the gram . . . I would laugh and say she was right. I was getting a little bit obsessed, wasn't I? I would suggest that we head straight to McDonald's for a quarter-pounder with cheese, large fries and a chocolate milkshake.

She would have agreed, I think. I can picture the scene down to the tiniest detail. We would have sat in our usual booth at the top of the stairs. We would have laughed off our pathetic attempt at being healthy as we slurped down the thick, cold shakes and munched on fries dipped in too much ketchup. Apple pie afterwards, for good measure.

That's how the story should have gone. And the weird thing is, if we'd had the conversation a week later, that's how it *would* have gone. I'd lost a bit of weight, and looked fine at Jackson Frith's party; his sister *hadn't* made an appearance. After that I sort of lost interest. It was boring. And I liked chips too much. And chocolate. And cheese.

While I was losing interest, the opposite was happening to Jenna. It was taking hold of her, this creeping sickness with a harmless nickname.

Ana was whispering in her ear, so softly that I couldn't hear.

FIFTEEN

Kirsty's the only one who knows it's the anniversary. The others don't remember and there's no reason for me to remind them. They've gone into the village, walking the two miles rather than waiting for the bus that ferries students after lunch on Saturdays. Kirsty and I head to the clay-pigeon range instead. Now that the outdoor pool is closed for the winter, it's the only time we have a proper chance to talk.

Kirsty may have only started shooting because of me (according to Rowan anyway) but it turns out she's a natural. She's as good as me already. It took me ages to get the hang of aiming in front of the clay rather than directly at it, so that the clay flies into the shot. But Kirsty picked it up fast; she has an almost eerie ability when it comes to recognising the kill zone. My secret hope is that she'll get good enough to beat Marcy Stone. That girl never misses an opportunity to brag about being Duncraggan's best shot.

I'm off my game today. A clear mind is the shooter's number one asset and mine is the opposite of clear. Jenna is all I can think about. I miss four clays in a row and even through my ear defenders I can hear Marcy's slow clapping. That's when Kirsty suggests we call it quits and go for a walk instead. Marcy watches us pack up before turning her attention back to the trap.

At the end of our walk, Kirsty and I sit on the bench on the headland, half a mile away from Duncraggan. You get the best view of the castle from here, with all the ugly modern additions hidden behind it. There's a sunset photo taken from this exact spot on the landing page of the website.

Today the North Sea is flat and pewter grey. The sky above seems indecisive, but I'd still bet on rain. When the memories of Jenna threaten to drown me, I concentrate on my breathing. I breathe in the salt-tinged air for a count of four and breathe out for a count of six. It calms me if I can keep my thoughts focused on the counting. In for four, out for six. Lily taught me that.

The breathing is starting to work when Kirsty asks me if I want to talk about Jenna.

'You know what it's like,' I say. I've tried talking to Kirsty about *her* sister, but she deflects my efforts every single time. It hasn't stopped me wondering about her scars and what it must be like to see them every day. I wonder if it's the same as when I look in the mirror.

Kirsty says nothing, staring out to sea. That's when I blurt out the words I never thought I'd say to anyone.

'It was my fault.'

'What do you mean?' Kirsty asks in that soft voice of hers.

I tell her. About Christmas, about my binge-eating, about me goading Jenna into exercising with me and eating less. Taking advantage of Jenna's competitiveness.

'If it wasn't for me, my sister would still be alive.' It's strange to hear this well-worn mantra of mine out loud. The words have lost some of their raw power, and to my ears at least, sound false and overdramatic. I force out a laugh. 'So anyway, what's new with you?'

She doesn't laugh. And she doesn't say that I shouldn't blame myself. Or that Jenna was her own person and I can't be held responsible for her actions. Instead, she asks a question. 'Did you think about suicide?'

'*What?*'

'If you think it's your fault she died. How do you live with the guilt?' She doesn't look at me. She looks out to sea, where a group of Duncraggan girls are kayaking a hundred metres from shore. Three green kayaks, two blue, one yellow. Three, two, one. I try to remember Lily's breathing exercise but I can't think straight.

'Guilt eats away at you. Hollows you out and fills you up with itself until it's the only thing left.' There's something trance-like about the way she speaks.

A seagull swoops down and lands in front of me, close to the cliff's edge. It's a great black-backed gull. You can tell by their pink feet; Rowan taught me that. This one struts along the cliff edge, back and forth like it's on patrol.

I get up and approach the cliff edge. The bird lets me get quite close before stretching its huge wings and launching itself into the air.

I look down to see that the tide is in, masking the rocks below. You could imagine diving right in and emerging from the waves unharmed. I shuffle so that my toes are right at the edge. It would be so easy just to lean forward and let myself fall.

Her hand on my shoulder startles me. 'Do you think that would do the job?' she says quietly, looking down at the drop.

It would.

Kirsty's hand moves to my back. All it would take is a gentle push. Barely more than a nudge. But her hand grasps the fabric of my hoodie and pulls me backwards. A strangled sob escapes me and I find myself on my knees on the damp grass. She crouches down next to me and rubs my back as I cry.

'I miss her so much.' I choke out the words before dissolving into tears again. She strokes my hair and says, 'I know, Harper. I know. I miss her too.'

My tears come to a sniffing standstill and I turn to look at her. 'Rhiannon?'

She has tears in her eyes as she nods. It hits me that maybe she wasn't talking about *my* guilt before. But how could a thirteen-year-old girl possibly be to blame for a car accident?

SIXTEEN

Half an hour later, we sit on her bed with cups of tea and I ask about her sister. She changes the subject yet again and starts talking about her mum. She says they're best friends. I've always thought that people who say that are weird, but it actually sounds quite nice, the way she describes it. Kirsty says she can talk to her mum about anything. I ask if that includes sex stuff.

'There's nothing much to say. I'm a virgin.'

I smile. In a school where everyone is always trying to outdo each other over how experienced they are, it's refreshing to hear someone come out and say that. 'But if I wasn't . . . Yeah, I'm pretty sure I could talk to Mum about sex. I tell her everything in my letters.'

'You write letters? Old school!'

A look of annoyance flashes across her face. 'I like letters. They're real. They have a weight to them,'

I'm not sure what she means, but I nod all the same.

'I've told her all about you.'

'Nothing bad I hope?' It's just what you say, isn't it? When you know someone's been talking about you.

'She's really happy that I've made such a good friend here. She says it's rare to find someone who understands you. A true friend.'

'You must have had friends at your old school though?'

Kirsty looks at me. 'No one like you.'

It's all a bit intense. I gulp down the rest of my tea and get up from the bed to put my mug on the desk. A fine drizzle meanders down the windowpane. I check my watch; the girls won't be back from the village yet.

'Ama's going to be so pissed off if the rain messes up her hair. Rowan told her not to bother with an umbrella.'

'Is everything OK?' asks Kirsty.

I turn to see the me-shaped depression in the duvet next to her. 'Of course. Why wouldn't it be?'

Her expression darkens. 'God, you think I'm a freak, don't you?' She hits her head back against the wall – hard. Then she does it again.

'Stop that!' I rush over to her, filling the me-shaped depression, perfectly. 'You're not a freak! What are you talking about?!'

Kirsty shakes her head. 'Mum always said I shouldn't

be so honest with people. That I should play my cards close to my chest until I get to know people a little better . . . But since . . . since Rhiannon died, I've just been so lonely. No one else seems to understand . . . But you do, don't you?'

'I do,' I say, taking her hand in mine. It takes ten more minutes to convince Kirsty that everything is OK and that I don't think she's a freak for not having a ton of friends. 'I never had many friends either, before I met Rowan and the girls. Your mum's right – it can take a while to find your people.'

'I'm glad I found you,' she whispers.

'Not just me – you've got Ama, Lil and Rowan too.' I'm not sure why I say that. It's the pressure, perhaps. Knowing that Kirsty is relying on me for support. 'Listen, I'd better get going. I said I'd help Hozzie set up for movie night.' Hozzie is Fairclough's resident movie nerd, specialising in choosing obscure foreign films for our Saturday night movie. It's tradition for us to whine about her choices, but more often than not we end up loving the films.

Kirsty asks if we need any extra help, but I tell her that we've got it covered. 'I'll see you at dinner though, yeah?' She nods vaguely, and I close the door behind me.

I don't actually have to meet Hozzie for half an hour yet, so I head back to my room and lie on my bed. I feel bad for lying to Kirsty, but I needed to get out of that room. Today has been too much; I feel flattened by it.

I do feel pressure, knowing that I'm the only real friend Kirsty has here. But it's still early days. I was just lucky that Rowan and I hit it off so quickly, and that Lily and Ama accepted me too. I wish it could be that easy with Kirsty, but for some reason it's not. So it's up to me to be there for her, like she's been there for me. Listening and understanding as best I can.

Kirsty clearly has more issues than she's letting on, but then who doesn't? Maybe I can help her somehow.

I try not to listen to the toxic whisper in my head, but it wheedles its way into my thoughts. *Like you helped Jenna?*

I was sure Jenna would be pissed off with me when I gave up on my New Year health kick. But I was wrong; she didn't seem to mind at all.

'Don't you think you're getting a little obsessed?' I asked one morning, when she was just back from a ninety-minute run.

She gulped from a bottle of water and flopped down on the bed. 'There's a difference between obsessed and disciplined.'

When we were getting ready for bed that night I

watched Jenna as she stood in front of the mirror in her bra and pants. Her eyes narrowed as she scrutinised her reflection from head to toe. I could tell she didn't like what she saw even though she looked good.

I knew I could look just as good, if only I could be bothered to keep up the strict regime. But you know that thing that people say? 'Nothing tastes as good as skinny feels'? Those people are dead wrong. They've clearly never been anywhere near a double bacon cheeseburger or a salted caramel brownie or pretty much anything involving melted cheese.

I often wonder if it was already too late, or if I could have made her see sense. Was it one of those moments when life is balancing on a knife-edge and you don't even know it?

SEVENTEEN

It's not my face I see reflected in the rock pool. It's hers. Just for a second. And then it's me again. I refocus my eyes to look beyond the reflection: seaweed, mostly. Sand, tiny stones and shells. A rock that I wouldn't have been able to resist turning over a few years ago, waiting for the sand to stop swirling and the beasties to show themselves. It was always my job, turning over the rocks. Jenna was in charge of the bucket. We took turns with the net.

Something darts across the bottom of the pool and hides among the fronds of seaweed. Jenna used to call it witch's hair. I put some on my head once, to make her laugh.

A scream shatters the peace, immediately followed by laughter. I look across the beach to see Ama gripping Rowan's arm as Lily crouches down to look at something on the sand. I hurry across the rocks towards them, careful not to slip on the slick green algae. It's just a jellyfish, even if it is the size of a dinner plate.

The four of us sit on the sand and watch the waves crashing on to the shore. The sand is damp and cold through my jeans but I don't mind. Rowan has her binoculars out and reels off a list of birds and we humour her because we're all nerds in our own way.

'Why don't we come down here more often?' asks Lil. 'It's so peaceful.'

As if on cue, shouts and laughter fill the air and a bunch of Year 7s and 8s come streaming on to the beach, accompanied by the PE teacher, Miss Frick. The girls run wild, like animals uncaged.

We decide we might as well head back up to school since Rowan and I have a Queer Soc. meeting. Last year that would have just meant me and her sitting in our room and chatting, but this year we actually have some members. Rowan went on a big recruitment drive at the start of term and it seems to have actually worked. A membership of eight may not sound like much, but in a place like Duncraggan it's pretty impressive.

We trudge up the path back to school. Sea buckthorn bushes crowd the path with their bright orange berries and sharp thorns.

'What's Kirsty up to this afternoon?' Ama asks, out of breath from the slow climb.

I shrug. 'Not sure. Maybe down at the shooting range?'

'She didn't fancy coming to the beach?' Lil asks. 'Nope.'

The truth is I didn't ask her. I wanted it to be just the four of us, like it used to be. But I don't want Rowan to know that. I don't want to give her the satisfaction of thinking she was right. She's *not* right; I just wanted a bit of a break after yesterday. I told Kirsty I had to work on a presentation for History. It's not technically a lie, because I will be working on it later.

Marek is hard at work when we pass the vegetable garden. 'I thought Sunday was his day off?' I ask Lil, expert on all things Marek.

'It is,' she says, not taking her eyes off him. 'Maybe he's picking veg for his dinner?'

'Why don't you go and ask, Lil? See if you can score an invite?' Ama teases.

Lily turns back to us. 'How's my hair? Teeth?' She bares them in a chimpanzee grin.

I shake my head. 'Your hair is shit and you have spinach between your teeth.'

Lil narrows her eyes and smirks. 'Fuck you, Kent. OK guys, cover me, I'm going in.'

Rowan grabs Lily's arm and yanks her back. 'Are you sure that's a good idea, Lil?'

'I'm just going to talk to him. What's wrong with *that*?'

'Nothing,' Rowan admits. 'Just be careful, OK?

You know what people are like round here. They'll latch on to any piece of gossip – doesn't matter if it's true or not.'

Lily laughs. 'Who cares about gossip? Anyway, I think it's my duty as head girl to check on the vegetable garden. I take the nutrition and wellbeing of the students *very* seriously.'

Rowan sticks her tongue out at Lily and says, 'Fine. Go embarrass yourself. See if I . . .' She trails off, looking behind me. 'Hi!'

I know who's there before I turn round. In this kind of situation it's *always* the person you don't want it to be.

I say a sheepish hello to Kirsty who ignores the others and speaks only to me. 'I looked for you in the library. I thought you might want some help with your presentation.' She crosses her arms against the cold. She really should be wearing a coat.

'Yeah, I decided some fresh air might help me think better.'

The silence that follows is more than a little awkward. Instead of helping me out, Lil strides off towards Marek and Ama and Rowan make themselves scarce, saying they'll catch us at dinner.

This silence is even more awkward.

'You went to the beach,' says Kirsty. A statement, not a question.

'Yeah, I needed to clear my head. How did you know we were at the beach?'

'Gabi saw you on her way back from windsurfing.'

Gabi Get Involved, doing what she does best. 'Look, Kirsty, I'm sorry. I should have asked if you wanted to come with us.'

'It's fine.'

I want to believe her, but I don't. 'Really? You're not annoyed?'

'Why would I be annoyed?'

She's got me there, because if I explain it to her she might *get* annoyed, even if she wasn't before. 'That was really nice of you – offering to help with my presentation.'

'That's what friends are for,' she says, smiling.

We walk up towards the castle and everything seems fine. We both act like nothing's happened, which suits me just fine.

It's only when we part ways outside the turret room that she says, 'I was worried. When I couldn't find you.'

'*Worried?* Why?' Duncraggan is probably one of the safest places in the country. It's too far from anywhere remotely interesting to attract criminals.

'After yesterday. You were so upset. I thought – I know it's silly – but I thought you might have done something stupid.'

'What?! God, no! Kirsty, I'm so sorry. I had no idea

that's what you might think. I'm fine today, honestly. Loads better.' Who am I trying to convince? Her or me?

'I'm glad you're feeling better,' she says, closing the door behind her.

It horrifies me – that Kirsty thought that was even a remote possibility. I should have invited her to come to the beach with us.

I should have made it clearer yesterday. I like being alive.

EIGHTEEN

The History presentation does not go well. I blush and mumble my way through it, but Mr Gilbert is nice enough to pretend I did a decent job. Rowan's presentation is brilliant; she doesn't even use notes.

At the end of the lesson Rowan is doing her best to reassure me that I wasn't completely terrible when Marcy Stone perches on the edge of my desk. Her presentation was crap too, but at least she was confident with it.

'Hi Harper!' Marcy smiles sweetly, showing off the gap between her front teeth. I often think about trying to slot a pound coin through there.

'A little birdie told me you've been keeping secrets from us.' Her voice is light and teasing. It could be mistaken for friendliness if you didn't know better.

I say nothing; Marcy needs no encouragement to be intensely irritating.

She looks around to see if anyone's paying attention,

but most people are chatting away or busy getting their books out for English. She coughs, loudly. 'So what I *really* want to know is . . . did your parents get one of those giant cheques?'

I go cold. 'What are you talking about?' Even though I know perfectly well.

'From the lottery people! You must have seen the pictures . . . the ones with the spurting bottle of champagne and the plastic glasses and the winners standing outside their poky little council house holding a cheque as big as a bath towel.'

'Fuck off, Marcy.' God bless Rowan, my knight in shining armour.

'I wasn't talking to *you*.' Marcy tries on a withering stare for size; it suits her much more than the smile.

She clears her throat and takes a quick glance over her shoulder. 'Why didn't you tell us that your dad won the *lottery*! He's a postman, isn't he?' Her voice carries across the classroom, halting conversations.

I'm not ashamed. I'm *not*.

People are looking at me; I can't stand people looking at me. A couple of them are laughing, some are whispering. Hozzie's the only one who looks remotely sympathetic – she aims a friendly, wincing sort of smile in my direction.

Tatiana starts humming the theme tune to *Postman Pat*. I'm surprised the daughter of a Russian oligarch has even heard of *Postman Pat*, let alone knows the theme tune.

I look up at Marcy, who's looking down her nose at me. 'What's your point, Marcy?'

Wide-eyed innocence, good enough to fool teachers but not me. 'Nothing! I was just interested, that's all. It must be so strange for you, coming from such a . . . *different* background. Don't get me wrong – I'm not saying it's a bad thing! It's fascinating. And you know my mum has always been a champion of the working class. "Hard-working families" and all that shit.' Marcy's mother is a politician, always on the news blethering about equality and social mobility while cheerfully voting against any legislation that would actually help people.

Beside me, Rowan is unnaturally still. A predator ready to pounce. I put my hand on her arm just to stop her doing anything rash.

'I don't understand why you'd want to keep it a secret though! It's such a great story, isn't it? Rags to riches! I love it!'

Mrs Woolfson comes in, slamming the door behind her. She's always in a mood on Tuesdays; no one is quite sure why. Marcy hops off our desk and hurries back to her own, secure in the knowledge that the damage has been done.

'Are you OK?' Rowan whispers, when everyone's

settled down and Mrs Woolfson is droning on about Shirley Jackson. I forgot to read the book.

I nod, keeping my eyes on the teacher. I don't want to look at Rowan and see pity in her eyes. Because I'm not ashamed. I will not allow someone like Marcy Stone to shame me. Who cares if people know? I shouldn't have tried to keep it a secret in the first place.

I'm proud of the fact that Dad didn't jack in his job after the win. Even if his reasons had more to do with Jenna than anything else.

I look around at the other girls in my class. Girls with parents who work in advertising, investment banking, law. Girls whose parents have never worked a day in their lives because money has flowed down like water down the generations. Hozzie's mum used to own a business manufacturing pipes for toilets. That's about as down to earth as it gets here. She sold the business last summer for ten million quid and is currently four months into a year-long round-the-world yacht trip.

My parents have jobs where you actually have to *do* something rather than telling other people to do things for you. That's what it's like in the real world. Most of these girls wouldn't know the real world if it snuck up on them and handed them a bill for their platinum card.

I know that Rowan cares, but she's never had to

watch her parents sitting with a pile of bills at the kitchen table, frantically tapping away at a calculator. Trying to make the sums add up, knowing that they never will.

Kirsty understands though.

The *Postman Pat* theme tune haunts me for the rest of the day. Someone – I'm not sure who – must have downloaded the track on to their phone.

It's not a big deal. It's just mildly irritating, like an itchy scab. Most people don't seem to care all that much – they have their own shit to deal with. The girls do a good job of distracting me during dinner. I don't know if they've been warned by Rowan, but none of them mention the lottery thing. I'm quieter than usual, but Kirsty's on good form, laughing and joking with the others. Maybe that's what it will take for things to work with the five of us. Someone needs to step back to give her space.

After banco, I grab a book that Kirsty wanted to borrow and head for the door. Rowan swivels round in her chair. 'How do you think Marcy found out?'

'How should I know? It's a miracle I managed to keep it secret this long.'

'Hmm,' she says thoughtfully, chewing on the end of her pen. 'It's strange though, don't you think? That it should come out after all this time.'

'I don't see what's strange about it . . . What are you getting at?'

Another thoughtful nibble on the biro. 'Nothing.'

I turn to leave and the door is half open when she says, 'You didn't tell Kirsty about the lottery, did you?'

I look at her, the light from the desk lamp casting half her face in shadow.

'Of course not.'

I shut the door before she can see the lie on my face.

NINETEEN

I forget to knock on Kirsty's door and she practically jumps out of her skin. She's sitting at her desk with a small cardboard box in front of her. Before I can see what's in her hand, she stuffs it into the box and closes the lid with lightning speed.

'You scared me!' She laughs, moving the box to the corner of the desk.

'I brought the book you wanted. Spoiler: the ending is shit.' I toss it on to the bed.

'Thanks. I was just tidying up.'

The room is spotless compared to mine and Rowan's. I sit on the bed and she spins her chair round to face me.

It's the first chance I've had to talk to her on her own all day so of course I go off on a rant about Marcy.

Kirsty shakes her head and sighs. 'You've got nothing to be ashamed of, Harper. You know that, don't you?'

I nod.

Her eyes light up and she scoots her chair closer to me. 'Maybe I should tell everyone about my scholarship? That would take the heat off you for a bit – give them something else to gossip about.'

'You don't have to do that. But thank you.' I'm touched by the gesture. 'They'll get bored soon enough. I just wish I knew how Marcy found out.'

Kirsty shrugs and reaches over to grab the book from the bed. 'Maybe I shouldn't bother with this then? I'll wait till the film comes out.'

I know I shouldn't do this, but I can't help myself. 'Kirsty? You didn't . . . mention it to anyone, did you?' She looks up, slowly. 'It's OK if you did. It's not a big deal, honestly. It's just that I'd like to know if—'

'You don't trust me,' she says evenly.

'No! I shouldn't have said anything. I *do* trust you. Of course I do.'

I meet her gaze, willing her to believe me. I don't even blink. And then her shoulders slump. She sighs and shakes her head. 'I didn't want to say anything.'

'About what?'

A troubled frown creases her features. 'It was Ama.'

'*What?*'

'Ama told Marcy.' Kirsty reaches out and touches my arm. 'Please don't be angry with her. She didn't do it on purpose. I think it just sort of slipped out.'

'How do you know?'

'I was passing by the music room yesterday afternoon. I overheard—'

'Marcy doesn't play an instrument.' Neither does Kirsty for that matter.

'I think maybe a teacher had asked Marcy to pass on a message to Ama . . . I'm not quite sure.'

'And Ama just blurted out that my family was broke until we won the lottery?'

She shakes her head. 'It wasn't like that. They just got chatting. I can't remember exactly what was said.'

It makes no sense. Ama doesn't hate Marcy as much as I do, but they've never been particularly friendly. 'And where were you when this was going on?'

She looks away, tucking her hands under her thighs. 'I was . . . OK, you're probably going to think this is weird, but sometimes I go and listen to Ama play the piano.'

'Ama never mentioned it.'

'She doesn't know. I listen outside – you know that alcove around the corner?'

'Why?'

'My mum played.' Kirsty looks embarrassed for some reason I don't understand. 'I loved it, when I was younger. But she . . . stopped. She had to sell the piano when we moved to a smaller house.' She shakes her head to rid herself of the memory.

'I'm sure Ama wouldn't mind if you sat *inside* the music room instead of skulking around in the corridor,' I say with a smile.

'No. I like to . . . when I'm outside the room I can imagine it's my mum playing.' I'm about to say something flippant but the look on her face stops me. 'Please don't tell Ama that I listen to her play. I wouldn't feel comfortable listening any more and I would . . . well, I would really miss it.'

'I won't say anything. I promise.'

If I keep my word it means I can't confront Ama about blabbing to Marcy, which is actually a relief. I'm terrible with confrontation.

I can't believe Ama told Marcy after all this time. I always thought Ama collected little kernels of information from around the school and brought them back to us like some kind of gossip squirrel. It never occurred to me that she might be collecting kernels of information about *us* and doling them out to the likes of Marcy Stone. It's annoying, but I'm sure she didn't mean anything by it. I bet she was kicking herself as soon as she blurted it out – sometimes she just can't help herself. But no real harm has been done. I'm not ashamed about where I've come from, and anyone who thinks I should be can go fuck themselves. I just won't be telling Ama any more secrets in a hurry.

Not that I have many secrets left.

TWENTY

Every week we gather in the TV room for our house meeting. By unspoken agreement, the senior girls get to sit on the sofas and easy chairs and the junior girls sit on the floor. I'm perched on the arm of a sofa next to Kirsty. After the usual announcements and telling off the Year 9s about the disgusting state of their rooms, Miss Renner announces the pizza party for the last night before the half-term holiday. From the reaction of the Year 7s and 8s you'd think she'd announced a surprise trip to Disney World.

Renner asks for volunteers to make the pizzas and a few people shout out Ama's name, because she's really good at it. Ama laughs and blushes and says she'll do it, but this time she wants some help.

She makes a big show of considering her options before her eyes alight on me. 'What do you say, Harper? Fancy being my sous chef?'

I'm surprised that she chooses me. Either she's

feeling guilty about blabbing or she's conveniently forgotten all about it.

A couple of days later I report for duty to find Ama plugging her phone in next to the giant food mixer. She's made a special playlist for the occasion. Music blasts through the kitchens as we mix and knead and manage to get flour all over ourselves. I thought it might be awkward, but it really isn't. It's actually pretty fun.

We're waiting for the dough to prove and the tomato sauce is bubbling away on one of the industrial-sized hobs when Ama says pretty much what I'm thinking. 'This is nice, isn't it?'

'Yeah. It is.' Now's the time. I could ask her about Marcy right now. Swear her to secrecy so that Kirsty would never know.

'When was the last time we did something, just the two of us?'

I remember immediately. It was April. Rowan was on a lacrosse trip and Lily was busy with rehearsals for The Crucible. Ama and I decided to have a picnic on the beach. The sea was dead calm and there wasn't a cloud in the sky.

At first we talked about the usual stuff, but then we went deeper. I told her what it was like being a twin. I remember it clearly because it was the first time I'd ever been able to talk about Jenna without crying.

Ama told me about her anxiety. Rowan had already told me, but I hadn't realised how bad it was, or that she'd had a big fight with her mum about whether she should see a doctor. Ama's mum thinks that people with mental health problems should try to cheer up.

I start chopping red peppers after Ama's shown me exactly how she wants them done. There's something oddly soothing about chopping vegetables. We line up the toppings in stainless-steel bowls and sing along to 'That's Amore', which earned its spot on the playlist purely because it has the word 'pizza' in it.

'You looking forward to going home tomorrow?' I ask. If I'm going to ask about Marcy, I need to approach with caution.

'Not really. The London flat doesn't feel like home, you know?' Ama's parents have homes in Nigeria, London and Paris. I have no idea what that must be like. Confusing, I guess? 'Plus I need to see my doctor about increasing my meds. Which sucks.'

'Is it bad at the moment?' I don't know why I don't say the word 'anxiety'. I hate it when people don't say what they mean.

Ama shrugs and I suddenly worry that I should have known somehow. Have there been signs that I've missed? 'It's fine. Most of the time. But when it's bad

. . .' She shakes her head. 'Sometimes I wish they could cut open my brain and scoop out the broken bits.'

'You're not broken,' I say, putting my arm around her and pulling her into a hug. 'It's good that you're going to the doctor though. Of course you could just try cheering the fuck up. I've heard that works wonders.'

Ama laughs. 'Maybe they should offer therapy sessions with my mother instead of meds. "You think you have it bad? You don't even know bad! You should talk to Aunt Femi if you want to know about bad but you can't because she is dead. Now *that* is bad."' Ama's impressions of her mum always crack me up.

When the pizzas are in the oven, I decide it's time. 'Ama?'

'Mmmm?' She's distracted, watching the seconds count down on her phone so she can take the pizzas out at the exact right moment – crispy crust and oozy cheese.

'You know the lottery thing? I was just wondering if you—'

The swing door slams open and Kirsty comes in. 'I thought you might need a hand carrying the pizzas up. The Year 7s are threatening to storm the kitchens if they don't get fed soon.'

Ama laughs and says that you can't rush perfection.

*

'Were you eavesdropping on us?' I ask, quietly. Kirsty and I are standing in the corner of Miss Renner's living room. The pizza has been devoured and Ama's been basking in praise for the last half-hour. Renner has gone down to the kitchens with Hozzie to see if she can dig out some ice cream. No wonder everyone wishes they were in Fairclough; the best you get in Balmedie is a stale iced bun and a cup of weak tea.

At least Kirsty doesn't pretend to be clueless. 'I was only there for a second. I was worried you were going to say something about me listening outside the music room.' She pauses to take a sip of her drink. 'It seems like I was right to be worried.'

It seems like she spends a little too much time listening outside doors, but I suppose I can't blame her this time. 'I wasn't going to drop you in it. I just wanted to see what she said, that's all.'

I look over to the sofa where Ama, Rowan and Lily have their heads together, avidly watching something on Lily's phone.

'It sounded like you two were having a good time in the kitchen. I thought you were annoyed with her?'

I shrug. 'She's one of my best friends. There's no point holding a grudge, is there?'

Kirsty doesn't answer.

Rowan looks up and beckons me over. I jump at the chance, squeezing on to the sofa between Ama and

Rowan. There's not enough room for the four of us but we make it work.

They replay the video for me, but I only half watch. I'm hyper aware of Kirsty leaning against the wall on the other side of the room, watching. A few minutes later I look up and she's gone.

TWENTY-ONE

The next day, I'm sitting in a brand-new car with its strange new-car smell.

'You didn't tell me you were getting this.' I can't stop shivering. There's a digital display so that I can adjust the temperature for my seat. The display next to Mum's seat is set on 'LOW'. I crank mine up as high as it will go.

'Do you like it?' Mum strokes the steering wheel as if it's covered in fur. (It isn't. Dad used to have a car with fake fur on the steering wheel; Mum made him get rid of it when they got engaged.)

'Um . . . yeah. It's nice.' I hate it. What do they need a Land Rover for? And why does it have to be white?

I stare out of the window as she pulls out of the parking space.

'Aw, love, what's the matter? Is it the car? Don't worry! We've still got the old one! We thought . . .

we wondered if maybe you might like to have it. We thought you might like to start driving lessons this week? There's a crash course I saw advertised in the local paper.' She laughs. 'Crash course! That's hardly ideal for driving lessons, is it?!'

'I'd booked an afternoon train.'

'Oh, OK. We just thought . . . it doesn't matter. It's fine.'

I glance over at her, and she looks like a child driving this monstrous car. I feel bad. 'Maybe next summer? So I don't have to rush it. And the weather will be better.'

'It's up to you, love. No pressure.'

'Thanks, Mum. I really like the car. It's very . . . tank-like.'

She laughs. 'Isn't it just! If anyone gets in my way I can just roll right over them.'

My fingers find their way to my neck, out of habit. But my neck is bare; the necklace is gone. I only realised after lunch, when I had one last check in the mirror. The others had already left. I'd booked an afternoon train. It's not that I didn't want to see my parents. I do miss them, in a way. But it's hard.

It's hard to sit next to Mum without Jenna behind me, kicking the back of the seat to wind me up. It's hard to drive past the cinema where Jenna and I snuck in to see a 12-certificate film when we were ten years old. The park where Jenna used to pretend to be Spider-Man, hanging off the monkey bars by her feet. The shop where Mum took us to get our first bras, both of us cringing with embarrassment and wondering why we couldn't just keep wearing vests.

Today it's even harder, as if the necklace held me together somehow. As soon as I realised it wasn't round my neck, my stomach dropped. I take it off every night and leave it on my bedside table. I put it on straight after my shower in the morning. That's what I do, every day. But I can't remember taking it off after the pizza party. I must have, obviously. But I can't picture it, no matter how hard I try. And why didn't I realise first thing this morning? It's like brushing my teeth – it's not something I could ever forget.

The chain must have snapped. Which means the necklace could be anywhere. That's the worst-case scenario. Then I have a horrifying thought, which takes hold of me and won't let go. Now that I really, really think about it, I'm not even sure I put the necklace on yesterday. Or the day before, for that matter.

I texted Ama on the train, but she couldn't remember if I'd been wearing it in the kitchens. She said she was sure it would turn up though. I thanked her and wished her luck with the doctor's appointment.

I'll just have to do a thorough search when I get

back to Duncraggan. There's not much I can do until then except try not to freak out about it. It's only a necklace. It is an object, a thing. Misplacing it doesn't mean I love Jenna any less. It doesn't.

My phone buzzes with a text: '*Are you home yet? Mum picked me up from the airport and took me for pizza on the way home. You can never have too much pizza, right? Hope you're OK. xxx*'

'Is that Rowan?' asks Mum, slowing down at the crossing next to the park. The top of the bandstand is just visible over the trees. I look away fast.

'Kirsty.'

'Which one's Kirsty again?'

'The new girl. I've *told* you.'

'Sorry, love. You know what I'm like – I can barely even remember my own name these days.' We both know what she means by 'these days'. 'So what's she like, this Kirsty? Have you taken her under your wing a bit? It's not easy being the new girl, is it? Although you seemed to fit in quickly enough, didn't you?'

This is typical Mum, asking so many questions you can't figure out which ones to answer and which ones are meant to be rhetorical. It's oddly reassuring. It's a glimpse of who she used to be.

I tell her that Kirsty's on a scholarship, and that she's more normal than a lot of the Duncraggan girls. Then I tell her about Kirsty's sister.

'Tragic,' she says, shaking her head. 'No parent should ever outlive their child.'

I make a non-committal 'mmm' sort of sound, because of course she's right, but it always seems to circle back to *her* grief.

'I'm sorry. I didn't mean to . . . It's good that you can talk to someone who understands. I'm glad.'

There's something different about Mum today. It feels like she's making an effort. Maybe it's about time I started making an effort too.

Dad's asleep on the sofa when we get home. He always used to say that he wasn't napping, just 'resting his eyes for a minute or two'. Jenna used to do an unnervingly accurate impression of his snoring.

I dump my bag and go over and tap my knuckles gently on his forehead. 'Wake up, sleepyhead.'

Dad goes from fast asleep to bolt upright and wide awake in less than a second. He gathers me up in a big hug. 'It's good to have you home. We've missed you.'

I'm about to say that I'm happy to be home and that I've missed them too, but different words come out of my mouth instead. 'What the hell have you done to your hair? Have you got *highlights*?!'

He brings his hand up to his head, like he needs to check that he still actually *has* hair. 'Your mother thought . . .'

'I've started going to this new salon that's opened up in town,' Mum says, and now that I look at her properly, I see that she's looking a bit more groomed than usual. The haircut is still basically the same, but it's sharper somehow, like it's in HD. 'Your dad came to collect me one day and my stylist suggested that he might want to do something to cover up the grey.'

'But I like the grey! It was . . . I dunno . . .'

'Distinguished?' Dad says, with a wry smile. 'That's just another word for old.'

'What happened to Shirley?' Shirley is a mobile hairdresser; she's been coming to our house every couple of months for as long as I can remember. She used to bring lollipops for Jenna and me, and a big pile of her old magazines for Mum. Dad got nothing, except a fresh trim.

Mum and Dad share an awkward look.

'She's not . . . dead, is she?'

That breaks the tension a little. 'God, no! I just thought it was time for a change, you know? And my salon gives you a glass of champagne while you're having your hair done! And a head massage.'

'Sounds expensive.'

'Well we can afford it, can't we?' Mum shrugs.

Something has definitely changed here. We sit round the kitchen table, drinking tea. At least my mug is still the same. I grip it with both hands, drinking my tea while it's still far too hot. Jenna used to wait until hers was lukewarm before her first sip.

'There's something we wanted to talk to you about,' says Dad, drumming his fingers on the battered old pine table. He's nervous, but why?

A shared glance between them and then Mum says, 'We've decided to move.'

'Move where?'

'We're not sure yet. Not far. We still want to be able to see our friends, and for you to keep in touch with your old school friends.'

I don't remind them that their social life is practically non-existent these days, and that I haven't stayed in touch with anyone from my old school. I cleared every trace of them from my social media accounts well over a year ago. I don't say these things because all I can think about is this house. My parents moved in when they got back from their honeymoon in the Lake District. Jenna and I were born nine months later. *This* is our home. Jenna's home.

'Why now?' The words don't form easily around the lump in my throat.

'It's time to start living again,' Dad says softly.

Mum reaches over and takes his hand. 'Your dad and I had a talk, on the anniversary. Something had to change. The way things have been . . . we couldn't

141

go on like that. I think – we *both* think – that Jenna would want us to be happy. Or at least try.'

'Where's all this come from?' I don't mean to sound accusatory. It's just that I've been waiting a long time to hear these words.

'I've been seeing a therapist. It's really helped.'

'Since when?! Why didn't you tell me?' The thought of my mum lying back on some couch and spilling her innermost thoughts is almost impossible to comprehend.

'I didn't want to worry you,' she says sheepishly.

'*Worry* me? I'd have been happy!'

Dad butts in. 'It's all water under the bridge now, Harper. So what do you think about us moving house?'

I look from Mum to Dad and back again. They need this. 'I think it's a great idea.'

The relief on their faces tells me I've done the right thing. Telling the truth isn't always the best option, not when there's a possibility I might just be getting my parents back.

They wait till dinner (fish and chips from Frying Nemo) to tell me the rest: Mum's quitting her job at the end of the month and Dad plans to stop working early in the new year. Mum leaving her job isn't a surprise at all – it's weird that she's stayed this long – but Dad?

'You love being a postie!'

Dad dips a fat greasy chip in a blob of ketchup and

pops it into his mouth. 'I do. I did. I mean, I still do, kind of. But things have changed, Harper. It's not the same without the rest of them, you know? All my pals left after the win. It's time to move on.'

I ask them what they'll do with their time. Mum says she's always wanted to get into gardening, which is news to me. Our back garden consists of cracked, weed-choked paving stones, a rickety bench and a couple of empty plant pots.

Dad says he wants to paint.

'That's brilliant. You could have your own painting and decorating business – be your own boss.'

He laughs and wipes his mouth with some kitchen roll. 'I mean watercolours, oil paints, that sort of thing. I used to love it when I was at school.'

This is also news to me. I manage not to make a sarcastic remark about Dad's long-lost hobby that he's never even mentioned before. Clearly my parents have been hiding their hopes and dreams from me.

Or perhaps it's that I've never asked.

I smile and say, 'That sounds great, Dad. I'm happy for you both.'

'Really?' Mum asks cautiously, the first hint of a smile playing on her lips.

'Really.'

We drink a toast, clinking our glasses of apple juice together.

143

'To the future,' Dad says, and we all try to ignore the fact that there are tears in his eyes. And Mum's. And mine.

TWENTY-TWO

'Fucking hell!'

The estate agent stifles a laugh. He's busy tapping away on his iPhone in the corner, supposedly 'leaving us in peace' to have a look round the place.

'Do you like it?' asks Dad, but he already knows the answer. He's got this grin on his face. A grin so wide it almost hurts to look at. This kitchen is the size of the whole ground floor of our house.

'It's massive!' I run my hand along the worktop – it's black and shiny, with little sparkles in it. If you look closely it looks like a whole universe of stars.

Mum perches on a stool at the breakfast bar. 'I can just see myself sitting here with my coffee in the morning.'

The rest of the house is just as amazing; it's like something out of a magazine. The rooms are light and spacious and the ceilings are high; it's the kind of house where you feel guilty for wearing shoes inside.

The only blip is when Dad opens one of the doors and says, 'We thought this could be your room.'

There's more than enough room for a double bed – maybe even a king-size – and a sofa and a desk; there's even an en-suite bathroom. The sun shines through the branches of the huge oak tree outside, making pretty shadows on the built-in wardrobe that runs along an entire wall. Jenna used to moan about the size of our wardrobe. I can't imagine myself sleeping in this room without Jenna.

We're heading out to look at the garden when my phone buzzes with a message from Rowan. I'm about to reply when Dad calls me over to look at the fishpond. It has actual fish in it.

I look back at the house. It doesn't look too fancy from the outside – red roof, cream walls. Not showy at all. But it is detached. I never thought I would ever live in a detached house. I turn to find Mum and Dad holding hands.

'I could build an art studio at the bottom of the garden,' says Dad.

'A shed, you mean?' Mum laughs, and Dad laughs too. It takes a while for me to register that I can't remember the last time I saw them laugh together.

'Well? What's the verdict?' Dad says as we drive away from the house.

I turn in my seat to look at the house one last

time. The estate agent is getting into his Mini Cooper, a satisfied smile on his face.

I pause to try to find the right words. 'It looks like a home.'

They put an offer in after lunch – for the full asking price. You could buy four houses on our street with that much cash.

A few minutes later the estate agent calls back and says that the offer has been accepted. We have a new house. Mum and Dad hug each other and Mum has tears in her eyes. They hug me and I hug them back. There's a bottle of Cava in the fridge, which Dad cracks open and pours into wine glasses.

Later that night, I text Kirsty about the house.

She replies straightaway. *'How do you feel about moving?'*

I tell her I feel fine about it, that it's the best thing for my parents.

'But what's the best thing for you?'

That makes me smile. *'Maybe it's the best thing for me too.'*

We talk about other stuff for a while. Kirsty's mum took her shopping today. She bought three tops and a pair of jeans from Primark. I bet some of the girls at Duncraggan have never even heard of Primark, let alone bought anything there.

I compose a message and then delete it. I rewrite it using different words and then delete it again. Third time lucky. I hit send before I can change my mind.

'I miss you.' It's not entirely true, but it's not a lie. I just wanted to say something nice, to show that things are fine between us. They seemed a bit strained at Renner's the other night, and Kirsty was super quiet at breakfast the next morning when the rest of us were chatting about our plans for the holiday. She didn't seem very excited about going home, but it sounds like she's having an OK time after all. I'm glad.

I can see that she's read the message, but her reply doesn't come through for a few minutes: *'I miss you too.'*

Jenna's bed is made up with the same sheets as mine – blue and floral, like a china cup. Mum still changes Jenna's sheets when she changes mine; it's not exactly healthy behaviour.

My suitcase is on the floor in between the beds. It would be much more sensible to put it on her bed, but I can't bring myself to do that. I can't bear to think of her bed as 'spare'.

Her make-up and perfume are still on the dressing table/desk (Jenna called it a desking table). The pictures she cut out of magazines are still on the wall next to her bed, and her clothes hang in the wardrobe all mixed up with mine. I get out of bed and start rummaging. We used to swap clothes all the time, until I got a little bit bigger than her. Until she started shrinking. There's a T-shirt of hers that I'm suddenly desperate to find. It was her favourite when we were about twelve. There's nothing special about it – red with a cartoon cat on the front. She wore it so much that it faded to a dusky pink and the cat started to crack and crinkle with age.

When Jenna was twelve, the T-shirt was baggy. By the time she was fourteen, it was tight but she still loved it as much as she ever had. A month before she died, the T-shirt was baggy again, swamping her tiny frame.

I find it right at the bottom of the pile. I bring it to my nose and inhale, but there's nothing left of her. It just smells musty and a little damp.

I spritz some of Jenna's perfume on to the fabric and bring it to my nose again. Better.

I remember when Jenna had the idea for us to choose our 'signature scents'. The perfumes we looked at weren't expensive, and the bottles were tiny – we couldn't afford to spend more than a tenner each. After sniffing what seemed like every bottle in the shop, I had a killer headache and my nostrils felt like they needed a holiday. But true to her word, Jenna did find me the perfect one – fresh and clean and zingy. I still wear it almost every day, even though Lily laughed when she saw the bottle in my room (*'Oh my God! I remember wearing this stuff when I was a kid!'*).

Jenna picked out the perfect perfume for herself too. Different from mine — spicy and rich and exotic. I smell it now and the memories hit me with such force that I have to sit down.

A tiny bottle of perfume on top of a white cabinet. A couple of 'Get well soon' cards. A jug of water with a green plastic lid, a full cup beside it, untouched. A bed, dwarfing the form under the sheets.

My twin, the other half of my soul, hooked up to a drip, looking like a child. A dying child.

TWENTY-THREE

The bottle of perfume and the T-shirt accompany me on my journey back to Duncraggan. There were other things of Jenna's I could have taken, but once I started, where would I stop?

In the car on the way to the station, Mum tells me not to worry. 'We won't be throwing anything away. I couldn't . . . I wouldn't.'

I'm relieved, but for some reason I choose not to show it. 'You know Jenna wouldn't care what happens to her things, don't you? It's just . . . stuff.'

'I know, but it's more than that to me. And to you, I think? I couldn't help noticing . . . At least, I hope you don't mind me asking, but you haven't been wearing her necklace.'

My heart plummets to the pit of my stomach and splashes into a pool of acid. *Of course* she noticed. 'I left it at school. I was worried about losing it.'

Instead of saying this makes no sense, because I've

worn it every other time I've been home, Mum just nods. 'Very sensible. Remember how upset I was when I lost Great Aunt Flora's ring on holiday?! And I never even liked it that much! Or her for that matter!' she laughs.

I laugh too. I perfected the art of fake laughter a long time ago.

As soon as I see Rowan, I remember. 'Shit! I'm so sorry, I forgot to reply to your message. I was just . . . there was a lot going on at home.'

Rowan nods slowly. Her lips are pressed together so hard that her chin dimples.

I try again. 'I'm really sorry, Rowan. I just forgot. I'm a terrible person, and a terrible friend, and I will do *anything* to make it up to you.'

'All right, all right, no need to go over the top. It's cool, I don't care.'

She's hurt, and I feel bad. But I'm tired after the journey – my train was delayed – and I've already had more than my fair share of guilt today from lying to Mum about Jenna's necklace. Then I notice the box of sweets sitting on my pillow and I feel terrible. I thank her for the sweets but she just shrugs and says they were lying around at home and no one else wanted them. She is the worst liar. I bet she made a special trip to the Korean supermarket, just for me.

I ask Rowan about her holiday and she says it was fine. I try again, pushing her for more details about what she got up to, but she's not budging. 'This and that,' she says.

I try a different approach. 'Wow, that must have been amazing! I've always wanted to try this. And that.'

'Ha. Ha.' Rowan turns her back on me and carries on taking clothes from her bag and neatly refolding them ready to go in her wardrobe.

'Ouch,' I mutter, but if she hears me she doesn't give any indication.

I put some music on to fill the silence between us. I quickly unpack my case, shoving things into drawers and on to shelves. The only thing I'm careful with is Jenna's T-shirt, which I fold as if it's made of the finest silk. I'm aware that Rowan's watching me, but she doesn't say anything, even when I put Jenna's perfume next to mine on the windowsill.

I'm about to ask Rowan about my necklace when she finally speaks to me. 'Have you seen Kirsty yet?'

'No. Why?'

Rowan shrugs.

'Why? Is she OK? Has something happened?'

Rowan just shakes her head and says nothing. What the hell is her problem?

*

153

I knock on Kirsty's door but I don't wait for an answer before entering the room. A choked cry escapes from my throat before my brain has time to process what my eyes are seeing. My sister is sitting on the other side of the room, curled up in the chair next to the window. Her hair falls in front of her face, just like it always used to.

She looks up and smiles.

Kirsty. It's Kirsty.

I shake my head slightly, trying to dislodge Jenna. But it doesn't work. I still see her, as if her image has been superimposed on top of the girl in front of me.

'You . . . you got your hair cut?'

Kirsty nods enthusiastically. 'Highlights too. It was Mum's idea. Her friend's daughter is a trainee hairdresser so we got a cheap deal. Do you like it?'

All I can manage is a nod, and she looks so pleased. She *must* realise, surely? Even if it wasn't her intention.

Then it hits me. *My* first thought was that she looks like Jenna, but that's not what other people will think. They'll think she looks like me.

Kirsty bounds over and hugs me. 'I missed you.'

'I missed you too,' I mumble into her hair.

The new haircut does suit her. Perhaps it's just a coincidence. And the more I look at it, the more I realise that it's not entirely identical to Jenna's – or mine. It's a couple of centimetres shorter, and maybe half a shade lighter.

She starts talking, telling me all about her holiday, and the things she and her mum got up to. They went to the zoo, a ritual they've had ever since Kirsty was a little girl. Kirsty's mum likes the penguins best; Kirsty prefers the meerkats. They went window shopping and got sandwiches from Tesco and sat in a park next to a pond even though it was freezing. It all sounds so *normal*.

She tells me about this old film called *Beaches* that her mum made her watch. 'You won't believe the ending . . . oh my God we cried so much. I can check if it's on Netflix if you like but then again maybe it's a bit too . . . What? What's the matter?'

I can't believe I didn't notice straightaway. Maybe because it's half hidden under her shirt collar. 'What are you doing with that?'

'With what?' She realises that I'm staring at her neck. 'Oh! I forgot to tell you!' Her fingers touch my necklace. Jenna's necklace. 'I found it just before I left for the airport. I didn't want to leave it here in case someone stole it. I know how special it is to you. I hope you don't—'

'Take it off.'

She struggles to undo the delicate catch at the back of her neck. I have to help her, sweeping her hair to one side to see the catch. There are three little moles on the back of her neck, just above where the necklace lies. They're lined up like three dots on a dice.

I'm shaking a little as I undo the catch. The pendant feels hot in my hand – warmed by her skin.

'You're not annoyed, are you?'

'No.' I put the necklace back where it belongs.

I'm not sure why I don't ask her the obvious questions. Where did she find it and why didn't she tell me? She must have known I'd be freaking out about it. And did she really think I would be OK with her wearing my dead sister's necklace?

'I have to go. I promised Rowan I'd help her with . . . anyway, I'll see you at dinner.'

'OK!' She smiles too brightly. 'See you then!'

I don't go back to my room. There's this little nook in the window of the east wing corridor. It's usually quiet, especially at this time of day. I sit on the window seat with my feet wedged against the opposite wall.

It's getting dark already, but Marek is still out there, working away in the vegetable garden. His grey hoodie is slung over the handle of a spade standing upright in the soil. It soothes me, watching him work. I wonder if he likes his job. It can't be easy, working outside in all weathers, freezing your arse off most of the time.

Marek stands up straight and stretches as a figure approaches. It's Lily. She keeps glancing over her shoulder as if she's worried someone might be spying on her, but she doesn't look up. She stops a couple of feet away from Marek and I see him smile. It doesn't look like this is the first time she's paid a special visit to the vegetable garden. Lily hands him a bottle of water and he gulps from it greedily.

I know I shouldn't spy like this, but it's irresistible. The wind whips Lily's hair across her face and she laughs and turns to face the wind. They chat for a few more minutes and then Marek gestures to the half-dug soil in front of him. I can almost lip-read as he tells her he should probably get back to work.

I'm still watching as Lily makes her way back towards the castle. I lean back in the alcove in case she looks up. She should be more careful. There are at least a dozen other windows overlooking the vegetable garden. In this place, you never know who might be watching. Rumours barely even need a spark before bursting into flames and rampaging through the school.

TWENTY-FOUR

Kirsty's quiet when we first sit down to dinner. She accepts the compliments about her hair, but other than that she's silent. Maybe I should have been nicer about the necklace. I probably would have been, if I hadn't been freaking out about the hair.

Ama asks about my holiday, and I tell the girls about my parents moving house. They all stop eating, but relax as soon as I say that I'm fine with it. Ama and Lily take that at face value and immediately start asking loads of questions about the house. Only Rowan still looks worried, which hopefully means she's forgiven me for not messaging her back over the holiday.

Lily asks what my new bedroom is like and I'm about to answer when Kirsty pipes up. 'Three times the size of her old one! Right, Harper?'

I nod and my skin prickles a little. It's OK though. For all Rowan knows I just gave Kirsty the lowdown when I was in her room earlier. But then she drops me right in it. 'I was SO excited when you sent me the pictures. It looks so nice, doesn't it, Rowan?'

Rowan finishes chewing a mouthful of chicken. She nods and says, 'Yeah, really nice.' I can't work out if she's covering for me being a shitty friend or if she's trying to make me feel guilty. Either way, I feel horrible.

What's needed here is a bit of distraction. 'So, Lil . . . was Marek pining for you over the holiday?'

Lily shrugs and takes a sip of water. 'How would I know? I haven't seen him yet.'

I don't call her out on the lie. It's odd though. She usually tells us about every single conversation – in painstakingly tedious detail. Why the change all of a sudden?

'Anyway,' she says, 'I'm pretty sure I'm over him.'

Ama's staring at Lily, clearly confused. It's obviously the first she's heard of it.

Rowan lets out an exaggerated sigh. 'Thank fuck for that. I was sick of hearing about him.'

'Thanks, Rowan. You're too kind. *Truly*.'

'Aw, come on, Lil. You must admit, you were getting a little bit obsessed.'

Rowan's smiling, but Lily's not. Ama's concentrating a little too closely on her plate, and Kirsty's watching, silent.

I decide to lighten the mood. 'Well, I for one am gutted. I totally thought you two were going to get married and live in a little eco-friendly hobbit house and have babies called Moonbeam and Starlight.'

Nobody laughs, probably because it wasn't funny, but Lil at least rolls her eyes and mutters a sarcastic 'Ha.'

Everything's a bit off-kilter tonight. It's sometimes like that after the holidays. It's almost like we need some time to adjust to being back here, together in this unnatural bubble of privilege.

'Connor! *Love* the new look! It really suits you!'

I close my eyes and hope that Marcy Stone disappears by the time I open them again. I used to do that when Jenna teased me about the monster lurking under my bed. I thought that as long as I kept my eyes tightly shut, nothing bad could happen to me. It worked back then because the monster under my bed was entirely fictional. Unfortunately, Marcy Stone is all too real.

She timed her move perfectly – it's just me and Kirsty left at the table. Marcy probably waited for Rowan to leave before she came slithering over. 'Thanks!' Kirsty can't help herself, and I suppose I can't blame her. Everybody likes getting compliments.

'The colour really suits you.' Marcy flicks a glance over at me. 'Who'd have thought you could ever take style inspiration from the postman's daughter?! You two could almost be sisters.'

A smile flickers across Kirsty's face but is extinguished when her eyes meet mine. It takes a second for me to understand the implications of what Marcy's just said.

'What did you say?' There's no mistaking the iciness in my voice.

'You look like sisters,' she speaks slowly, emphasising every word.

This is where it gets tricky. Either she knows about Jenna and is proving herself to be an even worse human being than I thought, or she doesn't know and just magically managed to stumble on the one thing that would make me want to punch her lights out. But there's no way to find out if she knows about Jenna without asking her, thereby effectively *telling* her about Jenna.

Marcy looks from me to Kirsty and back again. 'I mean it's uncanny, really. You could be twins.'

I push back my chair so fast she flinches and I'm right in her face, close enough to smell her shampoo. 'Say that one more time.'

Marcy doesn't step back. She couldn't be more delighted by this turn of events. I bet she'd like nothing more than for me to hit her and get myself suspended or excluded. It would almost be worth whatever punishment Maddox decided to dole out.

Kirsty's hand grasps my arm. 'Leave it, Harper. Come on, let's go.'

'Yeah, Harper. Why don't you listen to your little shadow?'

And coward that I am, I let her pull me away, leaving Marcy standing there looking impossibly pleased with herself.

I storm down the corridor with Kirsty scurrying to catch up. 'Who the fuck does she think she is? I swear she'll get what's coming to her one of these days.' A few Year 7s gathered round a noticeboard see me heading straight for them and plaster themselves cartoonishly against the wall.

Why is it that every corridor is filled with people just when I want nobody around? Gabi's face lights up, until she sees the thunderous look on my face. Whatever it was she was going to say to me, she's wise enough to keep her mouth shut.

I head to Kirsty's room because I can't face Rowan. Even my own room doesn't feel like a sanctuary any more.

'I feel like this is all my fault,' says Kirsty as soon as the door is closed behind us, shutting out the rest of Duncraggan.

'How could it possibly be your fault?' My words come out sharper and louder than intended.

'The hair,' she says quietly, looking down so that her face is hidden.

'It's not about the hair!' I slump down on to Kirsty's

bed, next to her suitcase. I trace my fingers on the pattern – the overlapping L and V instantly recognisable. 'OK, it was sort of about the hair, but that's not the point. She knows about Jenna. How the fuck does she know about Jenna?'

Kirsty sits on the rug in front of me even though there are two perfectly decent chairs to choose from. 'I don't know,' she says.

'It couldn't have been Ama. I can just about get my head around the lottery thing, but this? She wouldn't. She just wouldn't.'

'I didn't realise it was a secret. About your sister,' Kirsty says.

I open my mouth and then realise that she's right. I never told her not to say anything. 'It wasn't . . . you didn't happen to say anything to Marcy?'

'Of course not,' she says at the same time I realise exactly how Marcy found out. I bet she went online to look for the lottery story, maybe looking for a photo of my parents to print out and plaster all over the place. But she found another story instead, and another photo. My parents huddled on a saggy old green sofa, holding up a framed school photo of Jenna. A cautionary tale. Fucking Google.

I tell Kirsty my theory and she agrees that it's the most likely explanation.

I shake my head. 'It was stupid, thinking I could

keep a secret like that in this day and age.'

Kirsty's staring into space again and I have to remind myself that I'm not the only one with problems. 'Are you OK? You've been quiet since you got back. Missing your mum?'

'I . . .' She takes a deep breath and looks me right in the eyes and there's something strangely bright there. 'Yes.'

I tell her that it gets better – the homesickness. Then I do my best to distract her . . . by talking about Marcy again. But this time I try to keep things light – telling her about the time Rowan wrapped every single thing in Marcy and Tatiana's room in several layers of cling film.

Before long we're laughing and by the time I'm back in my room I'm beginning to think it doesn't matter that Marcy knows about Jenna. People *should* know about Jenna. She existed. She exists, in me.

I'm half asleep by the time Rowan gets back from dealing with some minor stage crew disaster – something to do with a light rig falling and nearly flattening Ruth Pilkington.

It's not a conscious decision to keep quiet about what happened with Marcy. It's just that I'm exhausted and the thought of going through it all again is even more exhausting. What's done is done. Marcy knows about Jenna and there's nothing I can do about it.

Marcy's not stupid though – she knows she's not going to win any popularity points by telling everyone else that my twin sister died. If anything, it could make *me* more popular, or at least more sympathetic, and that's the last thing she'd want.

I'm drifting off to sleep, replaying the Marcy conversation and imagining all the different ways it could have gone, when the image of Kirsty's suitcase pops into my head.

Louis Vuitton? Those things cost the best part of two thousand quid. How the hell could she afford that?

TWENTY-FIVE

On Monday, Marcy barely even looks in my direction through breakfast, lessons and lunch. Even when we're standing right next to each other, going through the safety checks with our shotguns at the shooting range, Marcy acts like I don't exist. It's unsettling, but I'll take unsettling over awkward-confrontation-in-which-I'm-too-pathetic-to-say-what-I-actually-mean any day. I shoot badly, but I'm always rusty after the holidays. Marcy shoots well, as always. If she doesn't want to follow her mother into politics, she can always fall back on a career as a sniper.

Kirsty asks if we can study together on Tuesday night, but I've already promised to hang out with Rowan. I suggest that Kirsty asks Gabi to test her on her French vocab. Gabi may be annoying, but she's always – *always* – willing to help.

'What are you up to with Rowan?' Kirsty asks, all casual, as if she doesn't really care. It's quite sweet, really.

'Unsure. She said she has a favour to ask me, but she's being super shifty about what it actually entails.' I tell her that I'll come and see her later, after the mysterious favour has been dealt with.

It's easier to look at Kirsty now; I don't have that brain-freezing moment whenever she walks into a room. She's washed her hair and it doesn't look so much like Jenna's (or mine) any more. She'd need hair straighteners for that, and I'm pretty sure she doesn't have any. And if she doesn't even have a pair of ghds, there's no way in hell she's got a Louis Vuitton suitcase. It must be a knock-off; she probably thought it would help her fit in with the rich kids. Someone should have told her that these girls can spot a fake at twenty paces.

Rowan wants me to shave her head. She's been going on about this for months now, and we've always managed to talk her out of it, but this time she's adamant.

'You're the only one I trust, Harper,' she says solemnly, holding out the clippers like Obi-Wan Kenobi handing Luke Skywalker his first lightsaber.

God knows why she wants me to do it; Ama would be a much better choice. She bustles around the room, putting newspaper down and finding some scissors, while I hastily look up some head-shaving tutorials on YouTube. Thank fuck for YouTube.

'So what look are you after? Ripley or Imperator Furiosa?'

Rowan gives it some thought. 'Furiosa, definitely.'

I sit on my desk chair and Rowan sits on the floor between my legs.

I reckon I'll start with the scissors, getting rid of as much hair as I can before using the clippers. 'Any last words?'

'Dude. It's a haircut, not an execution.'

I snip away, slowly at first then faster when I become more confident.

'So, going anywhere nice on your holidays?' I ask in my best hairdresser voice.

'You are ridiculous, Harper.'

'Ridiculously *awesome*,' I say, and she shakes her head, which means I narrowly avoid stabbing her ear with the scissors.

The best bit is when I lather up her scalp with shaving cream. 'So does this mean I have to do this every week? Is that what I've signed up for here?'

She leans back her head so that she's looking at me upside down. 'Yup, pretty much. So you'll have to come to uni with me too. Hope that's OK?'

The truth is I would love to go to uni with Rowan. If only I had a chance of getting into any of the same places as her. 'Sure. You can just pack me up in your suitcase and bring me out whenever you need.'

She sits up straight again, and when she speaks her voice is different – more thoughtful. 'Sometimes I wish we could just stay here for ever.'

'You hate it here!'

'I hate the game, not the players.' Her hand brushes against my bare ankle and I'm not sure if it's intentional. 'And you're my favourite player.'

'You know, that could be the nicest thing you've ever said to me.'

She shrugs. 'I'm just buttering you up so you don't fuck up my hair.'

It turns out that I'm a natural with the clippers. Seriously. I should just train to become a barber instead of stressing about my UCAS form. I leave a short fuzz of hair on Rowan's head, just like she requested.

I'm glad I can do this for her. I've been a shitty friend recently. I know that now.

I hand over the mirror so that Rowan can have a look. Her grin is spectacular. 'Bloody hell.'

'What do you reckon your mum will say?'

'What, you mean *after* she tells me how much I look like my uncle Jun? Seriously, it's uncanny.'

'You look good,' I say, and she tilts the mirror so that our eyes meet. I run my hand over her scalp and it's like petting a mole. Not that I've ever petted a mole.

169

'You like it?' And Rowan, who literally has no fucks to give about what anyone thinks about her – ever – looks shy.

'I *love* it.'

She closes her eyes as my fingers run over her scalp and it's the strangest thing. I know we should get a move on and clear up all this hair, but I can't bring myself to stop. And it seems like she doesn't want me to.

Then there's a knock at the door and Ama and Lily burst right in, with Kirsty behind them.

'Whoa!' says Lily. She hurries over and puts her hands on Rowan's head even as Rowan tries to clamber up from the floor. 'Ooooh! Fuzzy!'

Ama tilts her head. 'You look like one of those babies . . . you know, when the mum has to stick a pink bow on their head so people don't think they're a boy. It really suits you though!'

Kirsty lingers awkwardly in the doorway. 'Yeah, it looks nice.'

Rowan mutters thank you, then sets about clearing up the hair-strewn newspaper while Lily explains that we need to get sorted for Halloween and this is our first official planning meeting.

'Did Gabi give you a hand?' I ask Kirsty when she sits down next to me.

Kirsty shakes her head. 'I managed by myself.' I

wonder if that's a dig at me, but she doesn't seem annoyed, so perhaps I'm just being paranoid.

When we're all settled down and Lily is banging on about making this the best Halloween ever, Rowan catches my eye and smiles. She really does look good with her head shaved.

I figure it's got to be a positive sign that Lily and Ama want Kirsty involved in the Halloween planning. They didn't have to do that. It makes me think that maybe things are getting back to normal for all of us – a new kind of normal.

TWENTY-SIX

'OK, so Renner's given us the go-ahead to do what we want – within reason. We'll have the usual get-together in her flat but we wanted to do something a bit different beforehand.'

Halloween is a big deal at Duncraggan; each house does their own thing. Balmedie girls always have a fancy-dress competition. Roundhouse usually go on a torchlit walk through the forest. Fairclough's Halloween is normally quite low-key – creepy cupcakes, zombie punch and a bunch of pumpkins.

'What did you have in mind?' I ask.

Lily smiles smugly. 'A ghost tour!'

We all 'Ooh' obligingly. It's a good idea. After all, Duncraggan has more than its fair share of ghost stories. You can take your pick from the lord's son who was gored by a stag on a hunting expedition, the guard who fell from the ramparts (or was he pushed?) and the serving girl who died in the fire that ripped through the east wing of the castle in 1868.

Lily's clearly been doing a lot of planning already. The tour will just be for the lower-school girls; it's a manageable number and they'll be the easiest to scare. The older girls can get things set up at Renner's. Lily will lead the tour, dressed up as 'ye olde slightly slutty kitchen maid'. The rest of us will be lying in wait in various rooms, ready to scare the bejesus out of the poor kids.

'We'll need two people in the trophy room.' Everyone hates the trophy room. It's already a chamber of death, with stags' heads on the walls and stuffed animals of varying levels of creepiness displayed on every available surface. 'I was thinking Harper and Rowan, if that's cool with you guys?' We both nod our assent. 'Ama can cover the library – zombie librarian, maybe? – and I can ask Hozzie, Gabi and the others to come up with something for the east wing. We can raid the drama department for costumes. So that leaves Kirsty. I thought you'd make a perfect Lady Fairclough – big hair, heaving bosom, that sort of thing. You can roam the halls, searching for your lost love . . . or some bollocks like that. I'll make something up.'

We start discussing costumes and ideas for scaring the younger girls out of their minds. Ama tells us that

Gabi has a gorilla costume in her wardrobe and we spend at least ten minutes trying to figure out *why* she has a gorilla costume, and why Ama's the only one who seems to know anything about it.

'What about special effects?' says Kirsty, getting involved for the first time.

'What do you mean?' asks Lily.

'Well, wouldn't it be cool if there were sound effects and dry ice and that sort of thing?'

Lily wrinkles her nose. 'I don't know . . . it sounds like a lot of work.'

I think it's a great idea. 'Rowan could do it, couldn't you Ro? You're brilliant with all that stuff.'

'I didn't think! Of course! OK, so Rowan can roam the corridors – don't worry, you don't have to be Lady Fairclough! You can be . . . I dunno . . . a creepy bald ghost girl or something. If you stay one step ahead of the tour you can manage the effects in each room. It is a lot of work, but it'll be worth it.'

'What, so you can get credit for organising the best Halloween in the entire history of Fairclough?' Rowan says.

Lily smiles winningly. 'Pretty much. So what do you say?'

Rowan sighs. 'OK, OK, I'll do it.' I can tell her mind is already whirring with ideas; she loves this shit.

The revised plan is for Kirsty to be with me in

the trophy room. It's going to be such a laugh. We're all buzzing, throwing ideas around and generally feeling pretty pleased with ourselves. I sit back and listen to the others, and I feel something close to nostalgia. It's hard to believe we only have eight more months together before we all go our separate ways.

A couple of days later, Lily and Ama come bounding into our room when Rowan and I are getting dressed. 'Happy Halloween, bitches!' Lily shouts. 'Trick or treat?'

'Um . . . I'd settle for friends who knock on the fucking door before barging into my room,' says Rowan, rushing to pull her shirt on. She's never been comfortable with the rest of us seeing her undressed.

Lily gives us each a Halloween lollipop, and proceeds to pretend to give her lollipop a blowjob. 'Thanks for putting me off these *for ever*,' says Rowan, handing her lolly to me.

Ama's brought her teddy bear – a scruffy old thing with one eye missing. 'You promise you'll look after Mr Pickles?' she asks me.

'I promise. I'll treat him as if he was my own. Oh God . . . please tell me this isn't the bear that you masturbated with!'

'Don't stress, he's been through the wash a few times since then,' she says cheerfully, and cackles when she sees the horror on my face. 'I'm kidding! Mr Pickles is pure as the driven snow. Honestly.'

Rowan and Lily run through the plans for each room, then Rowan turns to me. 'So I was in the trophy room last night, trying to work out where to put the speakers, and I found the perfect place for you and Kirsty to hide. I can't believe I didn't know about it before,' she says, as if Duncraggan has been deliberately withholding its secrets from her. 'It's a bit of a tight squeeze though. What is it with this castle and small, enclosed places?'

Lily drapes her arm around Rowan. 'It's *symbolic*, darling.' She kisses Rowan on the cheek, mock-whispers '*Vaginas*,' and then she and Ama hurry off to see Miss Renner before breakfast.

'Just how small is this hiding place?' I ask, wondering why Rowan didn't tell me sooner.

'It's . . . cosy. Kirsty will be happy.' She looks at me in the mirror as she finishes the knot on her tie. 'She got what she wanted, I guess.'

'What do you mean?'

'Oh, come on, Harper. Don't tell me you didn't realise.' She pauses for me to catch on, but I keep my face blank. 'The only reason she suggested the special effects was so she could be with you tonight. *Obviously*.' She says the last word in her Snape voice. It usually makes me smile, but not today.

'Did it ever occur to you that maybe she suggested it because she wanted tonight to be a success? And because she knows you're really good at this sort of thing?'

She suppresses a smile and pats me on the shoulder. 'Sure, maybe that's it after all.' She's out the door before I can tell her not to be so fucking patronising.

I want to be annoyed with her and chase her down the corridor and tell her she couldn't be more wrong. Trouble is, I think she's right.

But so what if Rowan is right? What's so wrong with Kirsty preferring to spend time with me than tramping up and down the hallways on her own? If anything, I should be flattered.

TWENTY-SEVEN

Dinner is an hour early to allow plenty of time for Halloween shenanigans. Some of the teachers have dressed up as Hogwarts teachers and everyone agrees that Maddox's Dolores Umbridge costume is a little too good.

Lily is pleased with herself, having found out that the other houses have nothing special planned. She's really big on house pride, Lil. I used to take the piss about it, but today, on our last Halloween, I'm feeling it too. Boarding school has a tendency to bring out your competitive streak, even if you didn't know you had one.

None of the younger kids have a clue what's going on. One of the braver ones comes over during dinner and asks Lil, who shrugs nonchalantly. 'I wouldn't get too excited. We're just going to take a little walk.'

The kid isn't quite brave enough to voice her disappointment. She nods and says 'Sounds good!' and 'Thank you.' That's another thing about boarding school – it teaches you manners – or at least how to fake them.

We split up after dinner. Rowan still has a lot to do; she's managed to rope in Hozzie as her assistant. Ama is on make-up duty and has been mainlining episodes of *The Walking Dead* for inspiration.

Kirsty and I get ready in my room, not that we actually have that much getting ready to do. No fancy costumes for us – we have to wear black. But it turns out that Kirsty doesn't own a black top. She turns up wearing black leggings and a school hoodie.

'Have a look in my wardrobe – second shelf. I think there's a long-sleeved top at the back somewhere.' I'm pulling on my socks and tucking the bottom of my trousers in. We've decided not to wear shoes, for maximum ninja stealth.

Kirsty rummages through my shelves and I remember about Jenna's T-shirt at the same moment that she pulls it out, a smile on her face. 'What's *this*?' She holds it up against herself. 'Bit small for you, isn't it?'

I manage to keep it together. I don't rush over and snatch it out of her hands. Because it's Kirsty; she understands. 'It's Jenna's,' I say quietly.

She pauses for a moment, before carefully folding the T-shirt and placing it back on the shelf. She pulls out the black top and sits on the edge of the bed.

I sit down next to her. 'It helps, a little. Having

179

her things around me.' I expect Kirsty to agree, but she says nothing. 'Do you . . . have anything that makes you feel closer to Rhiannon?' I wish she would talk about her more, instead of keeping everything all bottled up. But you can't force it. I know how I felt when people tried to get me to talk about Jenna. You just have to wait.

Just when I'm sure that she's not going to answer my question, Kirsty stands up and pulls her hoodie over her head. Underneath, she's wearing a plain black bra.

'I have this,' she whispers. Her skin is milk pale and smooth. Except where it's not. There's an uneven, dull reddish scar right across her stomach and another scything up diagonally and disappearing under her bra.

I stare, for too long.

'Seatbelt,' she says, not taking her eyes off me.

Her fingers run across her skin, tracing the lines. I have the strangest desire to reach out and touch her, to feel the difference between the rough and the smooth.

This is her memento. She carries it with her every second of every day. It can never be misplaced or lost or forgotten. It stays with her, always.

Rowan wasn't kidding about the hiding place being small. God knows how she realised there was this nook behind the tapestry. There is literally no reason for it to exist except as a place to hide, listen or snoop. Maybe they used to draw lots about who got to hide in the Hole in the library and who got to hide here. I know which I'd have chosen – it's much warmer here. I could do without the smell though; it reminds me of Great Aunt Flora's mahogany wardrobe.

We waited until the ghost tour was well underway before taking our places. We ran into Miss Renner on our way down here, and she took one look at us and our props and said, 'It's probably better if I don't ask.'

Rowan was considerate enough to sling a couple of cushions in here, and Kirsty and I are sitting with our backs against the wall and our knees drawn up against our chests.

A few chinks of light leak around the edges of the tapestry, just enough so that it's not pitch black, and there's a tiny hole in the fabric through which I can see the rest of the room if I lean on Kirsty's knees a bit.

I check the time on my phone. We've got fifteen, maybe twenty minutes before Lily leads the girls down here for the big finale.

'So what was your best-ever Halloween costume?' I ask Kirsty. I whisper, even though there's really no reason to. I want to keep things light, since she made it perfectly clear she didn't want to talk about the car crash. When I tried asking, she said, 'I can't. I'm sorry,' and quickly covered herself up. My top is a little tight on her but she was kind enough to pretend it fits perfectly.

'I never liked dressing up at Halloween,' she says.

'Really? I used to love it.' I tell Kirsty about my favourite ever Halloween, when Mum dressed Jenna and me up like the twins from *The Shining*. Of course, we hadn't seen the film. We just thought the old-fashioned dresses were hilarious, along with the white knee socks and shiny black sandals. Mum had us standing at the top of the stairs, hand in hand, waiting in the dark for Dad to get back from the pub after work. We didn't think it was particularly scary or Halloweeny —until we saw Dad's face when he switched on the hall light. It took a long time for us to stop doing impressions of his surprisingly high-pitched scream.

Kirsty says she hasn't seen *The Shining*, and we fall into silence. I'm sure she's thinking about the car accident, and I want to snap her out of it. I want her to be here, with me, now.

'My first kiss was on Halloween.' I can't help smiling at the memory, before I remember that it was Jenna's last Halloween. I wonder if I'll ever be able to remember anything without that crushing sadness hitting me every time.

'Who did you kiss?' Kirsty asks, shifting a little so that our shoulders touch.

'Marvin Roth, when we were playing Seven Minutes in Heaven. You know those things you do when you're younger that seem really normal at the time and it's only when you look back that you see how fucked up they are? Like why on earth did I agree to go into a dark room with some random boy I didn't fancy? And why the fuck did I let him put his tongue in my mouth?'

'Because you wanted to see what it was like?' she asks.

'Well, yeah. I guess so. By the time that seven minutes was over I knew enough to know I wanted to try it again – with someone else.'

Kirsty doesn't laugh. 'Can I tell you a secret?'

'Of course.' It worries me though – scares me a little, even. How many more of Kirsty's secrets am I going to have to keep?

'Promise you won't tell anyone?'

'I promise. Cross my heart and all that jazz.'

She moves and her leg shifts against mine. 'I've never kissed anyone before.'

This really wasn't what I was expecting, and yet somehow, I'm not altogether surprised. 'There's nothing wrong with that.'

'I didn't say there was,' she says, and I think I can hear the smile in her voice. It's hard to tell in the gloom.

'OK.' This seems like the safe thing to say. Where's she going with this?

'How did you know that you like girls as well as boys?' Kirsty asks. So *that's* where she's going.

It's not that she's asked the question. I'm used to being asked the question; it's one of the joys of being bisexual. Funny that people never seem to ask it the other way round – how I knew I liked boys as well as girls – because that couldn't possibly be the case, right? I've never been able to get my head round people's obsession with sexuality.

There's something different going on here though. A couple of differences, actually. Her hand has magically appeared on my knee. The hand isn't doing anything, but it's very much *there*. And it doesn't seem to be going anywhere anytime soon.

The other difference is her tone of voice. You pay more attention to things like that in the dark. It's smoother, like silk. Less timid or awkward than you might expect, particularly after her admission about not having kissed anyone before. If I didn't know better, I might have described it as flirtatious.

But do I know better, *really*? For all I've poured my heart out to this girl, I don't know all that much about her. Except now I know that she's never been kissed. And instead of following that up with some stuttering explanation about not having met anyone she likes or that one time at that party where the boy she liked kissed someone else, she followed it up by asking me about liking girls. Why would she do that? Unless . . .

I reach out to move her hand from my knee, but something stops me. I don't want to hurt her feelings. She's probably just being friendly.

Kirsty shifts and her face is suddenly very, very close to mine. 'Well?' she whispers. 'How did you know?'

And then she's leaning in towards me and there is no mistaking this – there just *isn't* – and what the fuck am I going to do?

I don't want this to happen. It's not like that with her. I don't see her that way. So why am I staying silent? Why don't I lean away, make a joke, say something – *anything* – to stop what's happening here?

Why is my heart hammering in my ribcage like it's trying to escape right out of my chest?

Her face is millimetres away now, her breath warm on my cheek. This is going to actually happen, even though I don't want it to. I *don't*.

TWENTY-EIGHT

Sudden, clattering footsteps echo round the room. 'Guys! Psssst! Guys! They're on their way!' By the time Gabi's face peers round the side of the tapestry, Kirsty's hand is no longer on my knee and she's shifted away from me.

Gabi gives us a double thumbs-up and wishes us luck and then bounds out of the room again. The ensuing silence is vast, endless in its awkwardness. I feel almost faint with gratitude when Lily leads the girls into the room.

Everything goes to plan; it's even better than we'd planned. Lil puts her acting training to good use, spinning a tale about the hunters who 'needlessly killed all these glorious creatures, these noble beasts'. She tells them the rumour that once a year, on Halloween, the spirits of the animals come back to seek vengeance on the descendants of the humans who killed them. It's a nice touch when Lil scoffs at the idea, which encourages the girls to do the same. At that exact moment, the lights go out and the door slams shut.

Kirsty and I sneak out of our hiding place, keeping close to the walls and heading to opposite sides of the room. The girls are giggling and all talking at once and generally enjoying themselves, until I hit the button on the remote control and snuffling animal noises sound out from different corners of the room. There are a couple of half-hearted screams when I push the button to activate the bellowing stag noise, and total pandemonium when some of the girls feel the brush of fur against their faces.

Before things get out of hand, the lights come up and everyone laughs when they see what was going on. It was Rowan's idea – teddy bears dangling from the ends of fishing rods.

It's hilarious and silly and brilliant and exactly the kind of memory I should want to bottle up and store for ever, but all I can think about is Kirsty. I watch her from across the room, smiling and apologising to a couple of Year 7s who are still clutching each other in terror. She doesn't look over at me – not once.

It's not till much later that I get a chance to talk to her. The party's been going on for an hour or so and a bunch of people are dancing to 'Monster Mash', which is playing for the fifth time. Lily and Zombie

Ama are posing for photographs, and Rowan is talking to Gabi about horror films. Kirsty is alone, ladling some punch from the cauldron, so I hurry over to her, trying not to look like I'm hurrying over to her.

'Can we . . . talk?'

'Sure. What do you want to talk about?'

I shake my head. 'Not here.'

In the empty corridor, I try to order my thoughts before I speak. 'Listen, Kirsty, about earlier . . .' Her face is curiously blank, even though there's no way she doesn't know what I'm talking about. 'When you asked about me liking girls . . .' Kirsty nods, waiting for me to go on. 'What exactly did you mean by that?'

She shakes her head and frowns a little. 'What do you mean?'

She's not making this easy for me. 'I just . . . It felt like . . .'

'Felt like what?'

'I kind of got the feeling that you sort of maybe were going to . . . erm, kiss me or something.'

'*What?!* Why would you think that?' It's as if her face can't decide between smiling and frowning – it oscillates between the two. 'You're my *friend*, Harper.' And she couldn't put more emphasis on the word if she tried.

'I . . . yes, of course. Sorry, I didn't mean to imply . . .' I stare down at the rug. There's a fake plastic spider next to my shoe. At least, I think it's fake. It's hard to tell what's real and what's not.

Kirsty puts a comforting hand on my arm. A friendly hand of a friendly friend who would never try to kiss me in a million years. 'I'm sorry if you got the wrong idea. I was just making conversation. I was curious, that's all.' She pauses, and tilts her head. 'Is everything OK? You're acting a little—'

'I'm fine. Everything's fine. Let's go see if there are any cupcakes left.' I turn away quickly, so that she can't see how very not fine I am.

It turns out there are no cupcakes left.

How could I have misread things so badly? I play it over and over again in my head – the question, her voice, her face so close to mine – but the memory must be distorted somehow. I was wrong. It's that simple.

It's been a while since I've kissed anyone so maybe I just wanted someone to want to kiss me. It's hardly a satisfactory explanation, but it's all I can come up with.

I won't let myself picture what might have happened if Gabi hadn't come bounding in. Thank God for Gabi Get Involved.

TWENTY-NINE

'Come on, then. Are you going to tell me what's up, or am I going to have to bug you about it for days before you cave and tell me? May I suggest the former option, to save us both time.' Rowan cracks a smile and I know she wants me to smile too but I can't.

Kirsty didn't come back to the party and I couldn't decide if I was glad about that or not. Things were starting to wind down anyway – the music had been turned down, the lower-school girls had been packed off to bed and everyone else was sitting around chatting. Lily and Miss Renner were talking about Oxford, while Ama and Rowan discussed the practicalities of defending Duncraggan in the event of a zombie apocalypse. I sat in the middle, half listening to both conversations, contributing the odd word or two so no one would ask me what was wrong. I was relieved when Renner checked her watch and said we should call it a night.

*

The mattress dips as Rowan sits down next to me, perching on the side of my bed. 'Are you annoyed I didn't save you a cupcake? Would it make you feel better if I told you they were made by Marcy and Tatiana and actually tasted of sadness and shattered dreams?'

That makes me smile, but the smile crumples fast and, annoyingly, I start to cry.

'Oh shit, what's the matter? Harper? Talk to me.'

I tell her everything, and the act of talking makes me feel a little better. It helps that Rowan doesn't burst out laughing or look at me like I'm some kind of freak. I tell her about the conversation I had with Kirsty in the corridor.

'How could I have been so stupid?'

'Here's the thing, Harper. You're *not* stupid. Trust your instincts. If you thought she was going to kiss you, then she was going to kiss you. The more important question is *why*.'

I sniff and wipe my nose on my sleeve. 'What do you mean?'

'Well, either she fancies you and this is the first time she's ever shown it, or she was gaslighting you. And hard as it is to believe – irresistible as you are – I really don't think she fancies you. Or any girl for that matter.'

Rowan prides herself on her gaydar; she says it never fails. I'm not sure about that but she does seem to have an uncanny ability to identify queer celebrities well before they come out. As superpowers go, it's not particularly useful.

'She's not gaslighting me,' I say firmly.

'Come on. This is pretty much the definition of gaslighting. She deliberately manipulated you and then made you question your own sanity.'

'But why would she do that? I think maybe she's just confused. Like, for a second there she wanted to kiss me, just to see what it was like, but then she got freaked out and decided to deny the whole thing.'

'It's possible, I guess.' But she doesn't sound convinced. Maybe Rowan was the wrong person to confide in about this; she's never liked Kirsty.

'Did you . . . did you want to kiss her?' She looks away, and I'm surprised that the question embarrasses her.

'No! She's my *friend*, Rowan.' Rowan opens her mouth and shuts it again. 'What? What were you going to say?' I don't want her to edit herself with me.

'Why do you like her so much? She never seems to have anything interesting to say.'

'She says plenty of interesting things when it's just the two of us. You guys don't give her the chance. You don't know how hard it is, coming to Duncraggan and trying to fit in.'

'Um . . . hi. I went to boarding school when I was *eight*. You have no fucking idea.'

'I know, but that's different. Look, you wanted to know why I like her and I'm trying to tell you if you'll just listen. Kirsty and I have a lot in common.'

'Like what? What exactly do you have in common?'

The scepticism on Rowan's face is beyond infuriating. 'Well, for one thing, she wasn't born with a silver spoon in her mouth. Her family's normal — like mine.'

'Really? So how the hell can they afford the school fees?'

'She's on a scholarship!' I know it's betraying Kirsty's confidence, but I'm desperate for Rowan to understand.

Rowan barks out a laugh. 'Did she tell you that?'

I nod tentatively.

'There are only two scholarship places per year. Olivia Dixon got hers for music, and Sara Thorne is some kind of fucking maths prodigy.'

Why didn't I know that? Why does Rowan always know *everything*? 'Well, they must have decided to offer another scholarship.' I get up from the bed and start brushing my hair, trying not to look at my blotchy face in the mirror.

'Yeah? And what exactly would that scholarship be for? You know Kirsty's struggling in almost every subject, don't you? Ama says it's starting to be a real issue in their classes.'

I turn to look at her, still lounging on my bed as if everything's fine. 'I don't *know* what Kirsty's scholarship is for and I don't particularly care! All I was trying to say is that she gets where I'm coming from and you . . .'

'And I *what*?' She sits up straight and there's no mistaking the challenge in her eyes.

None of the words that pop into my head seem to be the right ones, but I have to try to make her understand. 'It's just that . . . it's not easy, being surrounded by all this privilege. People who've never known what it's like to struggle.'

'Oh for fuck's sake, Harper. Can you even hear yourself? You're rich too, you do realise that? So what if it only happened a couple of years ago?! And anyone would think you'd been living on the streets, the way you go on about it. You had a decent house and parents with decent jobs . . . you weren't exactly Oliver fucking Twist so why don't you just get over yourself?'

It's like being slapped, only more painful. I stand there, stunned.

Rowan's face softens straight away. 'I'm sorry. That wasn't fair. I just can't stand seeing you like this, being manipulated by this girl. Harper?'

I shake my head. I have nothing to say to her.

She goes over to her desk and opens her laptop. After a few seconds tapping away, she beckons me over to look at the scholarships page on Duncraggan's website.

Two per year, sponsored by alumni: one academic, one extracurricular.

I close the laptop lid without a word and start getting ready for bed. Rowan hovers the whole time, trying to catch my eye. 'I'm sorry, Harper. I don't know what else you want me to say.'

'I think you've said more than enough.'

I turn off my bedside light and turn to face the wall. A few minutes later Rowan turns off her light and says a quiet 'Good night.' I don't reply.

I know I shouldn't be pissed off at her for being right about the scholarship, but I have every right to be pissed off about everything else. There was no need for her to go off like that when I was just trying to be honest with her.

I should have realised as soon as I saw the suitcase that Kirsty was lying – I'm sure any idiot could tell it's not a fake. But why would she lie about something like that?

If I want to get to the bottom of this, I'm going to have to talk to her. And that would have been awkward enough even *before* what happened tonight.

THIRTY

It may be a cliché but a decent night's sleep really does put things into perspective. It helps that there are the beginnings of a gorgeous sunrise waiting for me when I open the curtains. It also helps that Rowan doesn't try to act like everything's OK. She apologises again and she's so sincere that I don't have the energy to stay mad at her. Plus there's the whispering voice inside my head telling me that she was right – maybe it's about time I accepted that I'm not some special snowflake here.

Rowan asks what I'm going to do about Kirsty, and I tell her the truth: I have no fucking idea.

'You should confront her.' This is so typical of Rowan that I can't help but smile.

'And say what?'

'Ask her a) why she lied to you about her folks being broke and b) why the fuck she tried to kiss you and c) why she's denying it.'

'Riiiiight, and should I do that before or after breakfast?'

'During. That way I can back you up.'

'You do realise there is precisely zero chance of my taking your advice?'

'Oh yes,' she says cheerfully. 'But that doesn't make my advice any less excellent.'

I love this girl, I really do.

I take the coward's way out, obviously. I pretend that everything's fine at breakfast, and Kirsty seems to be doing the same. Halloween is all anyone wants to talk about, and Lily is basking in glory. Rowan does a pretty good job of not being shifty around Kirsty, mostly by ignoring her, which is very easy to do.

When we're waiting to clear our trays, Kirsty asks what time we're heading down to the clay-pigeon range. I have to think on my feet. 'Sorry, I have to . . . I'm seeing Miss Renner to talk about my UCAS form.' The best lies are ones that *could* be true. Renner's been on at me for the past couple of weeks to come and see her if I need help with my personal statement.

'Right. Well how about we study together tonight then?'

'I said I'd help Rowan with something.' This lie comes out smoother, but the vagueness weakens it.

'OK then. I guess I'll see you at lunch?'

'Sure. Lunch. Yes.' Lunch is safe. Rowan and Ama and Lily make it safe.

Avoiding someone is pretty much impossible at Duncraggan but I give it my best shot, mostly by sticking to Rowan like super-strength super glue. I know Rowan thinks I'm being lame, but at least she hasn't said so. She's also promised not to tell Ama and Lily about Kirsty. Unlike me, Rowan can actually keep a secret.

I keep myself busy over the next few days. Outside of lessons, I help Lily in the vegetable garden, even though she said she didn't need any help. I turn the pages of Ama's sheet music when she plays piano, even though she can do it herself perfectly well. I even talk to Renner about my personal statement, which turns out to be really helpful; I should have done it weeks ago.

Saturday afternoon is one of my favourite times to swim in the indoor pool. The swim team is often away at meets, and everyone else is either busy with other sports and activities or heading to the village. The pool's never completely deserted, but I can always get a lane to myself and drift off into my own little underwater world. Today there's only the school secretary, Mrs Barton, swimming a sedate breaststroke and keeping her head above water so her hair doesn't get messed up.

Sometimes I swim the last length as fast as possible. It's a thing Jenna and I used to do, years ago. We'd pretend there was a shark chasing us and we had to reach the other end of the pool before it got us.

I slap my hand on the side of the pool and come up for air.

'That was really fast.' Her face is in shadow when I look up, the harsh overhead light haloing her head. 'No wonder Mr Tovey is annoyed you won't join the team.'

I boost myself out of the pool and she hands me my towel. I wonder if it's a deliberate move on her part, coming here to remind me of how we became friends in the first place. Or maybe it's just the only place she could talk to me without the others around.

'Thanks,' I say, wrapping the towel around myself.

'You've been avoiding me.' The words don't sound like an accusation, just a statement of fact.

'What do you mean? I saw you at lunch, and at breakfast.'

'You barely even looked at me, let alone talked to me.'

I'm about to deny it, but what's the point? She's here now; I can't avoid this for ever. 'I think we should talk.'

'I'd like that.' I look at her properly, for the first time in days. She has dark circles under her eyes.

Mrs Barton makes her way up the steps at the side of the pool and heads towards the changing rooms. Only a few strands of hair at the top of her neck are damp, and her make-up is still flawless. It's good timing, because I don't want to talk to Kirsty in the changing rooms. We need neutral territory.

'Meet me in the stand on the astro pitch in ten minutes?'

I don't bother to dry my hair even though Mrs Barton warns me I'll catch my death out there.

Kirsty's sitting right at the top of the stand, watching the junior hockey team practising penalties. There's no one else in the stand because who in their right mind would choose to spend their Saturday afternoon watching the junior hockey team doing anything?

I sit one seat away from her, and she says a shy 'hello' then goes back to biting at her thumbnail. I never noticed that she bites her nails; Jenna used to chew hers down to the quick.

'You're not really here on a scholarship, are you?' It's what Rowan would do – no messing about – and I'm oddly proud of myself for doing the same.

Her eyes widen in surprise. '*What?*'

'You lied about the scholarship. Why did you do that?'

She's silent for a minute and I decide not to push her. 'How did you find out?'

'Rowan told me.' There's a flash of something in her eyes, but it's gone before I have a chance to decipher it.

'I asked you not to tell anyone about it.'

'I know.' I don't feel the need to explain myself, and I'm definitely not going to tell her that Rowan knows all about what happened in the trophy room. 'Why did you lie?' I ask, more gently this time, because she looks pretty wretched. She's torn the skin next to her thumbnail and made it bleed.

'I didn't want you to think I was like them.' She watches the blood well up, then puts her thumb to her mouth. 'I wanted you to like me.'

'Why would you being on a scholarship make me like you?'

She smiles faintly. 'You talk about it all the time – how you're not like everyone else, and how spoiled and privileged they are. I didn't want you to think I was like that. I didn't mean to lie. It just sort of *happened*, and then it was too late. I wanted to tell you the truth, but I knew you'd hate me.'

It's exactly what Rowan said the other night. Was this my fault? Did I make her feel that she *had* to lie?

'I wouldn't have hated you.'

'You hate me now though, don't you?' She keeps

worrying at the same bit of skin with her teeth and I want her to stop.

'I just wish you'd told me the truth.'

'I'm sorry, Harper. I shouldn't have lied, I know that. But I was so desperate for you to like me.' She closes her eyes and takes a deep breath. 'I don't . . . it's not easy for me to make friends. Everyone makes it look so easy but it's never been easy for me. Sometimes I feel like the only one who wasn't given the instruction manual. It's always been that way and then I came to Duncraggan and you were so nice to me and I thought that maybe things could be different here, but of course they're not. I've ruined everything.' Her face contorts. 'I'm so *stupid*.' She punches her thigh and raises her hand to do it again but I grab it.

'You're not stupid,' I say, holding her clenched fist in mine. 'And you haven't ruined anything, OK?' She relaxes her hand, but I don't let go. 'I'm sorry you felt you had to lie. I'm sorry if I made you feel that way. I never meant to.'

The girls down on the pitch are playing a match now, half of them wearing green bibs over their T-shirts. The green bib girls are running rings round the other team. I liked hockey when I first came here – until I got hit in the face with a hockey stick.

'How can you ever trust me again?' Kirsty asks quietly, and I realise that I'm still holding her hand in mine, so I let go. I don't want her getting the wrong idea.

Her eyes are pleading. I don't know what to say.

'Harper? Please. What can I do to prove to you that I'm a good friend?'

'I could set a series of friendship challenges, each one more fiendish than the last . . .' This was meant to make her smile; it doesn't. 'You don't have to prove anything, Kirsty. That's not how it works.'

'So we're OK?'

I almost cave, but then I think about Halloween. 'Maybe it would be a good idea to give each other some space – just for a little while. Things have been a little . . . intense lately.'

'If you think that would be best . . .'

It's unbearably awkward, and I find myself saying that I really should be concentrating on my studies, and that I've sort of been neglecting Ama, Lil and Rowan – especially Rowan – and I know I should stop talking but if I stop talking then Kirsty might call me on my bullshit.

A shrill whistle from the pitch coincides with me finally running out of things to say. Kirsty doesn't look at me when she says, 'OK. I'll guess I'll see you around.' She stands and I have to move my legs so she can squeeze past me.

She starts walking down the steps. 'Kirsty, wait a

second.' She stops and looks back up at me, except she doesn't quite make eye contact. 'I don't want you to think . . . I just need some time, that's all. You can understand that?' She nods.

But I can't just abandon her like this; she doesn't have anyone else. 'And I'm here if you need me. I mean that.'

Finally, her eyes meet mine. 'Do you?'

'Of course.'

Kirsty stares at me for a few seconds, before carrying on down the stairs. She walks down the side of the pitch and starts on the path back to the castle.

She doesn't look back.

THIRTY-ONE

'So what's the deal? Have you two broken up?' Lily asks, looking across to where Kirsty is sitting with Gabi and Leah. I've been trying not to look in that direction for the past twenty minutes.

'Lil!' Rowan says sharply.

'What? What did I say?' She tears off a piece of naan and dips it in her dhal. 'Why isn't she sitting with us?'

'Why did you say "broken up"? We weren't *together*.'

Lil looks at me curiously. 'I *know*. I'm not a complete idiot, thank you. Why so touchy?'

I'm not in the mood for this. Because the strange thing is, it does feel a bit like a break-up. It hurts. I didn't mean for Kirsty to move tables. I would never have asked her to do that; it's not fair. But she was already sitting with Gabi and Leah when we walked in. I suppose I should be glad that she's making an effort with someone else.

Rowan looks at me questioningly and I nod, so she gives Lil and Ama an abbreviated version of the lowdown – that Kirsty and I have decided to give each other some space. They obviously want to know more, but that's all they're getting for now.

I told Rowan the truth – most of it anyway – when I got back to our room. Her reaction surprised me. She said she could kind of understand why Kirsty lied about the scholarship. Then she said that she felt sorry for Kirsty, which surprised me even more. I was surprised *and* annoyed, at first. But then she gave me a hug and said she was proud of me for confronting Kirsty and I hugged her back and told her not to be so fucking patronising.

Ama and Lily start talking about how friendships are so much more intense at boarding school. I think they're trying to make me feel better, and I appreciate the effort but I can't summon the energy to join in. They're right though. There's no escape here. My last school had sixteen hundred students – it was easy to avoid someone as long as you weren't in the same classes. And even if you were in the same classes, at least you got to head home at three-thirty. The people at a regular school might be a big part of your life, but here they're *everything*.

I actually do concentrate more on my work for the next couple of weeks. I even get my personal statement done, and make some tentative decisions about which universities to apply to. Rowan helps, and it's so much less overwhelming with her tapping away on her laptop next to me, pointing out that this uni is only an hour's train journey from her top choice, and this other one doesn't make you decide on your degree focus until the end of first year. She even creates a spreadsheet for me, because she loves spreadsheets, massive nerd that she is.

I still find it hard to think about next year. I can't imagine not seeing Rowan and Ama and Lily every day. The others talk about it all the time – about how amazing it will be to be in control of our own lives. But that's the thing that scares me most, I think. I don't want to be out in the big wide world, on my own. It was never meant to be that way. Not for me.

Kirsty seems to be doing OK. It's not too awkward when we see each other at mealtimes or in the corridors. I ended up sitting next to her for the Saturday night movie last week and she smiled when she handed me the tub of popcorn. We chatted about the film for a few minutes afterwards and I wondered if it was as strange for her as it was for me. I asked if she was still shooting, because I hadn't seen her down at the range. She said she goes on different days now.

'You don't need to do that.'

'I don't mind,' she said.

I was going to say something else, but Kirsty turned away and started talking to Hozzie.

Lily's the first of us to turn eighteen. We start singing 'Happy Birthday' at breakfast and loads of people join in. She's not embarrassed at all; she loves it. She proudly pins the oversized badge we got her on to her school jumper and carries her helium balloon around all day.

She insisted that we shouldn't get her a present, so we ended up clubbing together to donate to Lily's favourite charity instead. She was strangely reluctant to tell us what her parents got her, but we forced it out of her in the end. A two-bedroom flat in London. Soho, to be exact. 'It's an investment!' she said, when she saw the look on my face.

Kirsty comes over to our table at lunch and wishes Lily a happy birthday and there's this awkward moment when she asks if Lily's doing anything special to celebrate and Lil shrugs and says 'Not really.'

There's a pause before Kirsty says, 'Well. I hope you have a nice day anyway.'

Lily thanks her and Kirsty walks away. 'That was the right thing to say, wasn't it?'

I watch Kirsty sit back down next to Gabi. 'I think so.' Because *of course* we're doing something special tonight. There's no way we'd let Lily's eighteenth pass without a proper celebration. But it will just be the four of us, like old times.

We're bundled up in our warmest clothes but the cold still manages to worm its way under the layers. Lily is giddy with birthday joy and being a little less stealthy than usual. We have to shush her several times as we make our way through the deserted corridors and down the stairs.

I don't know what it is that makes me stop and look back up at the castle as the others run ahead. It feels almost like a memory of something that hasn't happened yet. The castle looks beautiful at night; blue-tinged lights illuminate the walls so that it's never in darkness. There are lights above each of the doors, and you can see dim lights from various corridors. Tonight, another light is burning, on the top floor of the west wing. The turret room. The curtains are wide open and a shadowy figure stands unmoving in the window.

'Oi! Get a move on!' Rowan shout-whispers, startling me.

I turn my back on the castle and run.

I don't tell the others that Kirsty was watching. It would just spoil the mood – it's definitely put a dampener on mine. If she was just spying on us, she wouldn't have put her light on and stood in the window like that. It's like she wanted me to see her. But why? To make me feel guilty for not inviting her? Because I don't. It's Lily's birthday and it's up to her who she wants to celebrate with — it's not my call.

The champagne opens with a loud POP and the cork ricochets off the cave walls, narrowly missing Ama's head. Lily grabs the bottle and puts it to her mouth to stop it spurting everywhere.

Rowan says, 'My dad reckons that when you open a bottle of champagne it should sound like a satisfied woman . . .'

Lily convulses with laughter, spitting out her mouthful. 'What the fuck?!'

'I feel sorry for your mum,' I say, taking the bottle from Lily. The champagne is so dry it makes the inside of my cheeks ache.

'What do you mean? Why would you feel sorry for Rowan's mum?' Ama asks, and the rest of us collapse into giggles. She stares at us for a moment before it dawns on her. 'Oh, right. I get it. Ha. Give me some of that,' she says, and I hand the bottle to her. She takes several gulps before letting out a tiny, ladylike burp.

We make quick work of the first bottle and move on to the second.

'So, Lil, how does it feel to be an adult?' I ask.

Lil leans back against the damp wall and shakes her head. 'I would try to explain it, but your tiny, childish minds would not be able to comprehend the complexities that await you.'

'You are so full of shit, Carter,' Rowan says, leaning against her.

Towards the end of the second bottle, I start feeling sentimental and it suddenly seems vitally important that I express my feelings. 'You know, I really love you guys.'

'Awwww, Kent is druuuuuunk.' Rowan swipes the bottle out of my hands. 'No more of that for you.'

'I'm not drunk! OK, I'm a little bit drunk, maybe. But that doesn't make it any less true. This is . . . this is really nice. Being here, with you.'

Lily turns to Rowan. 'Man, you're right. Totally hammered.'

'Fuck you guys!' I pout, and the others start laughing and doing impressions of me and I can't help laughing along with them.

I close my eyes for a second. I do feel quite drunk, but in a nice way. I feel nothing but love and gratitude. There's nowhere I would rather be.

'Lil, why don't you tell them about your gift from Marek?' Ama's voice is teasing, laced with laughter.

My eyes snap open again. Lily makes a big show of not wanting to tell us, which most likely means she really wants to tell us. 'It's nothing. Honestly. It's not a big deal.'

'He gave you a *birthday* present? That's . . . weird,' says Rowan.

'Why is it weird? Miss Renner gave me some chocolates.'

'She gives chocolates to *everyone* on their birthday. This isn't the same and you know it.'

'What did he get you?' I ask, at the same time as Rowan says, 'I thought you were over him?'

'Chill, guys. It's just a plant. He probably just nicked it from the greenhouse. And I *am* over him.'

'You've changed your tune!' Ama is indignant.

'Is there something going on with you and Marek?' asks Rowan.

'What's your problem, Chung?' Lil's still smiling – just about.

'No problem. I just asked you a simple question.'

I don't quite understand why everyone's looking so serious all of a sudden; I'm too drunk to be serious. 'Leave her alone, Rowan! Lil, I think it's *adorable* that Marek gave you a plant, but just remember we weren't allowed to get you a present and if we had it would have been nothing short of *amazing*.'

Lil laughs and ruffles my hair. 'I know, sweetie. I know.' She looks at her watch and sighs. 'I think we'd better get back. Ama, why don't we leave the last bottle here for next time?'

Ama stashes the bottle of champagne behind the

bar/rock and I wind my Gryffindor scarf round my neck. Rowan helps me tuck it inside my coat. 'One day you will accept yourself for who you truly are,' she says. 'Hufflepuff, through and through.'

Rowan helps me up the cliff steps, which is good, because I'm a little unsteady on my feet as well as distracted by having to defend my Gryffindor status. 'It's nothing to be ashamed of, Harper,' says Ama, linking arms with me as we cross the hockey pitch. 'Us Hufflepuffs should stick together.'

'I'm not a fucking Hufflepuff!'

We all stop in our tracks because there's no doubt about it – that was *way* too loud. Then, as one, we realise that stopping is a terrible idea and we make a run for it. I'm concentrating so hard on not falling flat on my face that I forget to look up at the turret window.

Rowan makes me brush my teeth before I slump into bed, because dental hygiene is very important to her.

'She didn't answer. Did you notice?'

The best I can manage is 'Huh?'

'Of course you didn't, Drunky McDrunkface. The bin's next to your bed if you need to puke. Wake me if you're choking to death.'

The last thought my drunk brain allows me before shutting down for the night is: remember not to have champagne on *my* birthday.

THIRTY-TWO

There's always a buzz around school in the run-up to a big production. Every year it makes me wish I was involved somehow, but I never get round to it. Rowan spends every spare minute on stage-crew duty and Lily spends more time freaking out about memorising her lines than she does memorising her lines. She's playing the baker's wife in *Into the Woods*, which she insists is one of the best parts, despite the fact the character is called 'the baker's wife' instead of having an actual name.

The opening night is a total triumph. When the whole cast come onstage at the end, Ama and I are the first to jump out of our seats for the standing ovation. It's a cool feeling, seeing one of your best friends on the receiving end of rapturous applause. Lily is beaming from ear to ear as she makes the whole stage crew get up onstage to share the applause. Rowan blushes hard when Ama and I start chanting her name.

Someone taps me on the shoulder as we all file out of the theatre. 'Did you enjoy the show?'

I slow down so that Kirsty can walk alongside me. 'Yeah, I loved it. Did you like it?'

'I had no idea Lily was such a good actor.'

'Sickening, isn't it? People should really only be good at one thing – save some talent for the rest of us.'

We share a quick smile before Ama grabs my arm and steers me away.

Three days later, Rowan and I are hanging out in Lily and Ama's room after lunch.

Rowan's curled up with her head on Ama's lap; her eyelids keep drooping closed every couple of minutes as Ama absentmindedly strokes her hair.

Lil's on her third cup of hot water and lemon, desperate to keep her voice going for one more night. 'Want me to go on in your place? I'm pretty sure I'd nail it.' I clear my throat and start singing one of the songs from the muscial.

Lil puts her hand over my mouth, muffling my voice until I stop. 'Thanks, but I think I can manage one last show.' Tonight's performance is open to the public. The locals pay three pounds (all proceeds to charity of course) to come and see a bunch of posh girls prancing around on stage. I think most people just use it as an excuse to nose around the school.

There's a knock at the door and Renner comes in.

'Was it Harper's singing?' Lily asks, laughing. 'Sorry Miss, we've told her a thousand times that her voice is a weapon of mass destruction, but she won't listen.'

'I like your trainers, Miss,' says Ama. 'Are they new?'

Miss Renner looks down at her feet for a second, as if she'd forgotten her blatantly fresh-out-of-the-box Nike Air Maxes. 'Er . . . yes. They are. Thank you.' Then she shakes her head and says, 'Lily, have you got a second?'

Lily sits up straight, eyes wide. 'Shit, I totally forgot! I'm so sorry! Can you give me another couple of days? I haven't even thought about the video yet.' Lily's supposed to be narrating a new video to go up on the school website to fool more unsuspecting parents into sending their daughters here.

Renner shakes her head and looks down at her feet again. Either she really likes her new trainers or something's up. 'The video can wait. Miss Maddox is waiting in her office.'

It's not an unusual thing, Lily being summoned to Miss Maddox's office. But on a Saturday, with Renner as go-between? Definitely unusual.

Lily stands up, puts her mug down on the bedside table and follows Renner out of the room without a word. She doesn't look at any of us, even when she closes the door behind her.

For a brief second I wonder if something's happened to Lily's parents. I've been that way since Jenna died – always assuming the worst. But whatever is going on here is different. Lily knows why Maddox wants to see her; I'm sure of it.

THIRTY-THREE

It was something about the look on her face as she put down her mug. There was a stillness – a sort of calm acceptance – that didn't make sense.

My suspicions are confirmed by Ama's shiftiness. 'Probably just head girl stuff,' she says, not meeting my eye.

I turn to Rowan, who's still gazing at the door. 'What do you think?' She ignores me so I chuck a cushion at her.

She shakes her head and shrugs.

'You were with Maddox earlier, Rowan. How did she seem?' Ama's forehead is creased with worry. I wish she'd just tell us what's wrong – we're going to find out eventually.

'You didn't tell me you saw Maddox today,' I say.

Rowan rolls her eyes. 'It might come as news to you, but I don't actually report back to you about every single person I talk to in the course of my day.' She reaches over and pats my knee. 'Maddox seemed fine. A bit antsy about tonight. She wants me to talk to a Japanese couple who are thinking of sending their kid here. She expects me to be the good little Asian poster girl, which is totally fucked up, but I couldn't exactly say no, could I?'

'I was on minority duty a couple of weeks ago. So tedious,' Ama sighs.

'As if she thinks that wheeling us out and putting us on display somehow negates the fact that there are more blonde white girls called Olivia here than minorities.'

'Is that true?' Ama asks, half laughing, half horrified.

The two of them proceed to count the Olivias. There's some debate about whether to count teachers or not.

I wait for them to start talking about Lily again, but instead they begin speculating about why Duncraggan is so white when other boarding schools aren't. Rowan reckons it's because 'you couldn't locate a school further away from anything remotely interesting if you tried'.

We head down to dinner, passing Maddox's office on the way. The door is closed, but that doesn't stop me staring and wishing for X-ray vision. Even then, Ama and Rowan don't mention Lily. She's been gone for nearly an hour.

'What if she's not back in time for the show?' I ask.

'She'll be back by then. Maddox needs to do her little speech before the performance,' Rowan says, checking the time on her phone.

After dinner, Rowan heads to the auditorium with Ama, who's supposed to be handing out programmes on the door. On my way back to my room I notice that Lily's door is ajar; I'm almost certain Ama closed it after us earlier.

I give the door a push and find Lily, splashing water on her face at the sink. When she looks up after drying her face, her eyes are puffy and red. 'Aw, Lil! What happened?!' I rush over to her, but she puts her hand up to stop me. 'Don't. The show starts in less than half an hour and I need to sort my face out so please don't be nice to me, I'm begging you.' She takes a long, deep breath and looks in the mirror. 'Fuck.' She splashes her face again.

'Are you going to tell me what's going on? What took you so long with Maddox? We were worried!'

She starts rushing round the room, grabbing clothes and make-up and stuffing them into a tote bag. 'We'll talk later, OK? I can't do this right now. I'm sorry . . . *The show must go on* . . . Can you believe she said that to me? The fucking cheek of the woman. If she's so worried about the fucking show she could have waited till tomorrow, couldn't she? We weren't . . .' She shakes her head angrily, then her shoulders slump. When she looks up at me, she's as sad as I've ever seen her. 'It's not like it's illegal or anything. We weren't doing anything wrong.'

'What are you talking about? Who wasn't doing anything wrong?'

'Me and Marek.'

Fuck.

The show *does* go on. I sit on the steps right at the back of the auditorium because the seats are all taken. I almost wish I hadn't come, but there was no way I was going to sit in my room and wait.

Lily's performance is almost as good as it was the other night. No one would know that anything's wrong. It's only at the end, when the audience is on its feet, that you can tell. Her smile is mechanical, and she rushes off the stage before the applause is over.

Twenty minutes later, the four of us are back in Lily and Ama's room. Lil doesn't cry when she tells us what happened in Maddox's office. It's all very matter of fact. 'She said *something troubling had come to her attention* and she wanted to ask me about it directly. She asked me straight out if I had become inappropriately involved with a member of the grounds staff.'

'What did you say?' asks Ama.

'I asked exactly what had come to her attention and how, but she just shook her head. Said I was in no position to ask questions. That's when I knew she *knew*. Then she said I should think very carefully before answering her question. She started on about this being such an important year for me, and me wanting to go to Oxford, and my position as head girl. Threatening me, basically.' Lil looks up as if she expects one of us to say something, but no one does. 'So I didn't have any choice. I had to tell her.'

'Tell her what? You haven't even told us!' It's impossible to hide my frustration.

Lil takes that on the chin. 'I'm sorry. There's not much to tell. I like him. He likes me.'

I sigh. 'Oh, come off it, Lil. There's got to be more to it than that. Did you fuck him?' Rowan winces at my choice of words, which is weird because she's no prude.

'No! We just kissed a few times . . . and stuff.' She actually blushes.

'I can't believe you didn't tell us!'

Ama puts her hand on my arm. 'Give her a break, Harper. Can't you see she's upset?'

'Well, it's OK for you, isn't it? She told *you*.'

They don't try to deny it. And why should they? They're best friends. *Best* best friends. That's what my rational mind is telling me, but whatever part of my mind isn't rational doesn't seem to care.

'Did you know?' I ask Rowan.

'Harper, you might want to chill out a bit. So what's happening to Marek? Has she fired him?'

I feel shamed, for a second. I hadn't given him a second thought.

'His contract is up at the end of term but I'll be surprised if she lets him stay that long. It's all my fault.'

'It's really not,' says Rowan. 'He's a grown-ass man. He could have resisted temptation if he wanted to.'

'I went after him.'

'So what? He could have said no. Simple.'

Lily sighs and shakes her head. 'What a fucking mess.'

'What about you?' Rowan asks. 'She's not suspending you or anything, is she?'

'No. But she's going to call my dad – as if he'll give a shit. I get to stay on as head girl though. Maddox was talking about replacing me, but she'd have to provide a reason and she definitely doesn't want to have to do that. They want to keep this under wraps.'

'So he loses his job and nothing happens to you?' I don't know why they all glare at me for stating a fact.

'She went on at me for more than an hour. It's not exactly nothing.'

I wrinkle my nose. 'It's pretty close to nothing. If something like this had happened at my old school you'd probably have been expelled.'

'Oh give it a rest, Harper.' Lily stands up and storms

over to the window. I'm about to apologise when she whirls round. 'See? *This* is why we didn't tell you. You're so fucking judgemental. I thought Rowan was bad – no offence, Rowan – but you fucking take the cake.'

'Don't get angry with me just because you were stupid enough to get involved with the gardener – and get caught. It's not my fault someone grassed you up.' I know that something bad is happening here, and that I'm making things worse, so it's particularly awful that I can't stifle my laughter over the grassed/gardener thing.

Lily goes ballistic, red face, eyes blazing. 'Fuck *you*, Kent! FUCK. YOU. Get out of my room.'

'*Seriously?*' I look to the others for back-up, but Ama looks furious and Rowan won't meet my eye.

No one says a word. 'Wow. OK. Guess I should have got the message about how much our friendship means to you when you started keeping secrets from me. Come on, Rowan. Let's go.'

I should have seen it coming, but I'm actually shocked when Rowan shakes her head.

I get up slowly, shakily. What the fuck just happened here? I take one last look at each of them, looking for a glimmer of something – a way back from this – but there's nothing.

There's nothing.

THIRTY-FOUR

Back in my room, I sit on the edge of my bed, knowing full well that they're talking about me on the other side of the wall.

My brain keeps replaying what went wrong, looking at it from different angles, turning up the volume on the worst bits. That little trickster voice in my head whispers that I deserved it. Because there's something wrong with me. There *must* be something very wrong with me to have acted like that. Rowan was in the same boat as me – she didn't know about Marek either – but she didn't bitch about it. She acted like a normal human being should act.

My gaze comes to rest on one of the photos pinned up next to Rowan's bed. It's one of Ama's; she's always taking photos. The rest of us seem to forget – too busy having fun to remember to record it. She usually prints off the best ones, giving us each a copy. It's old school, but we're always grateful – for something real that you can touch and hold in your hands. Something you can keep for ever. Or so I thought.

This particular photo was taken in the cave on the last night of summer term. Rowan and I are sprawled on the floor, our heads tilted together. I'm staring at the camera, eyes half closed. Rowan's looking at me, her mouth close to my ear as if she's whispering secrets.

Ama fretted when Rowan pinned the picture up on the wall. She thought Renner would notice it and find out about the cave. It took us a while to convince her that Renner isn't exactly Sherlock Holmes material.

My copy of the photo is tucked away inside a folder, along with letters from home (three in total), every single birthday card Jenna made for me (ten) and random bits and pieces I thought were worth keeping for whatever reason. The badge Rowan gave me on my first night is in there.

I might be pissed off with Lily and Ama, but I'm fucking furious with Rowan. Her loyalty should lie with me. Even when I'm being unreasonable.

I'm sitting up in bed with a book propped in front of me when she slinks in half an hour later. She was obviously hoping I'd be asleep.

There are so many things I want to say. Clever, cutting things. But I end up going for sarcasm. 'Thanks for having my back in there.'

She stops and stares at me. I stare back. I will not be the first one to look away. I will not.

I'm the first one to look away. Out of the corner of my eye, I see her shake her head. I bet she's rolling her eyes too.

I stare down at the book while she changes into her pyjamas. I turn the page as she brushes her teeth and washes her face.

'Are you really going to give me the silent treatment?' I say, as she gets into bed and turns off her bedside light.

I slam my book down on my table and some water sloshes over the side of the glass and on to my phone. I grab the phone and dry it on the corner of the duvet. It's still working. '*Fine.* That suits me just fine.'

For someone who talks so much, Rowan is surprisingly good at the silent treatment. There's no way I'd have been able to resist saying something back.

She's asleep within minutes, which makes me doubly furious. She obviously doesn't give a fuck. I close my eyes and try to sleep, so that if she wakes up she'll think that *I* don't give a fuck. It doesn't work.

I may not be able to sleep, but crying comes easily.

I try something different the next morning: I say nothing. The two of us move around the room in a sort of awkward dance – one in which you must stay at least three feet away from your partner at all times. One glance in the mirror confirms my suspicion that I look exactly how you'd expect someone who spent most of the night crying to look.

I can't tell for sure if she's still giving me the silent treatment unless I say something to check. She could just be waiting for me to make the first move. Perhaps she thinks it's my job to clear the air. She'll be waiting a long time for *that*.

When I come back from the shower room, she's looking out the window with her binoculars. She's even wearing the same T-shirt she was wearing the first night we met. It's faded now – soft grey instead of black.

She packs her binoculars away in their case and puts the case back on the windowsill. Then she checks her watch, which makes me do the same. Breakfast is in two minutes. A lot of the sixth-formers don't bother to go on Sunday, preferring to catch up on sleep. We always bother, because Sunday means pancakes.

Rowan fires off a message on her phone then pulls on a hoodie. She hasn't showered; she never does on Sunday mornings. She always waits till the evening and has the longest shower imaginable. I know she does a face mask then too, even though she would never admit it.

Something thaws in me, thinking of her with a face

mask on. I should apologise for being a dick last night. I don't want this to ruin the whole day. The four of us were planning to walk to the village to get pastries. I *really* want a pastry.

I brush my hair slowly and consider the phrasing. A straight-up 'I'm sorry' should do it, but maybe it would be better if I tried to explain, make her see things from my point of view.

I put down the brush on the shelf above the sink. Our toothbrushes stand together in a mug. The bristles on hers are splayed; I must tell her to get a new one from the tuck shop. It's always my job to remind her.

I turn around to see Rowan opening the door. She quickly closes it behind her. I tiptoe over and put my ear to the door. I hear Rowan's voice and Lily's. Then Ama's. I can't make out the words but I don't have to. It's enough to hear their footsteps receding down the hallway.

THIRTY-FIVE

I head straight to the pancake station without looking over at the tables. Three pancakes and three slices of crispy bacon, all slathered in maple syrup. I have the same thing every Sunday. I'm not in the least bit hungry, but maybe if I act like everything is the same as usual, things will be the same as usual. Freshly squeezed orange juice and a mug of strong tea, then I can't avoid it any longer. My fingers tighten on the edges of my tray as I walk over to our table.

Ama and Rowan are facing me, with Lily sitting opposite them. The chair next to Lily is empty. Ama's the first to notice me. Maybe she thinks she's being subtle, but her fake cough is anything but. Rowan looks up, and Lily turns around, her arm slung over the back of her chair. I keep walking and they keep watching. I'm ten steps away when Rowan shakes her head. Just once, so quickly that the other two don't see.

I'm grateful to her for that. I walk straight past

the table like that's what I'd been planning to do all along. I head towards the only empty table, put down my tray and pull out a chair. I sit with my back to them. It's the only way to avoid looking over there. Straight back, shoulders and neck. I will not let them see how this feels.

Two sips of orange juice confirms that my stomach has more than enough acid of its own sloshing around in there. Tea goes down better. The pancakes remain uneaten.

Some overly cheerful Year 11s sit down all around me. They act like I'm not here. There are four of them. I see them together all the time. I wonder if they know how fragile their friendship is.

I look around the room and try to tune out their talk. Everyone in the dining hall seems to be smiling or chatting or laughing, or eating at the very least. But there's one person who's doing none of those things.

Kirsty's looking at me, as I'm looking at her.

I get back to our room before Rowan. She would never let something as minor as falling out with her best friend ruin her Sunday breakfast.

I get on my laptop and send Mum a quick email. I hardly ever message her, so she replies straightaway, asking what's wrong. That's what you get when you tell your mum that you miss her when you have never,

ever said that in the whole time you've been at boarding school. I reply that nothing's wrong. I say that I'm heading into the village with the girls, and add two smiley faces for good measure. Mum's a big fan of smiley faces.

I deliberately don't look up when Rowan comes in. But she hovers awkwardly until I do. 'Thank you,' I say, sarcasm-free this time.

'For what?' she asks. The relief that she's finally talking to me is immense.

'Not making a scene downstairs. I bet Lily was dying for some drama.'

Rowan clenches her jaw and closes her eyes for a beat too long. I knew full well it was the wrong thing to say, but we both know it's true.

'So is that it? I'm not allowed to sit with you guys any more?' My voice sounds smaller than I would like it to, a little wobbly. She notices and for a second there I think she looks concerned, and I'm kicking myself. I don't want pity. 'I can't believe you're taking their side.'

There's no trace of pity now, that's for sure. Her face contorts. 'Grow *up*. This isn't about taking sides! Why can't you see that? It's about *you*.'

I slam my laptop lid shut. 'How is this about me? As far as I'm aware I didn't stick my tongue down the gardener's throat.'

'You seem to have forgotten that Lily's your *friend*. One of your best friends. She's *always* there for you, no matter what, and as soon as she needs you for a change, you treat her like shit.'

'If she's such a good friend, why didn't she tell me about Marek?'

'What? And have you go blabbing to Kirsty? You know that's the reason she didn't even tell me, don't you? Because she knows I tell you everything, and then you would tell Kirsty and the whole fucking school would know about it.'

'*What?* That's not why.' But there's truth in what she's saying; I see it. Clearly it didn't matter to Lily that I'm not even talking to Kirsty at the moment.

'It's exactly why.'

'But she told *Ama*, for fuck's sake. The biggest fucking gossip in the whole school.'

Rowan shakes her head angrily. 'Ama wouldn't talk about something like this, you know that.'

I get up and we're toe to toe, face to face. 'Oh really? Then why did she tell Marcy Stone about my parents winning the lottery?'

'She didn't,' Rowan says, and her certainty makes me want to punch something. 'Harper, you need to get a grip. I don't know what the deal is, but until you sort yourself out you'd better stay out of my way. I mean it.'

'How the hell am I supposed to do that? We sleep six feet away from each other in case you hadn't noticed.'

Two little red patches have appeared on her cheeks. She always laughs about being able to gauge her mum's level of pissed-offness from the colour of her cheeks. 'How about you pretend I don't exist? You were doing a pretty good job of that with your new little friend, so it shouldn't be that hard.'

Each word she spits at me is a body blow. The last jabs are delivered with less force, but that doesn't mean they hurt any less. 'You've changed, Harper. I don't even know who you are any more.' She's not done yet. She looks me up and down. 'But I don't like who you've become.'

The road is particularly quiet on Sundays. Some younger girls pass me on horseback and one of the horses lifts its tail and shits right in the middle of the road. A couple of Lycra-clad cyclists whizz past, oversize thighs pumping away.

The sky is overcast, but it's not too cold. Just as well, since I don't have my coat. You can't really stop for a coat when you storm out of a room – it ruins the momentum. I don't have any money, either, so I have no idea what I'm going to do when I get to the village. The pastries in the bakery are behind the counter so I can't even try to nick one. Not that I ever would. I've never stolen anything in my life. Jenna stole a packed of pickled onion Monster Munch when she was nine years old. The guilt was so bad that she could never eat them again.

Rowan likes Monster Munch. I gave her a massive box for her seventeenth birthday and she ate three packets before breakfast. I've already bought a present for her eighteenth – a leather bracelet with a tiny gold skull dangling off it. It's the most expensive present I've ever bought anyone. I got it six months ago so it's probably too late to get my money back. Rowan's birthday is still a couple of months away, but all the time in the world wouldn't be enough. There's no simple fix here. This isn't some minor bump in the road of our friendship; it's a gaping chasm.

Some sparrows flit in and out of the hedge next to the road. I stop to watch. There must be twenty of them at least. Rowan's always going on about sparrows; their numbers are declining, apparently. Fuck. I need to get Rowan out of my brain. I thought a walk would clear my head but it's doing the opposite. I stride out quickly and the sparrows scatter for cover.

Halfway to the village I find a dead fox at the side of the road, some of its insides on the outside. The blood is so bright it looks unreal. I kneel down to get a closer look. Its eyes are open, its teeth bared in a grimace. Unlucky, to be hit by a car on a quiet road like this.

I mutter a quiet not-quite-prayer and stand up.

'Poor thing.'

I whirl round to find Kirsty, leaning on the handlebars of a mountain bike.

'Me or the fox?'

She wheels the bike closer and stares at the fox. 'Both?'

I smile. 'At least my intestines are all in the right place . . . I think.'

'Are you OK?'

There's no point pretending. 'I've been better.'

She nods. 'I passed them on the way. They're maybe ten minutes behind you.'

I look back along the road, but of course I can't see them.

'Want a lift?' She gestures to the saddle. 'If we hurry we can be on our way back before they get to the village. We can cut through the woods if you don't want to see them.'

'I don't have any money.'

'I'm buying,' she says firmly, patting her pocket.

I don't know what to do. 'Why are you being so nice to me?'

'You looked . . . lost, when I saw you at breakfast. I know how that feels.'

'But I was awful to you . . .'

'No, you weren't. You had every right to be upset. I know that now. Anyway, it's in the past.'

I hesitate, before hopping on the back of the bike. We set off, a little wobbly at first, but the ride is smooth when she speeds up.

'Put your arms around my waist,' she says, and I do.

THIRTY-SIX

Kirsty buys me a pastry even though I say I'm not hungry. The music teacher, Mr Hennessy, is in front of us in the queue. He buys seven doughnuts.

'Want me to buy everything so there's nothing left when they get here?' Kirsty jokes. My smile is as weak as a bad cup of tea, but at least it's honest.

Kirsty wheels the bike and I carry the brown paper bag, already spotted with grease from the pastries inside. She hums the theme tune from *Into the Woods* when we reach the line of trees.

She tells me that she and her mum got lost in a forest once. They walked for hours, her mum telling stories the whole time to distract her. Kirsty didn't even realise anything was wrong until her mum burst into tears when they came across some campers just as it was getting dark.

We stop at the foot of a fallen oak, its roots torn from the ground. 'Do trees die of old age?' I murmur, putting my hand on the mossy trunk, as if I can feel a heartbeat.

'Do you want to talk about it?' Kirsty rests the bike against the trunk and hops up, sitting with her legs dangling.

I don't want to talk. At least, that's what I thought until I find myself talking. I can't explain what happened with the girls without mentioning Marek. I'd be lying if I said I didn't get a kick out of doing the very thing Lily didn't want me to do.

'I can't believe she didn't tell me. What did she think I was going to do? Go marching into Maddox's office and tell her that the head girl was giving head to the head gardener?' I pause, but Kirsty doesn't smile or laugh. 'You're not surprised, are you? That they got together?'

Kirsty shrugs. 'She didn't exactly hide how she felt about him. She should have been more careful.'

I tell her the rest, about Rowan blanking me, and what happened after breakfast. 'It's got to be some kind of record, don't you think? Losing all your friends in one fell swoop.'

'Not *all* your friends,' she says, with something not quite a question mark hanging off the end of the sentence.

I turn to her. 'Thank you.' My stomach gurgles loudly and we both laugh. 'Guess I'd better have a pastry after all.'

*

Kirsty goes quiet as we get closer to school. I want to ask what she's thinking, but I suspect she might be thinking I'm only here because I have no other options. I don't want her to think that, because it's not true. It's not that simple.

She stops outside the bike shed. 'I want you to know that I'm really sorry about what happened with the others . . .' She starts fiddling with the gears as if the gears need fiddling with.

'But?'

'What do you mean?'

I shrug. 'I dunno. It just sounded like you were about to say a "but" or maybe an "and". My best guess is a "but" though, and I'm sticking to it.'

She smiles at my nonsense. 'OK. I'm sorry about what happened with the others, *but* I've enjoyed being with you this morning.' She winces. 'Does that make me a bad person?'

'Not at all. It's been nice.'

'I suppose I'll see you around then.' She pulls open the bike shed door and starts to wheel the bike over the threshold.

I realise she thinks this was an aberration, and that I still want to steer clear of her. 'I'll wait for you. It's nearly lunchtime. We can go together . . . if that's OK with you?'

'Really?'

'Yes, really.' I laugh, grateful that she's the one who seems grateful when she's the one doing me the favour.

'And maybe we could head down to the range later, if you're not too busy? I feel like blasting stuff out of the sky.'

She puts the bike on its stand and comes out of the shed, smiling. 'I feel sorry for those pigeons already – even if they are made of clay.'

The look on Rowan's face when she sees me sitting in the dining hall with Kirsty is a particularly satisfying mixture of loathing and disbelief.

Instead of setting the clays to 'auto', we take it in turns to shoot while one of us mans the trap. I start to feel better as soon as I smell the gunpowder, and I'm grinning from ear to ear by the time my shoulder starts to ache from the shotgun's recoil.

We're packing up our stuff when Marcy Stone arrives.

'Good timing. I wouldn't want to show you up.' She can't resist. It's as if she's been genetically engineered to be hateful at all times.

'So I suppose the three musketeers have finally got bored of their little charity case? It was ever so kind of them, befriending someone from a deprived background.'

I make a show of looking over her shoulder, then in each direction. 'Who are you talking to, Marcy? Because I'm not listening.'

'It's OK, I know how difficult it must be. I feel for you, honestly. They let you believe that you fit in here, but the truth is that someone like you will never understand what it's like to be *someone*.'

It's a good thing my shotgun is locked away because I can picture it clearly: me calmly raising the gun to my shoulder and pointing it at her face, her cruel smile melting away into confusion, then terror.

'Come on, Kirsty, let's go.'

'*Come on, Kirsty, let's go,*' she sneers. Then she puts her hand on Kirsty's arm. 'You have terrible taste in friends, Connor, but there's hope for you yet. I expect you'll come to your senses soon.'

Kirsty grabs Marcy's wrist. 'If you touch me again, I'll break your fingers.'

Marcy laughs, but it seems forced. She backs away. 'I was just trying to be *nice*. I thought you were better than this, Connor. Guess I was wrong.'

I want to get the last word, but Kirsty's already walking away. Besides, I can't think of anything particularly clever to say.

Kirsty's storming down the path and I have to run to catch up with her. 'That was so hardcore! *I'll break your fingers?!*'

'I meant it.' She's breathing hard, nostrils flaring. 'She has no right to talk to you like that.' She's not slowing down, so I have to speed-walk beside her.

'It's just Marcy being Marcy.' Why am I making light of it, when the truth is that every word hit its target with pinpoint accuracy?

'Why does she hate you so much?'

'Who knows? I'm just lucky, I guess.'

'This isn't funny!'

I link my arm through hers to slow her down a bit. 'I'm sorry. I know it's not funny. And I do appreciate you sticking up for me back there. But Marcy doesn't matter. People like her always have to choose someone to go after – it's the natural order of the universe. If it weren't me, it would be someone else.' A memory bubbles up: a girl crying in the TV room while everyone laughed. I was laughing too. 'It *was* someone else before me. Who do you think gave Gabi that nickname?'

Kirsty stops walking and frowns. 'Gabi's nice. Someone should do something about Marcy.'

'Someone will, one day. In the meantime, I comfort myself with the thought that someone that poisonous can't possibly be happy.'

'Do you really believe that?' she asks quietly. 'That a bad person can never be happy?'

'I *wish*,' I laugh. 'Unfortunately the world doesn't

work that way. I think that terrible people can be deliriously happy.'

And good people – the best people – can die, leaving behind lesser versions of themselves to live lesser lives.

THIRTY-SEVEN

It's not easy, sharing a room with someone you're not talking to and living next door to two *other* people you're not talking to. It's awkward and uncomfortable, especially at first. And of course everyone in Fairclough has noticed – even Miss Renner. She calls Rowan and me into her office and asks what's going on, as if it's any of her business. I let Rowan take the lead and she says that everything's fine, so I go along with it.

Renner's right eyebrow shoots skyward. 'So you're happy to remain roommates? Even though I haven't seen you say a single word to each other in the last ten days?'

'Yes, Miss. After all, we should really be focusing on studying for our exams. That's the most important thing, isn't it?'

Renner knows Rowan's bullshit inside and out, but there isn't a lot she can do when we're both denying anything's wrong. She repeats her usual spiel about her door always being open, and adds a bit about boarding school being like a pressure cooker.

'Guess I should go and let off some steam then, Miss.' Rowan's grin is a contender for the most insincere smile I've ever seen. 'I'm late for lacrosse.'

We walk down the corridor together, because Renner's still watching from the doorway. 'Why did you do that?' I hiss. 'I'm sure you'd be happier with me out of your hair.'

Rowan turns back to wave at Miss Renner, her smile slipping as soon as she turns back to me. 'Why didn't *you* say something? If you want to kick me out of my room, you could at least have the balls to say it. I'm not doing your dirty work for you.'

It makes no sense, until I really think about it. The current arrangement isn't fun for either of us; it would be much easier if Rowan took the turret room and Kirsty moved in with me. Rowan *knows* that, but she wants me to be the one to bail out first. And there's no way I'm going to give her what she wants, so it looks like we're stuck with each other.

I don't tell Kirsty what happened in Renner's office. She wouldn't understand why I don't just ask for the room swap. It's about not letting Rowan win, definitely, but it's more than that. It's about something I try to ignore and try not to feel. Still, it wheedles its way in to catch me unawares at certain moments, like when

Rowan forgets that we're not talking and turns to me in lessons to ask something. That tiny sliver of time before she remembers and clamps her mouth shut. It's hope.

Later that night, I'm in Kirsty's room. We're supposed to be studying, but instead I've been teaching her to play chess. Dad bought me the set as a going-away-to-boarding-school gift and I didn't have the heart to tell him that whipping out a chess set wouldn't exactly help me make friends.

Kirsty's just about got the hang of the pieces and how they can move across the board, but the knight has totally messed with her head.

'He's on a horse! He can *jump*.' I show her what I mean, knocking out one of her pawns.

I manage to stick to chess talk for a good half-hour, before reverting to a topic I can't seem to leave alone. I return to it daily, picking the scab to make it bleed.

'It hurts, you know? Seeing the three of them acting like nothing's wrong. You should see Lily and Rowan in lessons, laughing and joking around. It's sickening. I swear they're only doing it for my benefit.'

Kirsty nods sympathetically even though she must be bored of listening to me. I'm lucky she's such a good listener; I would definitely have told me to shut the fuck up by now.

'I thought we were *so* close – that we'd always be there for each other. Even after we leave this place . . . I was sure that we'd go to each other's weddings and be aunties to each other's kids or whatever – not that I even want kids but that's not the point. Anyway, that was obviously bullshit wishful thinking. But I loved them, you know?' It's hard, to say those words out loud.

Kirsty picks up a black pawn and looks at it closely. 'I don't know,' she says slowly. 'Maybe it *was* wishful thinking, that the four of you would be friends for ever. People grow apart, Harper. It happens all the time. Things change.' She pauses, before adding, 'Perhaps you've changed.'

I would tell her that this is exactly what Rowan said, but she doesn't know the details of that particular argument. She doesn't know that it involved her.

'Changed how?'

'I don't know. But say that Ama's always been a gossip and Lily's always been secretive and Rowan's always been . . . Rowan. And maybe the old Harper knew all that and was OK with it. The old Harper didn't think she deserved any better. But now you know that you do.'

I find myself nodding. I *have* changed. And that's not a bad thing, no matter what Rowan thinks.

Kirsty picks up another chess piece and throws it

to me. 'Didn't you say that pawns get promoted if they reach the other side of the board?'

A smile edges on to my face. 'I did.'

'Well, then. Maybe it's time to accept that you've reached the other side of the board.'

The black queen is warm and heavy on my palm.

THIRTY-EIGHT

'I heard he was spotted by a model scout at Edinburgh Airport,' says a Year 10 with big hair and an even bigger attitude. 'My money's on a Calvin Klein campaign. God, what I wouldn't do to see that man in a pair of Calvins.' She heaps a second pile of spinach on to her plate, before moving on to the potatoes and murmuring, 'Mash or roasted . . . mash or roasted . . . fuck it, I'm gonna have both.'

In the three weeks since it happened, she's the first person I've heard speculating about Marek, but I'm sure she's not the only one. When the only attractive man under the age of thirty at a girls' boarding school mysteriously disappears, people are going to notice.

Kirsty and I exchange a smile as Big Hair's peroxide-blonde friend says, 'Nah, he probably got deported.'

I choose mash and Kirsty chooses roasted. I regret my decision immediately.

We sit at our usual table a couple of places away from Hozzie, Gabi and a few others. 'Calvin Klein! That's a good one. He's not even that hot. They just think he is because there are no other options. Straight people have so little imagination.' As soon as I say it, I think of Rowan. She would be holding up her hand for a high five right about now.

'Thanks,' Kirsty says dryly.

'Sorry. He did look good with his shirt off, I suppose.'

'Who are we talking about?' Gabi slides her tray over and moves seats so that she's sitting next to Kirsty.

I say 'No one' and Kirsty says 'Marek' at about the same time.

'Oh yes. He left, didn't he? I never liked him. He was more interested in perving over us lot than he was in gardening, if you ask me.'

Gabi asks if we're excited about Christmas and we both shrug, because it's far too early for normal people to be excited about Christmas. 'I can't wait. I *love* Christmas.' She looks down at her plate and blushes. 'Mummy insists on sending me an advent calendar even though I'm far too old for that sort of thing. Of course, it's Diptyque even though I'd rather have a chocolate one.'

I don't want to be mean to Gabi, I really don't. But why does she have to make it so hard? Somehow she manages to finish eating before us, even though she seems to talk non-stop. 'Right, must dash. Got to see a man about a dog.'

'What dog?' asks Kirsty.

'It's just an expression,' I explain, not bothering to add that it's an expression that I've only ever heard my grandfather use.

'I would love to have a dog though,' says Gabi. 'Except I'm super super allergic. Maybe a labradoodle would be OK though. What do you guys think?'

'You could try rubbing your face up against one and see what happens?' I'm not trying to be obnoxious, honestly.

'Good idea, H! Thanks! Now I just need to find someone who owns a labradoodle . . .' She walks away, muttering to herself.

I take my time over pudding; sticky toffee is my favourite. Lily and Ama are still at their table, but Rowan is gone. Even when I'm not actively looking at their table, I'm always aware of it.

I check over my shoulder that no one's close enough to overhear, then I whisper, 'Do you think she got to say goodbye to him?'

'Who?' Kirsty asks.

'Lily. Do you think she got the chance to say goodbye to Marek?' It still bothers me – that I don't know what happened.

Kirsty frowns and shakes her head. 'Who cares?'

'I was just wondering, that's all. She probably didn't, did she? I bet Maddox stood over him while he packed his stuff, then drove him to the station herself just to be sure.' I've found myself thinking about it a lot lately, wondering if Lily's feelings might have been deeper than I thought. It's not that she looks depressed or anything, but there's something off about her. It's most noticeable in assemblies when she's up on stage reading out the announcements — I can properly watch her then. She seems muted, a little less Lily somehow. It could be that she's on her best behaviour because she knows Maddox is keeping an eye on her, but what if it's more than that?

How hard would it be to fall in love with someone only to have them suddenly disappear? If I'd thought for one second that she actually *loved* the guy, I wouldn't have acted like such a brat.

Kirsty waves her hand in front of my face and I snap back to the here and now. 'What were you thinking about?' Her eyes narrow. She asks me that a lot lately, probably because I keep zoning out, brooding about what went wrong.

'Nothing.' She waits. 'Lily. I hope she's OK.'

'Lily's not your problem any more.'

'I know that. It's just . . .' I shake my head miserably. You don't stop caring about someone just

253

because you don't *want* to care about them. Kirsty's been so patient, letting me rant whenever I need to, but I'm not sure she gets that it's perfectly possible for me to be angry with Lily and worried about her at the same time.

She stares off into space for a moment, before refocusing on me. 'Look, it's not your fault that Lily got involved with Marek, and it's definitely not your fault that they got caught.'

I wince. Her voice is loud – far too loud. We're the only ones left on our table though so maybe it's fine. But then I check over my shoulder and someone's walking past.

The worst possible someone: Marcy Stone.

THIRTY-NINE

For a second I think Marcy's so engrossed in conversation with Tatiana that she didn't hear what Kirsty said. But that would be too good to be true and I've learned that things that seem too good to be true almost always *are*.

It's subtle, but it's there if you know the signs. Marcy doesn't look down at us as she walks by, but a small smile plays on her lips. There's no mistaking the look of delight – her eyes sparkle with it. The cat that got the fucking cream and then some.

I close my eyes and try to picture a way in which this doesn't play out badly. 'Shit. *Shit.*'

'What's wrong?'

'Marcy heard you.'

'What? *How?* But where . . .' She trails off as I point my thumb in Marcy's direction. 'Oh God, I'm so sorry! I didn't mean . . . Are you sure she heard though? Maybe she didn't. And even if she did, maybe she won't tell anyone.'

'It's OK, it's done now.'

'God, I'm such an idiot! I just wanted you to stop stressing about Lily and now I've made things worse.' She clenches her fist and knocks against her forehead. It would almost be funny if she didn't look so distraught. 'I *always* make things worse. Why do I always have to mess up?'

I reassure her that it's not her fault. It's not true, but she doesn't need me to make her feel worse than she already does. She keeps apologising over and over again as we leave the dining hall and head upstairs, only stopping when Ama passes us in the corridor.

When we're back in Kirsty's room I tell her to chill. 'There's no point worrying about it. We'll just have to wait and see what happens.' I sit down in Kirsty's armchair. 'It was bound to happen, when you think about it. Secrets are impossible to keep in this place – especially a secret like that. And for all we know Lily might have told some people. Or Ama might have. So even if word does get around, it's not necessarily our fault.'

Kirsty nods along with me and I almost manage to convince myself that it's going to be fine and even if it's not, Lily brought it on herself. So what if people start gossiping about her? It's not the end of the world. People will move on eventually, just like they did after they found out about the lottery win.

I'm actually glad when we're interrupted by my phone ringing. I head back to my room because I can't stand people listening to me talk on the phone. As I suspected, Rowan isn't there. She hardly ever is these days. She comes back in as late as possible and gets straight into bed. It makes things a little easier for both of us.

I can hear the sigh as Mum sits down at the other end of the line. 'It's been a nightmare, love.'

My heart stumbles. 'Why? What's happened? Is Dad OK? Are *you* OK?'

Mum laughs and my heart relaxes. 'You've forgotten, haven't you? We were packing up the house today! Well, I say "we" but the removal men did all the heavy lifting. You should see the place now, love. It's so much bigger without the furniture! It's sleeping bags on the floor tonight – reminds me of when I met your dad!'

I picture men – strangers – dismantling my bed, and Jenna's. Twin beds for twin girls. The beds will be going in one of the guest rooms in the new house. It seems a waste to have one room lying empty for at least 360 days of the year, let alone three of them.

I ask Mum if she's excited about the new house.

'Honestly? It's a little overwhelming. It feels like something we shouldn't be allowed to have. I never thought in a million years that we would end up living in a place like that.'

'You deserve it, Mum.' It's easier to be nice to her now that she's admitted it's weird for her too, but it's a struggle to get the next words out and inject them with the requisite enthusiasm. 'I'm looking forward to seeing it at Christmas.'

'Things will be better this year, love. I promise.' Clearly I didn't even come close to fooling her. Or maybe it's just that she knows how terrible the last couple of Christmases have been for all three of us. 'We were wondering about seeing if Annie and Mark wanted to come with the boys . . . although I suppose it's late notice. It's always nice though, isn't it? Having little ones around at Christmas.'

I'm not so sure if it's ever nice having these two particular little ones around. At Jenna's funeral, Callum started laughing hysterically as soon as he saw the coffin. Mikey puked at the reception afterwards. The thought of two brothers sleeping in our old beds is hard to swallow. 'I wonder if it would be better if it was just us, Mum?'

'Oh, I don't know. It used to be such a happy time.' She falls silent and I know she's thinking that filling this big new house with the noisiest, most annoying kids on the planet will be the key to a happy Christmas. Anything's got to be better than near silence at the dinner table.

'Anyway, what was I saying?' Mum never used to

forget what she was saying. It's as if when Jenna died she took parts of Mum's mind with her, as well as the smiles and the laughter and the giving a fuck about me. At least she's making an effort now though.

'It's OK with me if Annie and Mark come.' I almost sound like I mean it.

'No, no, you're right. Let's just leave it with the three of us. Give us some time to settle into the new house. Speaking of . . . can we schedule in a Skype call tomorrow? Around seven, maybe? We should have found the kettle by then!'

It doesn't occur to her that I might have preferred the Skype call tonight. That I'd rather see the old house – our *home* – than the new one. But it will make her happy if I do this, so I agree. Maybe enough tiny happy things can build up to create some semblance of the mother I lost when my sister died.

FORTY

I'm on my laptop at seven the next night, trawling the web for Christmas presents and waiting for Mum's call. I've been on edge all day, expecting to hear something about Lily and Marek.

Marcy *must* have told someone by now. Maybe even told them to keep it themselves – knowing that's a sure-fire way to guarantee the story spreads like wildfire. It's what I would do if I were her.

The call comes through just after quarter past seven. I click to connect and all I can see on the screen are a pair of brogues – cream and white. Whoever is holding the phone moves in for a close-up. 'What do you think?' It's Dad's voice; his face appears a few seconds later, filling the screen. 'Pretty swish, huh?'

'Wow,' I say, deadpan.

'What? The woman in the shop said they make me look like an English gent!'

'English wanker, more like.'

260

'Stop being mean to your dad!' They're both onscreen now, with the front door of the new house in the background. 'I think he looks very dapper.' Mum barely manages to get the word 'dapper' out before dissolving into giggles.

'Oi! Let's get on with the tour,' says Dad, and I see his hand reaching for the door handle and opening the door and it feels like I'm in a first-person video game – a boring one where you just wander around a deserted landscape looking for clues.

The house looks the same as when I saw it, except there are no pictures on the walls and the fancy furniture is gone. 'As you can see, we need to go shopping, pronto!' Mum laughs. The furniture from our old house doesn't look right in these rooms. Most of it is too small, and too shabby.

Mum runs me through her plans for each of the rooms, while Dad mans the camera. 'We want to have everything perfect by the time you come home for Christmas, love. Your dad thinks we should get an enormous tree for the hall.'

'Fifteen feet, at least!' Dad chips in, turning the camera on himself and giving me a thumbs-up.

I like the old Christmas tree. Small and plastic, with flashing multicoloured lights that give you a headache if you stare at them for too long and decorations that Jenna and I made when we were little.

She was particularly proud of the dried macaroni hearts we made when we were six. Mine was sprayed silver, Jenna's was gold.

'We're still going to have the old tree, of course.' says Mum. 'You can have it in your room if you like, or we can put it in the living room. It's up to you, love, just let us know.' It makes me feel better about things, knowing that she realises I don't want everything to be shiny and new. Some things are better when they're old and worn.

Last stop on the Skype tour is my bedroom. Not Harper and Jenna's bedroom, or the twins' bedroom, or the girls' bedroom. A room utterly devoid of memories. I can't picture Jenna here, doing her homework or lying on the bed or sitting cross-legged and painting her nails. She isn't here, and never will be.

There's no furniture yet, but Mum says they're going to buy me a double bed at the weekend and we can go shopping for a desk and bedside table when I'm home for Christmas.

Dad zooms in on the pile of boxes in the corner. Each one is carefully labelled in blue marker pen: Harper's school stuff; Harper's winter clothes; Harper's miscellaneous bits and bobs.

I know she means well, but I can already see that those boxes don't just contain my stuff. There's a toy magic wand sticking out of the box on top. Jenna got a magic set for her eleventh birthday and spent the next few months insisting that we all start calling her The Great Jennamundo. I was her assistant, which mostly involved standing next to her and acting amazed when the end of the wand suddenly sprouted a fabric flower.

You can't separate the belongings of twins – it's just not possible. Things that started out as mine became hers, and vice versa. We were always very good at sharing; it's probably the number one life skill you learn from being a twin.

Their landline starts ringing and Mum goes off to answer it. 'Better leave a trail of breadcrumbs so you can find your way back!' Dad calls after her.

He turns the camera back on himself and tilts his head back. 'Can you see the hairs in my nose? Your mum plucked one out the other day. I'm too young for nose hairs, don't you think?'

'I think . . . ewwww?'

He laughs. 'So what do you think of the house?'

'It's lovely, Dad.'

'It's . . . well, it's a big change, isn't it?'

'You deserve it. Both of you.'

'You don't think it's silly? The two of us rattling around in this big house? It wasn't an easy decision to make. I want you to know that.'

I don't want him to say her name. The happy mask will slip right off my face and crack on the floor. I'm not sure how many more times I can pick it up and glue the pieces back together.

'I know, Dad. You don't need to explain.' Please, please, please don't explain.

He coughs and clears his throat. 'Do you think . . . um . . . do you think she'd have understood? I had this dream . . . well, a nightmare really. That she came home and couldn't find us. There was another family in our house and she cried. I couldn't bear it if . . .' He chokes down a sob with another cough.

I won't let the mask slip. I can't. 'Of course she'd understand. You know she would. And—'

My door slams open with such force that it almost rebounds right back into the person who opened it. Lily storms in with a murderous look on her face. 'You fucking bitch!'

'What the hell?! Who is that?' Dad is peering close to the screen and looking left and right as if that will help him see what's going on.

'Gotta go, bye.' I slam the laptop lid down just as Lily moves to do it for me.

'How could you tell Marcy about me and Marek?!'

'I didn't!' It's not exactly lying.

'Liar!'

'OK, you need to calm down, Lil.' I don't like her towering over me like this so I put the laptop on the bed and stand up. 'I can explain.'

'Explain all you want. It doesn't change the fact that you fucked me over.'

'Look, I don't know where you got your information from, but you're wrong.' My phone starts ringing; it's Dad.

'She told me herself, OK? Said she thought I should know someone was spreading rumours about me. Acted like she was doing this big favour.' I can picture it clearly; it was a smart move on Marcy's part.

'Come on, Lil. You know me. Does this sound like something I would do? You know I can't stand that girl. That's not what happened at all. Kirsty and I were at dinner and Marcy overheard and it was terrible timing, but you have to know that it wasn't intentional.'

Lily's eyes nearly pop right out of her head. 'You told *Kirsty*?!' She's pacing up and down like a caged tiger.

I should have seen that coming. 'I had no one else to talk to! You three saw to that!' I can feel the anger stirring inside me now. 'I think you should come back when we've both calmed down.' That seems like the safest option all round, before things get out of hand.

'I'm not going anywhere until you explain why you thought it was appropriate to talk to Kirsty – someone you've known for approximately five minutes – about my business.' She crosses her arms.

OK, so we're doing this. 'Because Kirsty and I actually *share* stuff, like friends are meant to. You know, telling each other the important things like whether or not we've been getting off with the school gardener. And the length of time we've known each other is fucking irrelevant. You've known Ama for what? Six, seven years?'

'Leave Ama out of this. She's got nothing to do with it.'

'Oh, really? You know it was her who told Marcy about my parents winning the lottery?'

The door swings open again and Ama practically falls into the room. 'No it wasn't!'

I laugh and it sounds so cruel that I hardly recognise my own voice. 'Nice of you to drop by, Ama.' I turn back to Lily. 'See? Listening at the fucking door! I rest my case.'

It's two against one now, and I don't even care. 'I can't believe you thought that all this time. Why didn't you come to me? I didn't say a word to Marcy about your parents, I swear.' Ama's eyes bore into mine as if I'll believe her just because she's not blinking.

'I don't believe you.' Her shoulders slump, and the strange thing is, I *enjoy* seeing that happen.

'Harper, you have to. I'm begging you!' I don't know why it's so important to her. She's already decided whose side she's on and it's certainly not mine.

Lily puts a gentle hand on Ama's shoulder. 'Leave it, Ams. She's not worth it.' She looks at me and shakes her head. 'She never was.'

I launch myself at her, slamming her against the wardrobe. The wardrobe door collapses inward and Lily loses her balance and falls to the floor.

'Oh my God, Lily, are you OK?' Ama crouches down next to Lily. There are tears in her eyes when she looks back up at me. 'What is *wrong* with you, Harper?'

I'm sure Lily isn't hurt. She just doesn't know how to get to her feet while maintaining some sense of dignity.

'I suppose I'm finally living down to your expectations of someone like me,' I say flatly.

Ama stares at me for a second, then helps Lily to her feet. Lily is limping a little as they shuffle out the door. That girl will do anything for a bit of sympathy.

I don't know if they look back before leaving the room, because I'm already grabbing my phone to call Dad.

Nothing's wrong. Lily was just messing around. Rehearsing for a play.

He believes me. He even laughs and says it must be nice, living with my best mates 24/7.

'You've got friends for life there, Harper. There's nothing more precious.'

FORTY-ONE

It's not as if I hit the girl. It was a push, and barely even that. She just fell against the wardrobe because she was caught unawares. And she was definitely faking that limp.

'I can't believe she came barging into your room like that,' says Kirsty, after I tell her everything. 'Do you want me to talk to her?'

'There's no point. I don't want anything more to do with them. I'm glad it happened, actually. At least now I know for sure that I'm better off without them.'

'Are you OK though? I mean, I know today's a hard day for you – with the move and everything.'

'I'm fine. I'm *fine*.' I am definitely almost fine. You'd think I'd be more upset if they really meant that much to me.

Kirsty says nothing.

'What is it?'

'Nothing. It's just . . . they were your friends –

your *best* friends. Is that really something you want to throw away?' She looks down at the desk and runs her finger through the ring of condensation left by her Coke can. I don't know why she's saying this. She seemed happy about it before – that there's space for her in my life again.

'It'd be too late to do anything about it even if I wanted to. Those bridges are well and truly burned.'

'Things were fine before I turned up, weren't they?' she asks in the smallest voice imaginable.

'This has *nothing* to do with you.'

'I ruin everything.' Still with that same sad, lost voice.

'Bollocks. You're just about the only good thing in my shitshow of a life, so you can stop that talk right now. Maybe things seemed fine before you came here, but they very obviously *weren't*. Marcy was right. They never accepted me for who I am.' The thought of Marcy being right about anything is disconcerting. 'But you know everything there is to know about me and still want to be my friend. That's miraculous to me.' She looks up to meet my eye. 'I can't even tell you how glad I am that you came to Duncraggan.'

Before Halloween I might have hugged her or taken her hand in mine – some gesture to reinforce my words. But things are different now. Tonight, words have to be enough.

There's an extra layer of tension in the room when Rowan and I are getting ready for bed. We timed it badly, returning to the room within minutes of each other. Lily and Ama must have told her what happened, because I swear I can feel her watching me out of the corner of her eye. I bet they exaggerated everything and she's probably wondering if I'm going to Hulk out on her too.

My teeth get a less than thorough brushing and I don't bother with my moisturiser. I get into bed and put my headphones on, keeping the volume low so she can't complain about the noise. I have to keep skipping forward until I finally get to a song with no memories attached to it.

I close my eyes and try to let the music take me away, but tonight it seems that there's no escape. This final year was supposed to be about making memories to last a lifetime, squeezing every last drop of goodness out of this place before I leave. I'm not sure how I can make it to the end of term, let alone the end of the school year.

The only consolation is that I've been through worse things in my life. When the worst thing you can possibly imagine has already happened, everything else pales into insignificance. And if I keep telling myself that enough times, maybe I'll start to believe it.

'Harper?'

I ignore her, because that's what we do to each other now. The rules are simple.

'Harper!'

I take out one of the earbuds and open my eyes. 'What?! The volume is so low even *I* can't hear it, so don't try to tell me—'

'The volume's fine.' She's lying on her side, facing me. We used to lie like this, talking long after lights out. Whoever fell asleep first was the loser.

'Well? I'm *waiting*. Spit it out.' God, I sound like a child.

'I want you to be careful.'

'What the fuck is that supposed to mean?'

'It means you're making some bad choices right now and you're the only one who can't seem to see it. And it means I haven't stopped caring about you even though you're being an arsehole of epic proportions.'

Does she expect me to thank her? Get down on my knees and beg for forgiveness?

'I liked it better when you were ignoring me.' I put the earbud back in and turn the volume way up, watching her face the whole time. Her expression doesn't change, which is deeply annoying. What's even more annoying is that *she* doesn't look annoyed.

She looks like someone who cares.

FORTY-TWO

Kirsty stops and stares, and I can't help but smile. 'Bit bigger than your average Christmas tree, isn't it?'

'Just a bit.'

There's always an air of mystery to Duncraggan's Christmas tree; no one ever seems to see it arrive. You just wake up one morning in early December and there it is, standing proud on the front lawn – all fifty feet of it.

'Apparently it's donated by someone in the Norwegian government. I think his daughter used to go here, and I guess she must have *really* liked the place. Last year there was a huge storm and the tree fell over and hit Mr Hennessy's car.'

'How do they get the star on top?' Kirsty walks slowly around the base of the tree, the frosty grass crunching under her feet.

'The abseiling club do it – and put the lights on too.'

She thinks I'm joking, but it's true. I tell her the ridiculous rumour that the star has real diamonds in it and Miss Maddox stashes it in her safe for the rest of the year.

Our star at home is silver and gold, made of wire and tinsel. We have to bend it back into shape every year. Jenna and I used to fight over who got to put it on the tree so Dad decided we would take it in turns, year on year. It was my turn, that last Christmas, but I let Jenna do it. It's not like I had a premonition or anything. She was having terrible period pains and I thought it might cheer her up a bit. She said I was the best sister in the whole world, and that I could cement my claim to the title by getting her a hot water bottle and a mug of hot chocolate.

I open my mouth to tell Kirsty about it, but the words don't seem to want to come. Perhaps the act of sharing a memory dilutes it, making it paler and paler until it barely even exists any more. Keeping it for yourself concentrates the memory until you can almost taste it. This memory tastes of marshmallows.

Some Year 7s come barrelling down the front steps towards the tree, one girl trailing behind the rest. She slips on the grass and lands on her bum, but she's on her feet before I can blink. She dusts the frost from her skirt as she races to catch up with the others.

'Did Rhiannon like Christmas?' I ask Kirsty as we

make our way back up the steps. It's an inane question, but I'm curious to see how she answers it.

She stops at the top of the steps and looks back at the tree. 'Yeah, I suppose so.'

'You don't talk about her much.' It's never bothered me, that I'm always pouring my heart out and Kirsty seems to keep hers in a tightly stoppered bottle. Never bothered me *much*, anyway.

She says nothing, standing back to let me go through the door first.

I wait until we're in the breakfast queue before trying again. The background chatter is loud, but I lower my voice just in case. 'Have you ever tried talking to your mum? I know you two are close.'

She takes a deep breath like she's about to dive underwater. 'I *can't* talk to Mum.'

'It was the same with my parents – they totally fell apart. It just takes time, I suppose. Maybe you should give her another chance.'

Kirsty shakes her head and looks away. 'You don't understand.'

'I *do* though.' I nudge her and smile. 'Dead Sisters Club for ever, remember?'

Instead of returning my smile, she looks desolate. Somehow I've managed to turn a perfectly decent, festive sort of morning to shit. 'I'm sorry, Harper. I wish I could . . . Can we talk about something else? Please?'

I ask if she's started revising for the exams yet and her relief is palpable. Part of me wishes I'd not given up so easily though. Because I have the oddest feeling that there's something she's not telling me. And even odder, that it's something she *wants* to tell me.

Kirsty and I are studying together in my room that night. My studying looks a lot like online shopping, but Kirsty seems to be doing actual work. I figure that she'll tell me whatever it is when she's good and ready, and that it's not because she doesn't trust me.

There's music coming from Lily and Ama's room: a recording of the piece Ama's playing at the Christmas concert. She must have listened to it a hundred times in the past month; it's a wonder Lily hasn't throttled her by now. But Lily knows how important this is for Ama. Best friends care about that sort of thing, I suppose.

Kirsty slams her book shut. 'Can you ask them to turn the music down? I can't concentrate.'

'It's not *that* loud.' It's pretty loud. I'm surprised Renner hasn't complained. 'We could go to your room if it's bothering you?'

'Or you could ask them to turn it down? I bet they're playing it just to annoy us.'

'I thought you *liked* piano music.'

'I do. Just . . . not tonight.'

I explain about the concert, and how it's a big deal for Ama. 'It's the first time she's ever played in public. She's wanted to do it for years, but her anxiety was always too bad.' I realise that I never asked Ama how the new meds were working out, and now it's too late. 'I bet she's going to nail it at the concert. I hope so, anyway.'

'*Really?* After the way she's treated you?'

'Yes.' And I do mean it. 'She's just being loyal to Lily – I can understand that. The lottery thing was . . . unfortunate, but I'm sure she didn't do it on purpose.'

Kirsty swivels her chair round to face me. 'I don't understand you, Harper. How can you forgive so easily?'

'I haven't forgiven anyone.'

'It doesn't sound that way to me.' She stares at me. 'Some things are too bad to ever be forgiven.' Something tells me she's not talking about Ama any more.

I choose my words carefully. 'There's always a place for forgiveness.'

She stares at me for a moment or two longer, and I stare back, trying to work out what we're really saying here. She's impossible to read.

I do believe in forgiveness – for other people. If only it were as simple to forgive yourself.

276

FORTY-THREE

You can always tell when it's getting near the end of term. Mealtimes are that little bit more raucous and most teachers are more relaxed, letting us take it easy for the last couple of weeks.

Some girls put Christmas decorations up in their rooms – Gabi has so many fairy lights that it's got to be a fire hazard. Rowan and I didn't bother till last year when she bought me a plastic Rudolph complete with flashing nose. It was the tackiest thing I'd ever seen; I loved it immediately. Rudolph has remained in his box this year.

I've been waiting for the rumour about Lily to rear its ugly head, but there hasn't even been a whisper. No one's even talking about Marek any more. There's a new gardener – a ruddy-cheeked middle-aged woman called Rosie. I doubt she'll be inspiring any crushes anytime soon.

It's a relief that no one knows about Lily and Marek.

Not just because it would have been my fault, although I'd be lying if I said that wasn't a big part of it. But I'm also glad that Lily can get on with her life and concentrate on what's important to her: getting into Oxford. In class, she's more focused than ever, asking the teachers for extra reading and not caring when the others take the piss. She always seems to be in the library every time I go in, brow furrowed in concentration. Sometimes I think it would be nice to care that much about the future. I try to ignore the unpleasant thought that perhaps the reason she's focusing so hard on the future is to try to forget the past.

At first it surprises me that Marcy didn't do more with the Lily/Marek information, but when I give it some thought, perhaps it's not so surprising after all. Marcy's problem is with me, not Lily. And she dropped me right in it when she told Lily. The fact that she didn't bother to tell anyone else doesn't make her a good person, but I can't help feeling grateful that she reined in the evil just this once.

Ten days before the concert, I bump into Ama in the corridor. We do that awkward shuffle of both moving in the same direction to try to pass each other. It happens three times before she looks up and makes eye contact. Her laugh comes naturally and mine bubbles up to meet it – an unstoppable reflex. Before I can say anything, she's walking away. It's probably for the best, because what would I have said? *Hey, I know I should have asked two months ago but I was just wondering how you're coping with your anxiety?*

I have to come to terms with the fact that things have changed. I won't be one of the first people Lily tells if/when she gets her acceptance for Oxford, and I won't be there to hug Ama and congratulate her when she blows everyone away at the concert.

I don't belong to a group of friends any more; I'm one of a pair. You'd think that would come naturally to me.

A couple of days later I get a text from Dad when I'm waiting for the house meeting to start in the TV room. Miss Renner's running late because someone puked in the hallway. Kirsty's next to me on the sofa and Rowan's on the other side of the room. I can feel her eyes on us, but I won't give her the satisfaction of seeing me check.

I read Dad's message, expecting the usual link to some unfunny clip on YouTube. On the surface, the message is innocuous enough: *'Jurassic Park, Christmas Eve?'*

Instead of kisses at the end, there's a dinosaur emoji and a Christmas tree emoji.

I want to say no. I even type the word, my finger hovering over the send button.

He knows it was Jenna's thing, not mine. It was her idea to start the tradition, after she found out that her friend Kaz watched *Elf* with her family every Christmas Eve. I think *Jurassic Park* was the first movie that popped into Jenna's head and the rest of us just rolled with it. So that was that, a Kent family tradition was born, and for the next five years our Christmas Eve featured gradually improving versions of Jenna's velociraptor impression, exaggerated screaming at the first appearance of the T. rex, and the four of us swaying along to the sweeping orchestral music at the end.

I hit send, after changing 'N' and 'o' to 'O' and 'K'. No emojis.

It's going to hurt – two hours and seven minutes of memories. But maybe next year it will hurt a little less, and the year after that I might even be able to crack a smile at smooth-chested Jeff Goldblum with his shirt hanging open. Jenna said she thought he was sexy before she even knew what sexy meant; Dad laughed so hard he spilled red wine on the carpet.

I have to learn to deal with things like this. I owe it to her.

Kirsty must have noticed I zoned out for a minute there, because she asks me about the message. I tell her it's nothing. She doesn't believe me, but she doesn't ask again.

It's petty, but I figure it's only fair after her

weirdness yesterday. We were in the library, and I was counting down the minutes till dinnertime while everyone else was being studious. At least, I *would* have been counting down the minutes if someone hadn't forgotten to wind up the grandfather clock. I grabbed Kirsty's phone to check the time and saw there was a message from her dad – a long message. She snatched the phone from my hand, but not before I'd read the first line: 'Can we talk about Mum?'

Kirsty stared down at the phone for a second, then said, 'I forgot there was this thing I wanted to show you . . . wait a second, I don't think the wi-fi's working . . .'

'I was just checking the time,' I said. 'Is everything OK?' I want to ask what's up with her mum, but I don't want her to know I saw the message.

She kept tapping away on the phone; she wouldn't meet my eye. 'Sorry, the site won't load. I'll show you later though.'

I couldn't help noticing that she put the phone in her pocket instead of back on the table.

FORTY-FOUR

'Let's go to my room instead,' says Kirsty on Thursday night, when we realise that my room isn't empty after all.

I survey the scene and sigh. 'Do you need a hand with that?'

'No, I'm fine.' Rowan's standing in front of the mirror above the sink, holding a small mirror up behind her while she attempts to use the clippers with her other hand. From the look of the hair on the back of her head, things aren't going so well. She drops the clippers on the floor, swears and sneezes four times. She looks like shit – sweaty and pale, except for a nose redder than Rudolph's. The cold must have come on fast; she seemed fine this morning.

I pick up the clippers. 'Come on, I'll do it. I don't want Renner blaming me if you slice an ear off.'

Rowan blows her nose and looks at me warily. 'What's the catch?'

I roll my eyes. 'There's no catch. Just grab a towel and sit down. Kirsty, I'll come and—' But Kirsty's not standing in the doorway any more; she's already gone. I turn back to Rowan and I swear if she says something or even looks at me the wrong way, I'll leave her to it.

We don't speak, except when Rowan warns me she's about to sneeze so I can move the clippers away from her scalp. I'm grateful for the insistent buzz of the clippers, masking the awkward silence. I get the job done much quicker than last time. I'm not sure whether that's because I'm taking less care or because I know what I'm doing this time.

She thanks me and I shrug. 'There's some Vicks in the cabinet above the sink. And there's that extra blanket in my wardrobe if you're cold.'

'Thank you,' she says again and this time it sounds like she means it. I feel like if I stay in this room we will start talking about things I really don't want to talk about, so I leave.

I knock on Kirsty's door, but she doesn't answer. I knock again, louder this time, but there's still no answer. I open the door, just a crack, and the room is dark. The light from the corridor casts a shaft of light on to the bed and she's under the duvet, lying with her back to me. I check my watch and it's not even nine o'clock. 'Kirsty,' I half whisper. 'Are you awake?' There's no answer, and I don't want to speak any louder in case she *is* asleep. Asleep or faking, she obviously doesn't want me there. I whisper 'Good night,' and leave.

I can't go back to my room yet, and I don't want to go to the TV room. It would be weird to drop by someone else's room, because I never drop by anyone else's room. Gabi would let me hang out with her, no questions asked, but I don't want to use her like that. Lily and Ama's door is open; Lily's at her desk but Ama's not there. No prizes for guessing where *she* is.

It sounds exactly like the recording – until the clash of discordant notes followed by 'FUCK!'

When I enter the music room, Ama's forehead is resting on the keys of the piano and her eyes are closed.

'Hi,' I say quietly.

She raises her head. 'What do you want?' Not quite hostile, but hardly welcoming either.

'I don't know.' I wander to the far wall and pretend to study a poster of labelled percussion instruments. What would she say if I told her I wanted things to go back to the way they were?

Ama starts to play again; after a minute or two, my shoulders start to relax. I turn to watch her. She looks so different when she's at the piano – otherworldly, almost.

The sound washes over me and I slide my back down the wall so I'm sitting on the floor. There's nothing for me to do but listen. After the last notes die away, she sits with her hands resting lightly on the keys, her back ramrod straight.

'You're going to be brilliant.'

She shakes her head. 'I'm not ready. Nowhere near.'

'You are.'

I can tell she wants to talk, and after a couple of seconds, it all comes tumbling out in the most Ama way possible. 'So yesterday Mr Hennessy just happened to mention that he's invited an old friend of his to the concert. No big deal, right? But this old friend of his teaches at Goldsmiths, and Mr Hennessy's told him all about me. How the hell am I supposed to play well under that kind of pressure?' Ama has wanted to go to Goldsmiths ever since I've known her. 'And did you notice that chord progression at the start of the second movement? Disastrous. My brain knows what it wants my fingers to do but my fingers are all "*Nope*".'

It's as if she's forgotten how things are between us; it makes me want to forget too.

She turns back to the piano and plays a few notes. 'See?'

Of course I don't see – or hear. 'You're being too hard on yourself. You're ready. You've *got* this.'

She closes the lid of the piano, none too gently.

285

'Why the hell did I agree to play in the first place? I mean, it seemed like something I could maybe do, way back in September when it was still bloody months away. But now there's two bloody days. Two days! I should just pull out of the competition and spare everyone the horror of having to listen to me massacre one of the greatest compositions of all time.'

I burst out laughing. 'Yeah, I wouldn't be surprised if everyone's ears start bleeding from the trauma.'

Ama laughs too, but we both stop as soon was we realise that this isn't how things work now.

'I should go.' I get to my feet and dust off my jeans even though there isn't any dust to speak of.

'Harper—'

'I've distracted you for long enough.'

'I'm glad you came. I wish . . .'

Ama doesn't finish her sentence, but I'm as sure as it's possible to be that I wish for exactly the same thing.

FORTY-FIVE

'Morning! Did you sleep well? You look tired. Are you tired? I can get you coffee if you like. I'm going to have another cup – want me to get you some?'

It sounds like coffee is the last thing Kirsty needs. 'I'm fine with tea, thanks.' I put down my tray and slide into the seat next to hers while she gets more coffee.

'Hi!' she says perkily when she sits down again.

'Hi,' I say, bemused.

'Is everything OK?'

I start buttering my toast. 'I was going to ask you the same question. You were out for the count when I came by your room last night.'

'I felt like I might be coming down with something. I thought an early night might help – and it did. I feel fine this morning. Better than fine.'

'So you weren't annoyed at me for helping Rowan?'

'Not at all.' Her smile is a little too quick to arrive, and to leave. 'Is she feeling better?'

I shrug as if I couldn't care less.

Rowan isn't feeling any better. I know because I asked as soon as she woke up. She won't miss lessons though – she'd have to be practically dying to stay in bed. I turn round in my chair and sure enough, Rowan is sitting with Ama and Lily. She has two glasses of orange juice in front of her.

'It was nice of you, what you did for her.' Her smile functions a little better this time. There's real warmth in it.

'Anyone would have done the same.'

'I don't think so. You're a good person, Harper.'

'You say that like it's a bad thing.' I laugh.

'Not at all. It's why we became friends in the first place. Your kindness – that night. I'll never forget it.'

What would have happened if I *hadn't* given her the torch? Or if I'd told her it was Rowan's idea? You never know which tiny decisions will make a difference in your life.

There were no lessons after lunch today, so that people could get ready for the concert, and the carols beforehand. I was planning on having a nap. No matter how much I sleep at the moment, it's never enough. My plans were foiled by Mr Gilbert, my history teacher, who cornered me after lunch. 'Just a chat,' he said, in an effort to put me at ease. Then he got to the point: last week's test paper was 'not up to my usual standard'. My usual standard is the very definition of average, so that was just Mr Gilbert-speak for 'really fucking terrible'. He was really nice about it, because he's always nice. He asked if there's anything bothering me, and I was almost tempted to tell him, just to see his face, but I said I was fine. And now I'm stuck doing an extra test paper over the holidays, and I had to act grateful for the opportunity. So I was distracted when I got back to my room, busy kicking myself for letting things – *them* – get to me.

It took me a few minutes to notice: blank spaces where there used to be pictures. Four blobs of Blu-tack in each corner, even though Blu-tack is practically a banned substance at Duncraggan.

It was the blank spaces above Rowan's bed that I noticed first – and it hurt, but I understood. It didn't occur to me that it would be the same on my side of the room. But it was, and that's when the hurt turned to anger. I sat down to wait for her.

The photographs have been selected with care. Every single one with both Rowan and me is gone. Twelve photos in total, seven on her side, five on mine.

The door opens and Rowan comes in, sweating and mud-splattered after lacrosse practice. She wasn't really well enough to play lacrosse today but she did it anyway because that's the kind of person she is. She is also, apparently, the kind of person to do something petty like this.

'What did you do with them?' My voice is weary; I can't do this any more. I cannot have another confrontation – especially not with her.

Rowan just stands there, staring at the walls, so I repeat the question.

Her lacrosse stick clatters to the floor and she sits down on the edge of her bed.

'Well? Say something!' Maybe I can do this after all. What's one more confrontation between not-best friends?

'You tell her I want those photos back.' She has tears in her eyes, but her voice is hard and defiant.

Rowan never cries. I'm so taken aback by the tears that I'm slow to understand her words. 'Why would she . . .?' Rowan stares at me, but I don't understand.

And then I do. Suddenly, finally.

She turns to look at the wall next to her bed. 'Those pictures meant a lot to me. They *mean* a lot to me.' Then she turns to me, sniffing and wiping her nose on her sleeve. 'Which either makes me a total fucking idiot or . . .' Her face crumples and it feels like my heart follows suit. 'I *miss* you, Harper.'

I get up from my chair, but I don't go to her. I make for the door.

'She's not there.' Rowan sniffs again. 'I saw her heading to the shooting range on my way back.'

'Even better.' I look back at my friend – my *best* friend – as I open the door. 'Well? Are you coming or not?'

FORTY-SIX

I close Kirsty's door behind us and survey the room. 'You try the wardrobe, I'll take the desk.'

'Renner will kill us if she catches us.' There's no need to whisper, but we do nonetheless.

'She's not going to catch us. But let's be quick about it.' Even the contents of the drawers are neatly organised. Kirsty's extreme neatness should work in our favour. I rifle through the contents – notebooks and pens and a phone charger. I shake out each notebook in case she's stashed the photos between the pages. I'm extra careful to put everything back exactly as I found it.

'Christ, she should be in the army.' Rowan steps back so I can see into the wardrobe – impossibly neat piles of clothes, evenly spaced hangers.

'Try not to mess anything up,' I say, knowing full well that Rowan has never folded anything properly in her whole life. I have to help her pack at the end of each term because I can't bear to watch her make such a mess of it.

It doesn't feel wrong, doing this. Perhaps it should. It's a huge invasion of privacy after all. But it's our only option. If I ask her, she will lie. It's what she does. I try not to think about why I couldn't see that before. I can beat myself up about that later — *after* we find the photos.

I'm going through the pile of books on her desk when Rowan says my name.

'Got them?' I say, swivelling round in the chair.

But it's not the photos that Rowan's holding up for me to see. It's a T-shirt. Jenna's T-shirt.

Rowan hands it over and I clutch the soft fabric in my hands. I turn it this way and that, checking for signs of damage, but it's fine. Kirsty is very, very lucky that it's fine.

'I'm sorry,' says Rowan.

'You have nothing to be sorry about. We both know that. But thank you.' It's hard to look at her, standing there, pitying me.

All I can think about is that fact that I didn't realise the T-shirt was missing. I haven't looked at it for ages. Shouldn't I have felt its absence somehow? What the hell is Kirsty playing at? I don't understand it, and I'm not sure I want to.

I just want my life back.

Rowan tries the bedside drawers next. She's good at this, faster than me. She makes a joke about me being Watson to her Sherlock, but she doesn't seem to mind when I fail to laugh.

I can get my head around why Kirsty would have taken the photos. The other night when I helped Rowan with her hair, Kirsty could see what was going on. She saw that we were getting close to being friends again, and she was jealous. She figured I'd blame Rowan for taking the photos down and that would be that.

The T-shirt though? And the necklace; I almost forgot about the necklace. These things have nothing to do with Rowan or the others. How would she feel if I took something of Rhiannon's and hid it from her? I don't even know if she *has* anything of Rhiannon's . . .

I stop dead and stare at the T-shirt on my lap. I have so many things that belonged to Jenna. I even have her hairbrush in my spongebag; nobody knows about that. I like having her stuff around me, even when it makes me feel sad. I like looking at old photos of her on my phone.

Kirsty's never even shown me a photo of her sister. Surely there's no way . . .? My mind tries to reject the idea even as it starts to make perfect sense – a twisted, fucked-up kind of sense.

I don't voice my suspicions to Rowan – not yet. I want to find the photos and get the hell out of here.

'Nothing in here,' says Rowan. 'Apart from this.' She hands me a ring box, pale blue leather. I open the box as she carries on searching. Inside, there's a plain platinum ring on a thin chain. I'm about to put it back when the light catches something engraved on its inner surface. It's a name written in swirly writing, hard to read until I shine the desk light right on it. I feel almost dizzy with relief: Rhiannon. She didn't lie about her after all.

I put the ring back in the box and hand it back to Rowan. If she notices my hand shaking, she doesn't say anything.

'We should hold it for ransom until she gives us the photos back,' says Rowan, but she's already putting it back where she found it. She would never do something like that; her moral compass is unshakeable. I should never have doubted that.

My gaze falls on to a box at the back of the desk. There are books piled on top of it, and I check through each one. I remember the box – Kirsty hurrying to put something inside when I forgot to knock on the door.

'Pretty terrible hiding place, if that's where she stashed them,' says Rowan. But she's wrong. It's the perfect hiding place. There's nowhere better to hide something than out in the open, in plain sight. My sister taught me that.

It's a pale green Molton Brown box, slightly worn around the edges. I pull off the lid and peer inside. The photos aren't there – unless she's put them inside one of these envelopes. But there's no way to know for sure unless I break the seals. The envelopes are standard letter size, made of thick, creamy paper. Expensive. There must be at least twenty stacked inside the box.

I spread the envelopes out on the desk and see Kirsty's handwriting on the front of each one. The first few letters have the same name and the same address.

Rhiannon Connor
16 Miles Lane
Cobham
Surrey
KT11 2AF

'Who's Rhiannon?' Rowan whispers, startling me. I hadn't realised she was so close, leaning over me to see.

I can't speak. Why on earth would Kirsty be writing letters to her dead sister?

The last three letters just say 'Mum' on the front, with no address below.

'Isn't that a therapy thing? Writing letters and not sending them?' Rowan asks. A foggy memory surfaces. Aiden, the grief counsellor. A man whose face I can't picture, because I didn't look him in the eye, not even once. It was too soon; I wasn't ready to talk about Jenna, especially not to a stranger. I remember his socks. He always wore argyle socks, in various different colours. Must have got a multi-pack.

Aiden mentioned letters once, early on. He said something about me dealing with my anger towards Jenna. I hated him for that. I wasn't angry with Jenna, not back then. I was angry with myself, and I didn't need to write a fucking letter to deal with that. I'd just have to learn to live with it. Later, I found out it was possible to be angry with both of us – we could share it. Trouble is, we never seemed to share it equally; my anger with her could never quite compete.

I put the letters back in the box, making sure they're in the right order. Then I put the box back in place, with the pile of books on top. She won't know we've been here – unless I tell her. Rowan goes to the door and opens it a crack to check the coast is clear.

Back in our room, Rowan asks what I'm going to do.

'I'm going to talk to her.' I fold up Jenna's T-shirt and slip it inside my hoodie. It feels right there, next to my skin.

'*Now?* Why don't you wait till she's back?'

I shake my head. If I wait, the doubts will start to creep in. The sympathy too, maybe.

'I'll come with you then.'

'I don't think it will help, her seeing me with you. I need to do this on my own. It'll be fine.'

'Sure. Confronting a girl who's got a loaded shotgun. What could possibly go wrong?'

'I'm not stupid, Rowan.' She raises an eyebrow at that. 'OK, I *am* stupid about some things, and I seem to have gone out of my way to prove it these past few weeks. But I'm not stupid around guns, and neither is Kirsty.'

Rowan doesn't look convinced. I put my hands on her shoulders and look her in the eye. 'It will be fine. *We* will be fine.'

Her gaze flickers downwards. 'Is that *broccoli* between your teeth?'

'*What?* But I didn't have any . . .' I hurry over to the mirror.

'Nah, I'm just messing with you.' She grins, and God I've missed that. 'Now go find out where our fucking photos are. That Polaroid one is the only decent photo *ever* taken of me.'

'The beach one? But it's all blurry!'

Rowan nods sagely. '*Exactly.*'

FORTY-SEVEN

It would have been weak to let Rowan come with me, and I've had enough of being weak. All that matters is that she *wanted* to come. For some reason she's still got my back, after everything that's happened.

It's slippery underfoot, with slimy, rotten leaves clogging the path through the woods. The cross-country team seems to manage OK, thundering past on either side of me. It must be easier to keep your balance when your feet hardly even touch the ground.

Kirsty isn't alone at the range. Miss Whaite is running through the safety spiel with a couple of Year 9s. I remember barely listening my first time. I just wanted to get on with it; I wanted to shoot something. These two seem to be taking it seriously though. The red-haired one looks afraid, which makes me wonder why she's even here.

Kirsty's at the stand on the far side. The clays are being thrown fast — faster than I can handle. I lean against a tree to watch as she blasts clay after clay. Her focus never wavers; she reloads smoothly and quickly.

She misses some, but not many. Miss Whaite and the Year 9s even stop to watch. I can see her pointing out Kirsty's stance and showing the small red-haired girl how to stand the same way.

Kirsty's still going when Miss Whaite and the girls pack up to leave. Miss Whaite stops and smiles when she sees me. 'Your friend is good, Harper – exceptional, even. She could possibly compete nationally in a year or two. Talk to her for me, will you? I've tried, but she says she's not interested.'

I nod and say I'll talk to Kirsty. She believes me.

I grab a pair of ear defenders and head across to stand behind Kirsty. I'm not about to tap her on the shoulder to get her attention – a gut full of shotgun pellets would hardly improve my day.

Finally, she lowers the gun. She takes off her ear defenders and shooting glasses and stretches, the gun resting in the crook of her arm.

She doesn't seem surprised to see me when she turns round. She smiles. The smile is the same as it's been for the last couple of days – a touch too bright. 'I thought that might be you. You can tell, can't you? When someone's watching you.' It's a funny thing to say for someone who's usually the one doing the watching.

She maintains the smile as she takes cartridges out

of the pockets of her shooting vest, and when she asks if I've come to shoot. It only drops off her face when I don't answer.

'Is everything OK? Has something happened?'

'Where are the photos?'

She furrows her brow and shakes her head. When she opens her mouth to speak, I get there first. 'I know it was you. And I know you wanted me to blame Rowan, but we both know the truth here so can we just cut the crap?'

She swallows and looks left and right, as if she's working out an escape route.

'If you return them today, maybe I won't go to Renner about this.'

'Harper, why are you doing this? I'm your friend.'

'Really?' I unzip the front of my hoodie and take out Jenna's T-shirt.

'You've been in my room.'

'You steal something belonging to my dead sister and that's all you can say?'

You can practically see her brain working behind her eyes, frantically trying to come up with an explanation.

'I found the letters.'

She bends over like I've punched her. When she straightens up, she's breathing hard and fast. It looks like one of Ama's panic attacks. I should care, but it's too late for caring.

Finally, she speaks. 'I was going to tell you . . . I wanted to. I almost did. That morning, when the Christmas tree went up.'

'Going to tell me what?'

She takes a step towards me. 'You need to understand that I never meant for any of this to happen. It wasn't supposed to be like this.' I cross my arms, unimpressed, which makes her wince. 'I've never had a friend like you before. I would do *anything* for you.'

I shake my head. I won't allow myself to feel pity for this girl after everything she's done.

Another step closer to me, a hand reaching out. 'I *love* you, Harper!'

The sound of slow clapping echoes off the trees. '*I love you, Harper!* This is adorable. I wish I'd brought popcorn.'

My head snaps round to see Marcy Stone sauntering towards us.

'Leave. Now,' I say through gritted teeth.

'You're kidding, right? I wouldn't miss this for the world. Don't mind me. You won't even know I'm here – I'll be quiet as a mouse. Now where were we? Oh yes, Kirsty just declared her undying love so that means you're up next, Harper. What's your response?' She clasps her hands together in mock excitement.

'*Please*, Marcy. This is private,' Kirsty implores.

302

Maybe she thinks she can appeal to Marcy's better nature, but Marcy *has* no better nature.

'Oh, come on, there's no such thing as privacy at Duncraggan. You both know that. Secrets have a way of worming their way to the surface. There's really no point trying to keep them in the first place. Isn't that right, Connor?'

'What are you talking about?' I ask. I'm playing into her hands but I can't help myself. I glance at Kirsty to find her looking daggers at Marcy.

'Wow. You're even stupider than I thought. Who do you think told me your dirty little secret?'

'Shut *up*,' Kirsty says.

Marcy spreads her hands, eyes lit up. 'Harper Kent – the origin story! From *such* humble beginnings to the heady heights of Duncraggan Castle!' She smiles sweetly at me. 'Oops. Don't tell me you didn't know? Oh *dear*. I really should learn to keep my mouth shut, shouldn't I?' I swear I've never seen her look happier. 'Well this is awkward. Maybe I *will* leave you to it after all. Seems like you guys have a lot to talk about. Catch you later!' She turns on her heel and sashays towards the forest path.

My brain is sluggish. *It wasn't Ama. She was telling the truth the whole time.*

A sound brings me back to my senses. A loud snick-snack. Horribly familiar.

I whirl round to see Kirsty with the shotgun in her hands. The gun is pointed at Marcy's back. Steady aim, as always.

At first I think she might be messing around, even though she's breaking just about every gun safety rule there is. But I watch, horrified, as her finger slides the safety catch forward.

Marcy is oblivious. The girl is whistling, for Christ's sake. My first instinct is to shout, to warn her. But any sudden movement on Marcy's part could make Kirsty pull the trigger – by accident or on purpose.

My second instinct is try to tackle Kirsty, but it's too risky. Anything could happen. Before I have a chance to think about my third option, I'm already doing it.

Three steps and I'm staring down the barrels of a twenty-bore shotgun.

FORTY-EIGHT

Kirsty doesn't move a muscle; she doesn't lower the shotgun.

It's mesmerising, looking into the blackness of the barrels. You could fall inside there and never be found. There's something tempting about that. But the barrels start to move, ever so slightly. A tiny tremor that you might not notice if you weren't staring harder than you've ever stared at anything in your life.

Marcy is still whistling, but the sound is getting fainter. I can't turn to see if she's still visible through the trees.

'Put it down, Kirsty.' My voice sounds broken.

She says nothing, but the tremor continues.

I try to focus my eyes on her face, but it's hard to tear my attention away from those two black holes.

This has to end now. Before someone comes along and sees what's happening. I take a single step forward and the gun is centimetres from my face. 'If you're going to shoot, do it.' The words come out shakily.

'I didn't mean for any of this . . .' Kirsty sobs.

I lean into the gun so the barrels are pressing against my forehead, cold and unforgiving. It's madness, total madness.

'Do you want to die?' she whispers. The gun is suddenly still again.

I consider the question. I've thought about it more times than I can count. Anything to be rid of the pain of losing Jenna. Every day without her is hard. I never thought my life would be like this, but it's the life I've got. And there's no choice, really, but to live it.

'No.'

There's an emptiness in her eyes as she whispers, 'Lucky you.'

There's a moment where my brain catches on to what's about to happen. I can picture it – her brains splattered everywhere, the taste of her blood on my lips.

'Kirsty, no!'

I raise my hand to make a grab for the shotgun, but she moves faster. Instead of turning the gun on herself, she snaps the safety back on and lowers it to the ground.

Kirsty is shaking uncontrollably, eyes fixed on the shotgun. I think she's in shock. She looks back up, and it's almost as if she doesn't recognise me. Before I can say anything, she's running – sprinting towards the woods. She slips on wet leaves but scrambles quickly back to her feet, half running, half limping.

The girl needs help; I have to go after her. Or I could get Renner, or Maddox? What's the best thing to do? What would Rowan do?

My eyes are drawn to something red on the ground. Jenna's T-shirt, trampled into the mud. Kirsty's footprint obscures the image on the front. The sight makes my heart ache.

I don't even remember dropping it. I'll have to wash it, but that means it will fade even more. How long before the image on the front disappears completely?

Everything disappears. Cartoon cats. Friends. Sisters.

I crouch down to pick up the T-shirt.

The punch to my jaw comes out of nowhere.

It's more of a slap, to be fair. A hybrid punch/slap and it's a pretty weak effort. Rowan's breathing is fast and shallow; her face is leached of colour. She's got a vice-like grip on my shoulders and I can't escape.

'What the fuck, Rowan?' I move my jaw left and right even though I know there's no damage.

She wraps her arms around me and squeezes so hard that I struggle for breath. 'You're OK, you're

OK.' She says it over and over and I relax into the hug. My legs give way and she has to hold me up.

'You stupid, stupid, brave, stupid fuck.'

Now I'm the one shaking. And all of a sudden it's real. There was a loaded gun pointed at my head and I didn't even blink. That's not normal, is it? Not even close. And then I laugh. That's not normal either.

After the laughter, I vomit. Twice. That's probably normal.

Rowan rubs my back and tells me everything's going to be OK.

We sit on a bench while my stomach decides whether to go for round three. 'Did you . . . did you see?'

She taps the binoculars hanging round her neck. She's still wearing her lacrosse stuff, but at least she's got a coat on.

'Spying on me, were you?' I smile weakly.

'Got a problem with that, Kent?'

I shake my head. My own personal guardian angel watching over me, ready to punch me in the face if I step out of line.

'I'm sorry I wasn't close enough to help. She's gonna be expelled for sure.'

'She needs help, Rowan. We have to help her.'

'Please tell me you're joking.'

'She might do something stupid.'

Rowan snorts. 'More stupid than pointing a loaded gun at two of her classmates?'

'I think she might hurt herself.'

'*Shit.* Bollocksing fucking shitting shit.' She takes a deep breath and straightens her shoulders. 'OK, what are we going to do?'

FORTY-NINE

We decide the castle's our best bet. Kirsty was running in that direction, and with any luck she'll be in her room, mortified about what's happened. That's what Rowan thinks anyway.

I have to put the shotgun back in the shed; it takes me three attempts before my fingers stop shaking enough to enter the combination for the lock. I spot Kirsty's bag lying in the corner so I grab it and sling it over my shoulder. I check the bag, hoping she still has her phone on her, but it's there nestled at the bottom. Of all the safety rules, why did she have to comply with that one?

The sun is starting to set as we make our way back to the castle. Rowan says we should go to Renner if we can't find Kirsty. She thinks for a second, and then adds, 'We should go to Renner if we *do* find her too.'

I know she's right, even though my brain rebels

against the idea. You don't grass people up – you just *don't*. But the rules changed as soon as Kirsty pointed a loaded gun at Marcy.

I agree that we should go to Renner *after* we've found her, but not before. Renner will go straight to Maddox – she has to – and then the shit will hit the fan. I should be the one to talk to Kirsty, not some teacher who doesn't even know her.

You don't know her either.

I want to believe Rowan – that Kirsty won't do anything stupid. But I can't quite manage it.

Because you know that look. The emptiness in her eyes. You've seen it in the mirror.

They're already getting things ready for the carol service. There are lanterns dotted across the front lawn and the brass band are setting up their chairs and music stands next to the tree.

We pass Mr Hennessy in the foyer, shaking hands with a man in a brown bobble hat. He must be the lecturer from Goldsmiths. I hope he has better taste in music than he does in hats.

We run up the stairs, against the flow of people heading for an early dinner. In our corridor, Renner is standing in the doorway of Lily and Ama's room. She beams when she sees Rowan and me. 'Now *that's* what I like to see. I knew it was just a matter of time before you two kissed and made up.' She blushes as she realises that as far as she knows, the bi girl and the lesbian could actually be kissing. She turns back to Lily. 'Is Ama getting in some last-minute practice? I can't wait to hear her play.'

Lily isn't listening to Renner. She's staring at me and Rowan, clearly baffled.

'I'll just go and see if Kirsty wants to come for dinner,' I say, and head off in the direction of her room.

'Oh Christ on a bike, is that the time? I'm sure there's something I'm supposed to be doing. I'll see you girls later.' Renner hurries off down the corridor and I double back.

'Can one of you two please tell me what the hell is going on?' asks Lily, stepping out of the room.

Rowan shoos me away. 'Go! See if she's there. I'll explain everything.'

I touch Lily's arm, and she looks down at my hand, surprised. 'I'm sorry, Lily.' And I have no idea if she knows that I mean it, because I don't wait to see her reaction. There's so much I want to say to her but now's not the time. I rush down the corridor to the turret room and don't bother to knock.

She's not here, but she was.

*

The missing photos are neatly laid out on the bed, in the exact same configuration as they were on our walls. It makes me think that she must have studied those photos a lot when she was in our room, which makes me feel unaccountably sad.

I look around the room but nothing's changed since earlier. What was I expecting? A map, with 'X' marking the Kirsty? I should have known she wouldn't be here. But where the hell is she? She could be anywhere. *No. Think.*

A buzzing at my hip startles me. Another message from her dad, and she's not here to stop me reading this one. It shows up on the screen even though the phone is locked: *Please, angel, pick up the damn phone. I know it's hard — it's not easy for either of us. We have to move on.*

Another message comes through as I'm rereading the first: *You can't ignore me for ever. What about the wedding??? Hope you didn't mean what you said.*

The phone starts ringing and I look at the photo that comes up onscreen. He looks like a dad, anyone's dad. He could play the role of Dad in the John Lewis Christmas advert. My finger hovers over the green phone icon. I could talk to him. I'm sure he'd be able to answer at least some of my questions. But the phone stops ringing before I can make a decision.

Who's getting married? And what did Kirsty say that her dad hoped she didn't mean? My mind flicks back to that day in the library – the message from her dad that she didn't want me to see. Something about her mum?

The answers are on the phone in my hand. It's a total invasion of privacy, but I don't care. I try Kirsty's birthday for the passcode. No go. If it's the same set-up as my phone I've got two more tries before the phone locks itself. It feels massively egotistical, even as I'm typing, but no, my birthday isn't the answer either. One more shot. I look around the room, hoping for inspiration. If it's Rhiannon's birthday, I'm screwed, because I have no idea when that is. It might not even be a birthday. It could be random numbers for all I know, but this is Kirsty – there's nothing random about her. She's methodical, precise. Ever since that night in the Hole she's planned and plotted to . . . to what? Be my friend? Make me hate the others and the others hate me so that she was my only friend. It makes no sense. There's nothing special about me. It was all down to me giving her that fucking torch . . . Could it be that simple? I type in four numbers – the date of Kirsty's ordeal in the Hole – and the phone unlocks.

I go straight to the messages. I have pages and pages on my phone; Kirsty does not. According to this, there are only three people who message her.

Her dad is first in line – the most recent message showing up first – then me.

The last person is Kirsty's mum. I'm about to click on her dad's name to look at his messages when something odd strikes me. Her mum shouldn't be below me on the list; Kirsty says they message every day, and I haven't messaged Kirsty in a while. Has she been ignoring her mum as well as her dad? Is it something to do with this wedding?

I read her mum's message: *OK, I'm coming to pick you up. But we need to have a SERIOUS talk.*

Coming to pick her up? I thought Kirsty was booked on the early flight next Wednesday. Then I notice the date: the message was sent nearly a year ago.

There are other messages – lots of them. But they're all over a year old. Where are the messages about *DIY SOS* and *MasterChef* and all the other shit TV shows Kirsty's mum texts her about every week? She could have deleted them, I suppose. But why?

Something's not right, but what? I read her mum's message again, and the answer smacks me in the face. How could I not have seen it before? The truth was there all along, if only I'd been paying attention.

The messages from Kirsty's dad – and Kirsty's replies – fill in the rest of the details. I run from the room, stuffing the phone in my pocket as I go.

FIFTY

Ama's there with Rowan and Lily. From the look on her face, she knows the score too. She's dressed for the concert: white blouse, long black skirt, black ballet pumps. Her face is ashen – whether from nerves or finding out about Kirsty and the gun I can't tell.

'She wasn't there.' My heart is hammering what feels like a thousand beats a minute.

Rowan sighs. 'I was sure she . . . Wait, what took you so long if she wasn't even there?'

'I found the photos.'

'I don't give a shit about the photos. Well, I do, but you know what I mean. What are we going to do?'

'We have to find her.'

'But she could be anywhere!' says Lil. 'This place is fucking hide-and-seek heaven.'

'We should tell Renner,' says Ama, and Rowan nods. 'This is serious. What if she's gone back to the shooting range? We have to tell someone.'

Ama and Rowan discuss whether it would be best to go straight to Maddox, or whether we could keep it low-key by going to Renner.

Lily's looking at me. 'You know where she is, don't you?' she asks, cutting through Ama and Rowan's debate.

'No, I mean maybe. I'm just thinking about where I would go – if I wanted to be alone. If I wanted to . . .' I shake my head, not wanting to follow that thought to its conclusion. 'I'm going to get her. We can't tell Maddox or Renner – not yet. Rowan, have you got that torch?'

'I'm coming with you,' says Rowan, her tone of voice leaving no room for debate.

Lily stands up and walks over to the door. 'Guessing I'll need my coat?'

Why would they do this? After everything Kirsty's done. After everything *I've* done. They're still here, with me. I'm lost for words.

'OK, let's go,' says Ama.

'No!' all three of us say, not quite in unison.

'Yes,' Ama says firmly. She grabs her scarf from the back of her chair.

The other two look at me helplessly. 'Ama, you have to stay. The concert's in less than an hour.' I don't mention the carol service – no one cares about the carol service.

'There's plenty of time,' Ama says, all serene as if we're not talking about the scariest thing she's ever done.

'But don't you want to get some last-minute practice in?'

She smiles. 'Nah. Like, you said the other night, I'm ready. I got this.'

I look at Ama, at Lily, at Rowan. These miraculous girls.

Rowan puts her hand over my mouth. 'Save the big speech till later. We get it. You were a dick but now you see the error of your ways and we see the error of *our* ways and well, that pretty much covers it. Yes?' I nod. 'Good. Now let's get going.'

We head through the kitchens, and I fill them in on the stuff they don't know – they need to be prepared. One of the cooks is standing by the fire exit, smoking a cigarette. 'Up to no good, girls?'

Lily winks at him. 'Always.'

The entire school is gathered in a semicircle round the giant Christmas tree, and the lower-school girls are, predictably, singing 'O Christmas Tree'. I usually enjoy the carol service, even though I'd never admit it to anyone. It feels hopeful, somehow – like you're a part of something.

We creep down the side of the building, sticking

to the shadows when we can. It should be fine as long as none of the teachers turn round. We make a run for it down the side of the walled garden and we're out of sight by the time they move on to 'In the Bleak Midwinter'. It's always a downer, that one.

The temperature must have dropped ten degrees since the sun set; she must be freezing. Unless she's not where I think she is. I picture her sitting in the shed at the range, knuckles white as she grips the shotgun harder. No. I have to be right.

The singing fades as we move further away from the castle, replaced by crashing waves. Ama does her best to keep up, but her long skirt isn't exactly helping matters. 'Ama?' My breath puffs a white cloud in front of my face. 'I don't expect you and Lily to forgive me. After tonight, you don't have to . . .' I shrug.

'Don't have to what? Be friends with you?'

'Yeah.'

She shakes her head and laughs. 'You're not getting rid of us that easily, Kent. You made a mistake. Because you're a person, and that's what people do – they screw up. We *all* screw up. Life goes on, you know?'

But what happens when you make a mistake and life doesn't go on? What then?

It's a starry night, the moon hanging low in the sky. I hesitate at the top of the cliff steps and Rowan puts a hand on my shoulder. 'Come on, let's do this.'

'What if we're too late?' Lily whispers.

'We're not,' I say, with a confidence I don't quite feel. Being here, looking down at the black water crashing on to the rocks, bad things seem possible. Probable, even.

'What are you going to say to her?' Ama asks, with an involuntary shudder.

I take a deep breath of cold, salty air. 'I'm not going to say anything. I'm going to listen.'

FIFTY-ONE

We make our way silently down the cliff steps, me first. *What if you're wrong? What if you're wrong? Wrong wrong wrong.*

I know it as soon as I enter the cave, even in the inky blackness: I wasn't wrong. 'Kirsty? It's me.' My voice bounces off the walls.

The others wait at the entrance while I take a few tentative steps inside.

'I know you're in here.'

Silence. And then, 'Leave me alone,' spoken so softly that it sounds like it comes from inside my head.

A few more steps, and then I see her. Right at the back of the cave, curled up into an impossibly small space. Her knees are pulled up to her chest with her arms wrapped round them. She blinks against the light from the torch. 'Leave me alone. *Please.*'

'I'm not going to do that.'

Behind me, one of the girls switches on the fairy lights and Kirsty flinches. Maybe it's too much, the four of us. I should have come alone.

'Can we talk?' I ask, still hanging back a bit. I don't want her to feel trapped.

'Did you call the police?' Her voice is limp. She won't look at me.

I want to laugh, because that's exactly what you should do when someone points a gun at you. 'No, I didn't. And I haven't told any teachers if that's what you're worried about.' There's no need to mention that we'll have to tell them later.

'What are you doing here?'

'We wanted to see if you were OK. We were worried.'

'Worried? About me?' She looks at me, finally. 'I could have *shot* you, Harper.'

'Yeah, but you didn't. So that's something to be cheerful about, right?' Joking about it makes me nauseous.

'Kind of a shame you decided to spare Marcy though.' Lily steps forward and I wince. I should really be the one handling this. Lily's a bit too full-on for this sort of thing. Except . . . perhaps she's not.

Kirsty tilts her head. 'Why are you here? You hate me.' Her voice is flat, stating a fact.

'Look, I'm not going to pretend to be delighted that

you told Maddox about me and Marek, but it's done now.' She shrugs. 'No point crying over spilt semen.'

'Lily! Shut *up*!' Ama gives Lily a gentle shove, but I'm the one reeling.

'That was you?!' There seems to be no end to my obliviousness. 'Why?!'

'It's OK, you don't have to explain. The whole Marek thing was a bad idea anyway. You did me a favour, really.' Lily's breezy tone doesn't fool me, but I'm not the one it needs to fool.

'I wanted to hurt you.'

Lily crouches down in front of Kirsty. 'Why don't you come out of there so we can talk properly?' She holds a hand out to Kirsty and a memory jolts me. Lily pulling Kirsty out of the Hole, playing twin roles: tormentor and rescuer.

Kirsty looks at Lily's hand for a second or two, before reaching out. Lily hauls her up and she stumbles into Ama, who steadies her. We all sit down, and I realise we've unconsciously taken the same places as last time.

'Right, who brought the vodka?' Rowan claps her hands together and looks around at us expectantly. Lily and Ama laugh; Kirsty and I do not.

Lily's voice is unusually gentle when she asks Kirsty why she wanted to hurt her. 'Was it payback for the Hole? I can't say I blame you.'

Kirsty looks around at all of us, understandably hesitant.

'You can tell us.' I try an encouraging smile on for size; I'm not quite sure it fits. 'We just want to understand.'

'But you won't! You won't understand! No one ever does!'

'Try us,' says Rowan, with the same gentleness as Lily. It shocks me, that they're able to put aside their anger like it's nothing.

Kirsty looks at each of us in turn. 'It was the four of you – it was too much. I couldn't stand it.'

No one speaks, so Kirsty continues. 'There was this group of girls at my old school. Everyone wanted to be friends with them. They invited me to a party. I thought they liked me. I actually believed that was possible even though they'd never shown the slightest interest in me before.' She shakes her head and closes her eyes. 'They humiliated me.'

'What does that have to do with Lil?' I ask.

'It wasn't *about* Lily.' She turns to her. 'I don't have a problem with you. Or you, Ama. But I had to . . . groups of girls have always frightened me. They always seem to want to hurt you and put you down. They're . . . *cruel*.'

The words are gushing out of her now. I don't think the others have ever heard her talk this much. 'I don't fit in. I never have. Mum said it was good to be different – said I marched to the beat of my own drum or something – but it *isn't* good. People don't like it when you're different. They like you to be the same as them and I try *so* hard but it never seems to work.' It lands like a physical blow. All this time, she thought I wanted her to be like me. And the worst of it – and I could never admit this to the others – is that I think she was right.

'When I came to Duncraggan, all I wanted was a friend. I didn't think that was too much to hope for – one friend.' Kirsty turns to me, and her smile is unbearably sad. 'And then you gave me that torch. No one has ever done anything like that for me before. I . . . I thought that maybe you wouldn't hurt me.'

'Wait, what torch?' asks Lily, leaning forward.

Kirsty answers before I get the chance. 'Harper gave it to me before you put me in the Hole. That's why I didn't use any of the matches.'

Lily bursts out laughing and elbows me. 'You sly little . . .' She shakes her head, smiling. 'We thought you were such a badass.'

Kirsty responds with a Mona Lisa smile and it feels like we might be getting somewhere. Unpicking secrets and unwrapping lies until we're left with the truth.

I should have told her the truth a long time ago.

'It was Rowan's idea to give you the torch. I didn't want to.'

Whatever trace of a smile was on Kirsty's face has been wiped away by my confession.

'I didn't see why you should get special treatment.' I'm not saying it to hurt her; she needs to know. 'I'm not the person you thought I was.'

Kirsty looks to Rowan for confirmation and the truth is written all over her face. She's even holding the torch. Rowan says sorry even though she hasn't done anything wrong.

Would everything have been different, if she'd known the truth from the start? Would she have followed Rowan around and copied her hairstyle and tried to separate her from the group? No. Rowan would never have let it happen.

There's one lie left – the biggest one of all. 'I know about Rhiannon.'

Kirsty's head snaps up and I expect to see anger or fear or confusion, but I see none of those things. At first I can't decipher her expression, but then I realise what it is. It's relief.

'You're an only child, aren't you?' I ask softly.

Kirsty nods.

'And the car crash wasn't four years ago.'

A shake of the head, then a deep, juddery breath. 'Last Christmas.' If I knew anything about scars I might have realised that there was no way hers were four years old.

'Your mum was driving.' I reach for her hand; it's so very cold. 'She died.'

FIFTY-TWO

Finally, she cries. Silent tears streaming down her face. She grips my hand tightly, and it feels like she's hanging off the edge of a cliff. I won't let her fall.

There's nothing to do but wait. I catch Rowan checking the time; crying always makes her uncomfortable.

After a couple of minutes, Kirsty lets go of my hand. 'When you told me about Jenna, it shocked me. I couldn't understand how you were able to say the words out loud, like it was nothing.' She frowns and shakes her head. 'No, that's not right. It felt like you were able to accept what had happened. And I could *never* . . . I still can't believe that my mum is . . .'

She knows she has to say it. Sometimes you have to say the words even though it feels like they'll choke you. ' . . . dead.' The word comes out hard and flat and final. Her eyes widen, as if she can't believe she was the one to say it.

'So I said I had a sister. And it was a terrible lie to tell and I knew that as soon as I said it, but it *felt* like the truth. Mum was . . . her name was Rhiannon. I wanted you to know that I understood what it's like to lose someone.' She pauses, her eyes scanning my face for a reaction. 'I'm not trying to excuse what I did, because it's inexcusable. But you deserve an explanation.'

The others are looking at me. I know I should say something, but what? I can't tell her that it's OK.

The silence stretches out until Kirsty breaks it. 'The accident was my fault.'

'What happened?' Ama asks, and I'm grateful to her.

'We were arguing. I'd never seen her that angry – not with me. She was driving too fast, looking at me instead of the road. A van pulled out in front of us and she swerved. We hit a wall. The driver's side of the car was . . . There was no way . . .'

Lily reaches over to put her hand on Kirsty's knee, but Kirsty doesn't seem to notice. She's staring into space and I'm glad I can't see into her head.

'She'd been at the ballet with a friend. She thought I was at home in bed.'

'Where were you?' asks Lily.

'At a party that didn't exist. I thought it was strange, when those girls invited me. But they were being so nice, making suggestions about what I should wear and saying there was this boy who liked me. So I let myself believe them. I thought it was my big chance to change the way they saw me.' Her laugh is hollow. 'I was supposed to meet a couple of the girls at an address in east London. I knew the deal as soon as I got there – the windows of the house were boarded up. Then a taxi drove past – really slowly. They went out of their way so that I could see them laughing at me.'

I exchange a look with Rowan and I know we're both thinking the same thing. No wonder Kirsty hates groups of girls.

'I texted Mum to come and pick me up, but she didn't get the message until she was back from the ballet. I should have got a taxi or walked back to the tube station, but all I could think was that I wanted my mum. Everything would be all right if she was there. I sat on that doorstep in the freezing cold for two hours.' Her eyes refocus and she looks at me. 'I'll regret that for the rest of my life.'

She knows I understand. We have something in common after all. 'It wasn't your fault, Kirsty,' I say, and the others murmur their agreement. But I know she doesn't believe us. Nothing anybody else says can make a dent in guilt like this.

'Dad says I shouldn't blame myself. We have to

move on with our lives, according to him.' She snorts in disgust. 'He's moved on quick enough – he's getting married on New Year's Eve. And I'm supposed to go the wedding and smile and act like it's perfectly OK for him to marry one of Mum's friends a year after she died.'

None of us tries to hide how appalled we are. The news of the wedding has subtly altered the atmosphere, and I think we all feel the difference. Maybe Kirsty was worried we would take his side and try to convince her that her dad deserves to be happy. But as Rowan says, 'Getting married to her *friend*? Fuck that noise.'

Kirsty sheepishly admits that she stole her dad's wedding ring when she was home at half-term – he'd stopped wearing it when he got engaged. Lily shrugs and says, 'Good. Fucker doesn't deserve to keep it.'

The thing is, maybe Kirsty's dad is an OK guy but right now that doesn't matter. What matters is the look on Kirsty's face as she listens to Rowan and Ama's suggestions of how to ruin the wedding. They're not being serious, at least I don't *think* they are, but what they're doing is vital. They're managing to make Kirsty smile, in spite of everything. And then she remembers, and the smile vanishes. 'Why are you being so nice to me, after everything I've done?'

'Everyone deserves a second chance,' says Rowan, and it's the perfect thing to say and perhaps I should have been the one to say it. But I would have to believe it first, when all I can think is *not everyone*.

'Not *everyone*,' says Lil, and while I don't actually believe she can read minds, it still freaks me out. 'Take your dad, for instance. He sounds like a monumental asshole.'

Kirsty smiles, but again, it disappears before it's had time to settle. 'Oh my God, what time is it? The concert!'

Rowan, Lily and I all swear, but Ama just shrugs and checks her phone. 'I'm on in . . . nineteen minutes.'

Lily jumps up and hauls Ama to her feet. 'Go go go! You need to do your warm-up and your *Eye-of-the-Tiger* shit or whatever it is you do.'

This time, Ama's shrug is accompanied by a smile. 'There's plenty of time. Anyway, they'll wait for me. I'm the star of the show after all.' She brushes imaginary dust from her shoulders and the gesture is so alien that I have to laugh.

Kirsty looks more worried. 'You should hurry. This means a lot to you.'

'My friends mean more.'

Lily slings her arm around Ama's shoulders and addresses Kirsty. 'In case my girl here wasn't quite clear enough, that includes you.'

I don't know if they're being entirely honest – if

my friends are really willing to forgive and forget so easily – but it doesn't matter right now. What matters is that Kirsty is smiling. And that it's a real, genuine smile that shows no sign of disappearing.

FIFTY-THREE

Ama decides that we need to have a 'moment', whatever that means. So the five of us are standing on the cliff-top, staring out into the blackness.

'Are we supposed to be thinking deep thoughts?' Rowan whispers, earning an elbow in the ribs from Ama.

'We're *supposed* to be appreciating what we have,' says Ama, breathing deeply.

Lily is fidgety as hell. 'I would *appreciate* if you would get your ass over to the auditorium so that I don't have a fucking heart attack.'

As Ama, Lily and Rowan bicker and joke around I edge closer to Kirsty. 'Are you OK?' I whisper.

She doesn't look at me when she replies. 'I don't know.'

It feels like an honest answer to a stupid question, but even stupid questions have to be asked sometimes. 'What you said earlier, about me being lucky for wanting to live . . .'

'Dad wanted me to have therapy . . . maybe it's not such a terrible idea.' Perhaps her dad's not a one hundred per cent total douchebag after all. 'Do you think, one day, maybe we could be friends?' she asks shyly.

I turn to look at her – really look at her. The girl I thought I knew doesn't even exist. She was a mirror girl, reflecting back what I wanted to see. It turns out that I don't know much about the real Kirsty Connor. But I do know that she is grieving and vulnerable and scared. I know that she's in desperate need of a friend. Or four. I slip my arm through hers. 'There's no maybe about it.'

Ama coughs an attention-seeking cough. 'Um, guys? I know I'm acting all chilled about it, but I'm on in seven minutes so could we—'

Rowan's grinning face appears over Ama's shoulder. 'Make like a tree and leave?'

Lily groans. 'That was bad, even by your standards, Chung. Make like a banana and split would have been a *far* better option.' She smirks and Rowan rolls her eyes.

'Guys? I'm freaking out over here.' The fact that Ama looks like she might puke is oddly reassuring.

I turn to see Kirsty watching the four of us. I wonder what she sees. A group of girls who will stick with her, no matter what? That's what I hope we can be.

The five of us run towards the castle. Together.

EPILOGUE

'I'm definitely Team Velociraptor,' says Dad, leaning forward in his chair to take a sip of his tea, which must be cold by now. 'They're quite cute . . . when they're not, y'know, ripping people apart.'

'No way, it's all about the T. rex. Big teeth, tiny arms.'

'Rubbish at press-ups though,' says Mum.

And then the credits are rolling and the music is still as epic as ever and there are tears in my eyes. But it's OK because there are tears in Mum and Dad's eyes too.

'Thank you,' Dad says quietly.

'For what?'

'This. I know it wasn't easy.'

He's right. It wasn't. But it felt like it was important. For us, and for Jenna. She would be happy about us starting our little Christmas Eve tradition again. I know that for sure.

*

Christmas Day is just about bearable, which is all we can hope for right now. It's strange, sitting at the fancy new dining table in the fancy new house. But it was always going to be strange, and it was always going to be difficult. It always *will* be difficult, without Jenna. I have to learn to accept that.

I asked my parents not to go overboard on the presents this year, and they actually listened this time. A new pair of swimming goggles was the only thing I really wanted, but they also get me some books, a dressing gown and a pair of socks with sparkly Christmas puddings on.

The girls and I scheduled a Skype call for five p.m., and one by one their faces pop up on my laptop screen. Ama first, then Lily, then Rowan (complete with orange paper hat). It's good to see them. Really good.

We chat for a while, and take the piss out of Lily who can't stop moaning about the temperature in Barbados. 'You try eating Christmas pudding in this heat. It's hell, I tell you!' A sly look appears on her face. 'So anyway, Ama has some news to share with the group . . .'

Ama protests, but then blushes her way through telling us that she got an email from the Goldsmiths lecturer saying how impressed he was by her performance. We decide that it must have been the mad dash up to the castle that added the extra special something to her playing that night.

Rowan's the first one to mention Kirsty. 'Is she OK?'

I shake my head. 'I don't know. I haven't heard from her since . . .'

A new window pops up on my screen. 'Sorry! Sorry I'm late!' Kirsty's face is red and she's out of breath. She unwraps a long stripy scarf from her neck and smooths down her windswept hair before peering closer. 'I look like shit.'

She doesn't though. She looks good. *Alive.*

'You been out for a walk?' asks Rowan. 'What is it with parents and their obsession with getting some fresh air on Christmas Day?'

'We went to visit Mum's grave.' She waves away our sympathy before any of us can express it. 'It's OK, honestly. It was the first time, and it was hard. But I'm glad I went. I took some sprigs of holly from the garden. Mum always loved holly.'

The five of us talk for a few more minutes before Ama says she has to go and play *Monopoly* with her cousins. Lily and Rowan sign off too, leaving Kirsty and me.

As soon as it's just the two of us, her shoulders slump a little.

'How was the anniversary?'

She sighs and shakes her head. 'Awful. You were right about that.'

'It will get easier – or at least a tiny bit less awful. I know it doesn't feel like it right now, but it's true. How are things going with your dad?'

'Better, I think. We've been talking more. About Mum, mostly. I'm still not sure if I can face going to the wedding, but we'll see. I've got my first appointment with the therapist on Monday – I reckon Dad thinks she'll convince me to go. I don't think he knows how therapy actually works.'

After a silence that lasts a little bit too long, Kirsty says, 'So I've been thinking . . .'

'Thinking about what?'

'Nothing. Forget I said anything.'

'*Kirsty* . . .' I say in a mock-stern, teacherly voice. We talked about this, before we said goodbye at the end of term. Total honesty from now on – that was the deal.

'OK . . . you should think about talking to your parents about your sister.' This wasn't what I was expecting – at all.

'I can't,' I whisper as if my parents might hear me, even though they're on the other side of the house.

'You *can*,' Kirsty says firmly.

'It'll only upset them.'

'Maybe it will, but maybe that's OK. You have to stop blaming yourself for what happened to Jenna.'

'It was my fault!'

'No. It wasn't. Just like you said what happened to Mum wasn't *my* fault. Anorexia is a disease. You *know* that. And they know it too.'

'I have to go . . . I'll message you tomorrow, OK?'

'Harper . . .' she says in the same stern tone I used on her. 'Talk to them. Please.'

After we exchange goodbyes, she says something else, clicking to end the call before I have a chance to reply.

'You gave me the benefit of the doubt. You gave me a second chance. Don't you think you deserve the same?'

'What shall we watch now?' asks Mum, bringing in a fresh round of tea. 'Ooh, maybe we could get started on the *Downton Abbey* box set you got me.'

Dad stands up and stretches. 'I might have to excuse myself if you're going to watch that drivel.'

'You just want to go and play with your new toy. Go on, admit it.' The new toy in question is a bright blue electric guitar. The midlife crisis continues.

Dad laughs. 'You've got me there. Still, I think I'll leave you to it.'

I think of Kirsty's words. I don't know what *I* deserve, but I know that my parents deserve the truth.

'Actually, Dad, there's something I want to talk to you about.' My words come out in a rush and they can see straightaway that it's something serious.

Dad sits down next to me on the sofa and I say the words out loud, quickly, before I change my mind. 'It was my fault that Jenna died.'

They both protest, but I beg them to let me talk. And they do, even though I can see how much it's hurting them. Before long, Mum is sitting on the other side of me, holding my hand in hers. All three of us are crying.

I tell them everything. Every nasty little secret I've kept inside since Jenna's diagnosis. And then I run out of words, and the silence is unbearable.

I stare down at my hand and wait for Mum to let go. I wait for her to tell me she's ashamed of me. I wait for Dad to say he wishes I'd been the one to die instead of Jenna.

I wait, but none of those things happens.

Dad says it first. 'It wasn't your fault.'

Both of them say the same words, again and again and again. They tell me that they love me. Mum shakes her head and says she can't believe I didn't talk to them about this sooner. 'It breaks my heart to think of you carrying this with you every day. Harper, I want you to listen to me, OK? You *listen*,' she says, fiercely. 'What happened to Jenna was *no one's* fault, least of all yours. And I will tell you that every damn day if I have to, until I'm sure that you believe it.'

It wasn't my fault. I know that they believe it, but I don't. Not yet. Still, a hope flickers inside me, and the hope grows with every word they say.

After three years of the guilt clinging to me like a shadow, I can't quite bring myself to part with it just yet. But one day, I hope to leave the shadow behind me. I choose to believe in the possibility, and that's enough. For now.

ACKNOWLEDGEMENTS

Huge thanks to Julia Churchill, agent extraordinaire and voice of reason.

Thank you to Hélène Ferey, Jennifer Custer, Allison Hellegers, Sarah Lambert, Ruth Girmatsion, Sinem Erkas, Michelle Brackenborough, Sarah Baldwin, Anna Bowles, Nina Douglas, Glenn Tavennec and Fabien Le Roy.

Thank you to Kirsty Connor and Hozzie Bareham for bidding to have their names featured in *Girlhood*, in aid of Authors for Nepal and Authors for Refugees. I hope you approve of your namesakes.

As always, thank you to the Sisterhood, for sharing the highs, lows and absurdities.

I will be forever indebted to Jonni Rhodes for introducing me to 'Muffins for hands or squirrels for

HELP AND ADVICE

If you need help or advice, please think about reaching out to one of the organisations below.

Childline

A private and confidential service for young people up to age 19. Contact a Childline counsellor about anything – no problem is too big or small. Available 24hrs.
Call free on **0800 1111** or talk online at **www.childline.org.uk**

LGBT Youth Scotland

From questioning your sexual identity, coming out, relationship issues, bullying to sexual health – this is a private place designed for you to comfortably chat online with a youth worker.
Find them at **www.lgbtyouth.org.uk**

The Mix

Offers counselling to those under 25. Open 24/7 and 365 days a year.
Call free on **0808 808 4994** ot talk online at **www.themix.org.uk**

Samaritans

Confidential and emotional support for people who are experiencing feelings of distress, despair or suicidal thoughts. Lines open 24/7 and 365 days a year. If you need a response immediately, it's best to call on the phone.
Call free on **116 123** or find them at **www.samaritans.org**

Hope Again

Offers confidential help to young bereaved people. Mon-Fri 9.30am-5pm.
Call free on **0870 808 1677** or find them at **www.hopeagain.org.uk**

Papyrus

Young suicide prevention society. Mon-Fri 10am-5pm & 7pm-10pm. Weekends 2-5pm.
Call **0800 068 4141** or find them at **www.papyrus-uk.org**

Beat

Offers support and information about eating disorders. Helplines are open 365 days a year: 4pm-10pm.
Call free on **0808 801 0711** or find them at **www.b-eat.co.uk**

feet?'. Those of us who were lucky enough to hear the original song version will never be the same again.

Thank you to Ciara Daly, Victoria Schwab, Cate James, Anna Frame, Sam Meredith, Steve Wood, Sarah Crossan, Isobel & Graham Fisher and Robert Clarke.

Last, but never, ever least, thank you to Caro Clarke. I couldn't do it without you, nor would I want to.